THE ROCK WON'T MOVE

A Love Story

WM. HANK PERRY

Foreword by
Randy Packett, President and CEO
Chesapeake Capital Management LLC

xulon PRESS

To Alex and Jacob,
my two greatest gifts

CONTENTS

Foreword

In the course of a lifetime, we meet many people who either inspire or discourage you. Then you meet a person whose unique personality and ability to deal with trials and tribulations is so inspiring that it impacts your everyday life. This is Hank, the author, who became a fixture in my life over thirty years ago, as my brother and my friend. Even though we are brothers from different mothers, our lives are led by our beliefs in our Savior, our Lord, Jesus Christ.

I met Hank when both of us were working at a J.C. Penney® department store. We quickly became friends and roommates, while we both attended college. Almost immediately, we found that we had a common bond: not only in attending the same college, but also attending the same church, St. Martin Catholic Church. I knew right away that our Savior, Jesus Christ, had brought us together. Only through His mercy and grace are we both able to work and serve Him. The more I spent time with Hank, the more I realized his uniqueness as an individual and his love of Jesus Christ, and his willingness to serve Him and be more like Him. I remember a couple of occasions, in one of those college years, when Hank spent most of his free evenings volunteering to sell Christmas trees to raise money for the church. I also remember him winning a frozen turkey for being an exceptional employee, and he donated the turkey to a local soup kitchen.

Hank loves to help people. Whatever the problems they may have, he always finds ways to get involved to become a cog in the wheel, helping solve their problems and issues.

This book is another example of his way of sharing and helping those of us who might have either offended, or not cared for, the Lord's flock. Hank's unique and insightful approach in writing his thoughts destroys one's façade and pretense. He masterfully uses the two main characters, Professor Hutchinson and Professor Lewis, to illustrate our shortcomings. He further uses his incisive wit, biting insights and his ability to research to allow this book to be written in a most enjoyable manner.

This book represents the beginning of a major event in the life of Hank Perry. It's my hope that this book will start his amazing, God-giving gift of writing such thought-pro-voking books. I hope you enjoy reading this book and look forward to reading his future books.

Randy

Letter from the Author

Pardon me while I chuckle...

Sorry, it happens each time I think of myself as an *author*. This would be the first book with my name attached to it, and if you knew anything about me, you would chuckle, too. Furthermore, I really do not consider myself the sole author of this book; the author-in-chief, I believe, was God. I'm not suggesting that this book was God-breathed — more like the story was meant to be written, and I was merely obedient to write it. There could be no other explanation. I began writing down the words to this book during one of the deepest and darkest periods of my life, when I could have easily been swallowed up by self-pity. I won't deny the torrent of tears, but the Lord was good and He was in control... and evidently had other plans for my life.

Has that ever happened to you? One day everything was sunshine and lollipops, and the next day, you find yourself in a cold and lonely place, asking yourself, "Where was God?" You pray and you pray, but the only prayers that seem to get answered are those against you... and against God's Word. Soon you realize the Lord was there with you the whole time. The only way you were able to resist the devil's temptations for so long was by leaning on Him. Then, when it pleased Him, He presented the *gift*. Whatever form that gift may take, it filled the self-made void that separated you from Him.

You should also know that I did not intend to write a prologue. That's because when this book was still in its infancy, and no one took me — or it — seriously, my closest friend Randy asked if he could write the Foreword when it was finished. (I actually consider Randy more of a brother than a friend. He understands the flaws and limitations that make me human... and what only a quintessential brother would endure.) After the event that would change my life forever, it was Randy (and his precious wife Suzy) that would take me into their home. For over a year, I lived in their basement without doing much more than going to work in the morning and coming back to write. (Please don't feel bad about this... the basement was equipped with pool table and home theater room.) In fact, this book might not have been written if not for Randy's inexhaustible kindness. So, of course, what else could I say but, "Randy, you understand that means you actually have to read the book, right?"

Which reminds me... if you have been given a story to tell and are considering becoming a first-time *author* (hee hee... oops, there's that word again), forget asking your friends and family to read and critique your work. I can assure you that they will either not read it, or they will read it but give you nothing helpful (in an effort to be polite rather than be honest). You must appreciate they have better things to do than read your mistake-riddled, incoherent stab at writing... and then hope you won't come around too often asking them about it. After soliciting a dozen people, whom I love and respect, only one gave me feedback worth using (thank you, Barbara).

Anyway, this introduction came about as a direct result of my request for an initial critique by my soon-to-be publisher, Xulon Press. This critique finally came back to me as an email attachment. The day I received word that it was ready to download was a particularly busy day for me. I only had time to glance at the first page and then send it to my computer printer for review later; but from that quick read, I could tell the lovely people at Xulon loved my book, loved me and loved God.

I must have been awfully naïve to think that things I had done well would continue beyond this first page because, to my surprise, it was followed by three pages of things I had not done so well. Have you ever had anyone criticize your politics, your religion or, heaven forbid... your child? Then you know where I'm going with this: they hate my book, they hate me and they hate God!

Of course, this foolish overreaction could not have been further from the truth, and the observations and recommendations my editor (now lovely again) provided were exactly what I needed to make this book as enjoyable for you to read as it was for me to write.

In addition to my disregard for such things as punctuation and sentence structure, there were other issues brought to my attention. In the book you are now holding in your hand, I make references to Hillary University's Christian heritage and Civil War Era figures, buildings, battles and battlefields. There is good reason for that; the original manuscript contained two stories going on simultaneously. That's right: two stories in one book.

It was supposed to work like this: Chapter One "Intro to Opposites" would introduce the reader to the main characters, who are living in our modern times. In other words, they could be your neighbors. Chapter Two "The Battle" (no longer a part of this book) would take the reader back to the 1860s. The characters in this American Civil War setting were just as real as their modern-day counterparts... they just happen to be living in a different era than ours. This juxtaposition of two stories was not some goofy, paranormal, parallel-universe trickery. I simply had two tales to tell: one set the scene for the origins of Hillary University, while the other depicted life on Hillary's campus, as it exists today — both separate and distinct — yet they were bound to one another by the appearance of a magnificent rock.

In an effort to make two concurrent stories somewhat easier to read, I added some basic structure to the book. There were going to be, after the introduction of the main characters in Chapter One (modern era) and Chapter Two (Civil War era), two "modern era" chapters followed by one "Civil War era" chapter. This structure was to continue throughout the book. For example, Chapters Three and Four would take place in our modern times, then Chapter Five would take place back in the Civil War era; Chapters Six and Seven... modern era, Chapter Eight... Civil War era; Chapters Nine and Ten... modern, Chapter Eleven... Civil War; and so on.

Confused yet?

I thought this "twist" was ingenious... my editor called it "flip-flopping" and thought it would drive you, the reader, crazy.

At over 100,000 words and a confusing story *arc* (in book-editing lexicon), I was promptly advised to divide the story into two separate books; but that would have to be my decision, since I was the *author* (hee hee... oops).

So, two it is.

I have decided to publish the modern-era story first, since it is the more complete of the two. If you recall, it had two chapters for every one of the Civil War story. The Civil War era story, or prequel, will follow soon after this book is published... God willing. To whet your appetite (and plug my next book), the Civil War storyline was actually my favorite to write, because I love American history and its uniquely Christian heritage.

My apologies go out to those who find it difficult to listen to, or to read, curse words, especially the more vulgar kind. I agree with that sentiment and, as a rule, don't curse – except in that unguarded moment when self-control abandons me. With that being said, one of my secondary character's whole image was built upon the brutally profane language he uses. This was a concern of mine early on, but was informed that if this character was to remain true to his nature, then he must be given license to say what he will... regardless of my distaste for it. I was able to conceal his disturbing vocabulary until Chapter 7 (Great Awakenings). At this point, if I had used less offensive words here, you might have thought "Oh... that wasn't so bad"; when, in fact, the character's speech was rotten... very rotten. In any event, there are not many of these foul words, and you have my permission to black them out.

Now, as you are reading, I hope you will think on each one of the characters as being real and important enough to tell a story... just like you and me. I could have gone on and on about the two kids that run into Jack behind the stage (Chapter Six). As it was, I didn't even give them names... but you have seen them in your life. Take the time to talk to them about Jesus and what He means to you. We have far too many of our children being led astray.

Well, I've rattled on long enough, and I'm sure you want to get to the book, but one last word if you please.

I meant to be diligent in the way I describe the various love stories in these two books, but they all pale in comparison to Jesus Christ and His great love for us. If you don't already have a personal relationship with Him, may I suggest you start with the New Testament's book of Romans... just as the apostle Paul did in the first century, and just as Charlie did with Hitch in the Sanctuary (Chapter Twelve). Then find a local church that teaches the Word of God, concerning the Blessed Trinity from the Holy Scriptures... nothing more, nothing less. Be sure to lift up your pastor constantly, but do not be afraid to challenge him if you should see him backsliding to conform to this world. You are not of this world!

So, grab a cup of coffee and slide down into that comfy chair. Then read, laugh, cry, imagine... this is my gift to you.

In Him alone,
Hank

1

Intro to Opposites

S ummer had all but expired, and so too its freedoms. These summer breaks gave his mind a chance to mend itself from the exhaustive effort of educating this generation of unappreciative underachievers. It had not always been this way.

How is it that the vast majority of this student body, and even some of our younger faculty members, can't understand the price that was paid to reform this country's finest universities? he lamented.

This was in reference to the radical countercultural revolution that occurred on many campuses throughout the country in the sixties and seventies, an attitude and ideology he had proudly helped accelerate on this campus.

Much like Harvard, this university was mired in the theology of its founders when I arrived here, he mused.

He was familiar with Harvard's slow metamorphosis from Puritanism to Unitarianism to secular humanism back in the late nineteenth century. One need only pin point the date when Harvard truncated the motto on its shield from

17

Veritas pro Christo et Ecclesia (Truth for Christ and Church) to simply *Veritas* (Truth) to know exactly when their transformation to a reliance on man was complete.

He also knew, however, that for those who did not take part in the early struggles, there would always be an opportunity for apathy and indifference to set in. This, in turn, could lead to a shift backwards, even as far back as to resurrect a reliance on something as infantile as faith in God. The idea disgusted him.

I have fought too long and too hard to make this university a haven for enlightened human reasoning, in addition to being a powerhouse for advanced academics, he thought with some aggravation. *Yet, in spite of these strides, I have so little from which to choose among so many self-centered dimwits and slackers*. This brought to a close his train of thought with a relenting sigh.

It frustrated him to see the majority of today's best young intellectuals still falling over themselves to get into those mainstream "Ivy's." Then again, it was one of those Ivy's that had given him his education and, with it, his prestige and power. The only solace was that his dimwits and slackers were from very wealthy families.

These had become the recurring ruminations of Harvard-educated Dr. Edmond Hitchinson, professor of science and physics at Hillary University, an exclusively private college in the foothills of Pennsylvania. Professor Hitchinson, also known to a few close friends and colleagues as Hitch, had begun his hugely successful teaching career at Hillary fresh out of Harvard over twenty-five years ago. He had achieved tenure twenty years ago, soon after his first work in particle physics was published and became an instant best seller—at least within the ranks of those who could understand it. Since then he had authored or coauthored at least a dozen books—each book more commercially successful than the last—and hundreds of scientific and technical papers. This voluminous amount of work had become financially rewarding not only for him, but also for the university.

Hitch had always been a brilliant thinker and good at what he did. For this, he had become highly esteemed (and somewhat feared) by peers, faculty, and students. In recent years, he had even become sort of a celebrity in that he had developed a professional relationship with several cable news organizations. They invited him in to be their guest "expert" whenever the topic turned to astrophysics, human intelligence, or hot political issues such as global warming. Even the occasional discussion on the existence of extraterrestrial beings was acceptable, but only if he was in a lighthearted mood.

Hitch came to Hillary much like a prized first-round draft pick in football or basketball went to the pros—lured by a ton of money in anticipation of doing great things for the team. Unlike most overpriced jocks, however, he had not disappointed. Life at Hillary had been a mutually beneficial relationship, and he enjoyed all the perks of becoming the big fish in a relatively small pond, especially when that pond was flush with cash to support his pet projects.

With the overwhelming acceptance from the university's board of directors, Hitch spent a substantial amount of the school year traveling around the country and abroad. Hitch had even been invited to lecture at his alma mater, Harvard, from time to time. Whether the trips were to promote his books or to make a mainstream media appearance, the board considered it invaluable advertising for the school. When he was not traveling or authoring another book of superb thought and analysis, his only instructional obligations to Hillary were two lecture classes. Both met in the historic two-thousand-seat Walker Auditorium close to his office.

The first so-called lecture was, for the most part, a dog-and-pony show, a gesture of goodwill of sorts. It met only once, on the first day of the fall semester, and was offered to all freshman students, but did require an invitation; this was due to its popularity and the limited available seating. Its true purpose, however, was to showcase both professor and university to the wealthy parents who were also encouraged to attend. The topic of this little meet-and-greet was on whatever Dr. Hitchinson chose. However, it typically deteriorated into a personal rant on some random issue of the day and leaned towards the left politically, but it was usually quite entertaining for those who could keep up. Hitch believed that if they wanted a dazzling exposition of one or more of his trademark, esoteric theories on the perturbative formulation of string theories or the quantization of superstrings, scattering amplitudes, supergravity and mirror symmetry, they could buy his books. Still, most students and parents enjoyed listening to the ramblings of someone they perceived to be a genius.

Regardless of whether one leaned left or right, this ceremonial opening to the new school year in no way prepared anyone for Dr. Hitchinson's advanced physics class. It was here that the true "introduction to a genius" took place. The result was that more than half the class would find it incomprehensible and drop out or fail. In fact, some students wouldn't even make it through the first day. It was on this day that Dr. Hitchinson would begin his class with the same exhortation he had made for the last twenty years: "If you believe there is a God who is the sovereign governor of the universe, it is highly unlikely you will pass this course, and I suggest you drop it today."

This provocative introductory statement had the intended effect of prompting at least one or two defiant young Christians to defend their faith. Unfortunately, these poor souls would immediately find themselves on the receiving end of a relentless vilification of their Savior. Hitch was careful not to malign the students. They were free to believe whatever nonsense they wished, but their God was open game in his classroom, and he wanted to make damn sure they knew it. It was inevitable that after twenty years, this intimidation was not as satisfying as it once was.

Hitch presently occupied what had been for the last 150 years the original president's quarters in Turner Hall. These quarters were actually a conglomeration of tastefully decorated rooms of various sizes and shapes as was the design of the Civil War era in which they were constructed. All the rooms connected in some fashion by a series of hallways or appendages. Most of these intertwining hallways were well lit and wonderfully adorned. They were then separated from their destination by large beautifully sculpted hardwood doors. It sometimes appeared as if these great doors were there simply to separate hallway from hallway in some of the longer runs. As it would happen, two of these hallways would converge into one of the more spacious rooms, giving it the false appearance of having more closets than it actually had or needed. There were lesser passages, narrower and dimly lit, with no apparent destination at all, most likely leaving many to find themselves unwittingly back to where they had started. One can easily imagine this was all planned by the architect to confuse the unfamiliar so that the familiar could make a great escape.

The crown jewel of these many rooms was the president's study. This room was not necessarily the place in which the university president received business guests, or wanted to discuss administrative matters at all. Rather, it was a comfortable place to read, think, and restore oneself. It was the largest of all the rooms, with many magnificently tall windows, and somewhat secluded by means of those many hallways and doors. Unless a person knew the way there, or was plain lucky, it would take many attempts to arrive at one of its entrances.

The study contained thousands of first-edition books, manuscripts, and fine art. Many of these items had become so rare and valuable that the university transferred them to local museums on permanent loan. The accommodation that Hitch appreciated most, however, was the fine tall windows. These faced in a southeasterly direction and therefore captured all the sunlight the day provided. This was perfect lighting to read by or to write in, without requiring any of the horribly dull illumination that dripped reluctantly from artificial light sources. Occasionally, Hitch would find himself awakening from a quick daydream that would come about while looking out these windows and onto the meticulously groomed courtyard. This wide grassy field was the Grand Courtyard, or as it was affectionately known, the Yard.

The appropriation of this office space was an amicable decision between Hitch and the current university president, Dr. Peter Stansbury. The transition finally came after the long- awaited completion of the new administration building, which was the first of many buildings to be added as part of the new and extensive Hillary University Campus Complex Project begun several years ago. The intent of this aggressive project was to eventually replace the old buildings as places to conduct university business and return the historic section to its earliest condition, with only the four original buildings left standing: Turner Hall (the old administration building), Walker Hall (classrooms and auditorium), Samuel Hall (student dormitories), and the Sanctuary (with library and dining hall).

The newer buildings were fabulously modern and equipped with the newest green technology available. This, of course, made them fabulously expensive—and fraught with problems. Perched on the very top floor of the administration building sat the opulent offices of the president, in which Dr. Stansbury wasted no time occupying. Aesthetically, the contrast between these newer buildings and the older historical buildings was so uncomplimentary that it was determined from the beginning that all new structures would be constructed as far away from the older structures as possible. This decision put Dr. Stansbury's office on the opposite side of the vast Grand Courtyard and more than a mile away from Hitch's offices, which suited both men fine.

It could be said that scholastically, Hitch had the Midas touch, but then, not all his enterprises turned to gold. As is often the case with the exceptionally gifted (and the exceptionally self-absorbed), love—the kind that lasts—eluded him. He was, in fact, the product of three failed marriages. His first wife, Sunshine (a pseudonym, he suspected), was the quintessential eighties college pacifist from his graduate days. How they stumbled into a marriage when the sex-without-commitment thing suited him fine, he would never know. Nonetheless, she disappeared one day, and that was the end of that. His second wife, Aubrey, was the proverbial trophy wife. She was not only beautiful on the outside, but she was also caring to his needs from the inside. After several blissful years, however, Aubrey turned to religion. This made his life so unbearable that he had no choice but to divorce her for irreconcilable differences.

Hitch had high hopes for the third wife, Gloria. She was a well-educated, high-ranking executive for several regional women's clinics, and an active community organizer. Life was good once again. She made a lot of money and ran in all the right circles. As a Harvard-educated professor and a feminist executive, they made quite an impression at all the liberal gatherings. Unfortunately, the abortion industry in general, and Gloria's clinics in particular, experienced a sharp downturn of the number of "procedures" they performed. Added to this, an unwelcome congressional scrutiny of her parent organization caused a drastic reduction of her clinic's funding. These events quickly tarnished Gloria's once bulletproof image, and she struggled to keep her clinics open. Rather than look to her husband for support and comfort, she occupied all her time with fund-raising and damage control with the media. As a consequence, they found less and less time for each other, and their marriage soon faded unnoticed out of existence.

Hitch was not without feeling. Each divorce hurt deep within him where quantum theories provided no comfort... well, except for maybe Sunshine. But now, in his mid-fifties, with both parents long since deceased and no siblings or children to console him, for the first time in his life, he felt suddenly... alone.

* * * * *

Summer had an altogether different meaning for others. *Good riddance,* Jack thought.

A wonderfully creative and energetic wife and two very active young boys made the summertime schedule one unresolved butt-kicking after another. It was the school year that actually provided the chance to mend his mind and body. Oh, but if not for his precious wife, MJ, he would be another easy-chair-sitting, dead-white-guy-reading bookaholic. Her actual name was Joy, but the romantic poet inside of Jack had to add *"My"* to this, making his new love-induced name for her "My Joy"—and she truly was his joy in life. Because this new name was somewhat cumbersome to say, especially in public, it morphed naturally into simply "MJ." This reminded him:

Pick up flowers for MJ to let her know you are thinking of her. Oh, and don't forget this time, moron!

These were the endearing thoughts of Stanford-educated Dr. Jonathan Lewis, professor of English and American literature at Hillary University. Professor Lewis had begun his career at Hillary four years ago and enjoyed it, mostly. Since he was a kid, one of his greatest passions had been the written word, and he consumed every superhero comic he could get his hands on. When these comic book heroes became... well... comical, Jack's interests gravitated towards the classics like *Beowulf* and *Battle of Maldon* and then Homer's *Iliad* and the *Odyssey*. These works taught him early on that heroism was virtuous. It was innate and intoxicating; it was its own reward, and yet, deserving of praise. All his young life he wanted to be the hero, to come to the rescue, to save the day. Unfortunately, as he grew older, he noticed that heroism was almost always misunderstood by the cowardly, the selfish and those having trouble differentiating right from wrong. But to him, these intrinsically masculine exploits caused him to want to read more and more.

As a young teen, he developed a passion for Old English poets such as Geoffrey Chaucer and William Langland. Whereas Chaucer was rich and famous, Langland was poor and obscure, yet both influenced him greatly. His understanding of how to apply meter and rhyme grew exponentially by committing to memory vast amounts of poetry from eighteenth-century geniuses like Samuel Johnson and Alexander Pope. As Jack matured physically and mentally into young adulthood (raging hormones, more likely), he developed a passion for the great nineteenth-century Romantic poets like John Keats and Oscar Wilde.

Jack often wondered if there was any human condition meaningful to him that could not be put into words. Whenever he sensed there might be such an oversight, he would go to his literary hero, Shakespeare. Shakespeare's characters were not all heroes necessarily, but they were all breathtakingly real with every known strength and weakness God gave to fallen man. In the early years of college, Jack found himself playing the part of Othello's lieutenant, Michael Cassio, in a summer theater group. His enjoyment was not so much in the acting, but rather in his growing familiarity with the people he had been reading about for so long. It didn't hurt that his character was also a lady's man and he was able to kiss several beautiful women three nights a week for an entire summer, either.

Jack applied this same logic of living vicariously through Shakespeare's characters by committing many of his 154 sonnets to memory. Again his desire was not so much to impress or beguile a girl he liked, but to understand more intimately the poem's true meaning. Well... okay... so that wasn't exactly true. Jack soon discovered that other than the angriest of Stanford feminists, most women were moved by his honorable attempt to touch their hearts simply by reciting Shakespeare from memory, like quoting from his eighteenth sonnet: "Shall I compare thee to a summer's day?"

Especially if the deliverer was a hot guy like himself, Jack remembered.

Now, to be able to share this passion for great literature with a classroom full of young people for a living had truly been a gift from God Almighty. In fact, the past two years had been most extraordinary in this respect because Jack finally realized for himself what the majority of his teachers had realized in him: the inexpressible joy of watching the "lights come on" when a student finally comprehends the true intent and meaning of the author. Or even better, when the student finally understands why the author chose this word and not that word, and why it's used here and not there. Jack couldn't remember where he had picked up this word analysis technique, but it had become a great conversation-starter for the apathetic, ear-bud-wearing video-gamers that frequently showed up in his classes.

Still, his failures to inspire his students had far exceeded his successes, and it was beginning to take its toll on him. Amazingly, the greatest challenge to teaching this whole process of truly understanding great literature was not in the mechanics. Instead, it was in keeping his students from corrupting the story to fit their own postmodern preferences and biases. That is to say, it was not unusual for him to spend far too much of his time undoing a deceitful ideology thrust upon his students by some politically correct buffoon (disguised as an English teacher) who had come before him. It was hard to admit, but it only took four years for these hopelessly indoctrinated zombies to wear him down.

Jack's office had always been in the same marvelous group of old historical buildings as Dr. Hitchinson's, only he resided underground, on the basement floor of Turner Hall. However, as a lover of old American poetry and even older English poetry, these wonderfully archaic buildings resonated within him. So when the mad dash by his fellow professors to acquire office space in the new administrative buildings began, Jack actually preferred to stay where he was. To his amazement, permission was needed to maintain an office in the historic section. This procedure turned out to be somewhat pointless, however, after it became apparent that space in the new complex was being gobbled up so quickly that demand exceeded supply within days. Fortunately for people like him, the vacuum created by his neighbors' exodus provided an ample supply of available office space in his building, and his request was quickly granted. In the shuffle, he even managed to move from the basement to a second-floor office with several tall windows overlooking the Yard.

Even though Hitch and Jack continued to maintain their offices in the same building, the two professors rarely met. This was in large part due to the fact that Hitch walked less than a block to get to his classrooms that, for the time being, still met in Walker Auditorium, while Jack was forced to hike the mile across the Grand Courtyard and hillside to get to his first class, which was held in the recently completed humanities building. If they ever did meet, they rarely shared more than the innocuous salutation one receives from a minor acquaintance. Jack knew of Dr. Hitchinson, of course, and his iconic reputation. Even before being hired, he made it a point to attend as many of the controversial professor's welcoming lectures to the incoming classes as he could, even if it was without invitation.

Jack's voracious appetite for great literature had certainly groomed him well for life as an English literature professor, but this had not always been his first choice in careers, and Stanford had not been his first choice in graduate schools. He felt back then, and continued to believe today, that the greatest book ever written was the inspired word of God in the Holy Bible. He was convinced that pastoring a church was the more God-honoring of the two careers; therefore, Dallas Theological Seminary had been his first desire for graduate and doctorial work. Jack always knew he had a gift and desperately wanted to use it for the glory of God.

God had other plans.

Like in all great Shakespearian tragedies, Jack's process of chasing his dreams was filled with guilt, doubt, and sorrow. Unfortunately, like in many other American households whose parents grew up in the sixties and seventies, Jack was told that he lived in a Christian home, but other than celebrating Christmas (for the gifts) and Easter (for the food and gathering of family), the love of an actual Savior was virtually undetectable. His dad eventually cheated on his mom and left when Jack was ten, and to add to Jack's sorrows, his mom remarried a man soon afterwards who made no pretense of being a Christian. The best that could be said of this whole mess was that his parents were no longer living in their hypocrisy, but it was difficult to see that either was any happier now than before they divorced.

Jack was a broken and faithless kid when he first met Joy in his early teens. Although her outward appearance attracted him at first, it was Joy's tender heart that actually held his attention captive. She was different from the other girls. She also had something he desperately wanted in his life at that moment, and it was greater than youthful lust. That something was actually someone—Christ Jesus. With Joy by his side, he eventually accepted Jesus into his heart at age sixteen.

It had taken some doing, but Jack finally forgave both of his parents for putting him through hell on earth. He understood that his anger toward them was keeping him prisoner, and the only key that would unlock his cell door was forgiveness. He continued to talk to his mom and dad about Jesus and his wonderful gift of grace and mercy, but they would simply roll their eyes at him and quickly change the subject. This reaction made no difference to him; they were his parents, and as long as he had breath, Jack would pray for their salvation.

Perhaps it was Jack's inability to convince even his own mom and dad of the atoning sacrifice of Jesus Christ that led him to decline Dallas Theological Seminary's acceptance and offer of enrollment. Or perhaps it was simply God's "calling" for him to be at Stanford. Then again, Stanford's generous offer of a full scholarship didn't hurt either.

This should qualify as God's provision, Jack thought in a clever attempt to justify his decision to attend Stanford.

In any case, it had always been Jack's most fervent desire to be an ambassador of Christ. If that had something to do with him teaching English literature at one of the most renowned secular college institutions on the planet, well then, who was he to question God?

So why is it that every bone in my body is telling me I could be saving more souls pastoring snake handlers in a church in the Appalachian Mountains somewhere? Jack wondered, not fully grasping the sanctimonious undertone of his heart.

2

Hitch's Visitor

Loneliness was no simple emotion to be underestimated or ignored. Like fear, guilt, jealousy, hate, love and faith in a god, it was one of those misunderstood sentiments that had taken down some of the most capable and intelligent of human beings, before they ever had a chance to fulfill their destinies in life. Once one or more of these curses to the human mind took root in the subconscious, there was no stopping the malignancy. Like water to rock, they wore down, broke apart, and eventually destroyed their mark. Without a definitive remedy in mind (besides a fourth attempt at marriage), Hitch had no choice but to cope with this miserable distraction for now: but it caused Hitch to feel particularly ornery going into this new school year, and unless his melancholy subsided, the first semester students—and some faculty—were in for a horrifying ride.

Hitch immediately determined the best antidote for this type of ailment was a healthy dose of reality. Fortunately, the remedy he was seeking should be coming through his door any moment now. That was because almost every morning for the past five years, his personal secretary arrived at his door precisely at 7:00 a.m. to review his schedule. The action clause *arrived at his door* was quite inadequate, however, for the abrupt intrusion into his office after a somewhat meaningless rap upon the door by the aforementioned personal secretary. But he has grown accustomed to her intensity and no-nonsense aggressiveness. Of course, if she ever overheard him refer to her as his "personal secretary" again, his life would become a living hell. His indifference to her job title infuriated her. Early on, she insisted on a professional job title and the reasonable amount of respect it represented. Unfortunately for him, her title had been amended so many times he found it impossible to keep up with.

Was it "administrative coordinator" or "administrative support manager" now, or maybe "executive administrative director"? he thought. *Yes, that's it. The title definitely has "executive" in it.*

In any event, he would never make the terrible mistake of using such terms as *personal* or *secretary* in her presence again. As a result of this quandary, he never addressed her by anything other than "Ms. Brown," in public or elsewhere.

Ms. Brown was in her mid-twenties, and she was beautiful, brash, and brilliant. He would readily admit that much of his public success was a direct result of how well she managed his career, his time, and him. Nonetheless, for the life of him, he could not remember hiring her. She had showed up as his life began to spiral out of control, restored balance, and never left. Not being very sensitive in these matters, he only recently became acutely aware of how valuable she was. Through other sources, he learned that soon after he and Gloria divorced, Gloria attempted to steal Ms. Brown away from him and even offered her ten thousand dollars more a year than what he was paying her—an offer she respectfully declined. It upset Hitch a little to admit that not long before this treasonous proposition by his ex-wife took place, the thought had actually crossed his mind that he might be paying Ms. Brown too much. Following the discovery of Gloria's villainy and to make amends for his slow-wittedness, he immediately increased her salary a thousand dollars a month without explanation—an offer she humbly accepted.

For having worked so closely for so long, it was amazing how very little Hitch knew about Ms. Brown. As far as he knew, she had never been married and had no kids, although this was pure speculation. This made positively no sense to him because she was perfectly lovely and without a vice that he could tell, reminding him of his second wife, Aubrey. Her dress was always modestly professional, yet on her, stunningly beautiful, and her speech clear and concise. She had an undergraduate degree of some sort from some obscure college somewhere, though he couldn't recall ever seeing a résumé or even performing a routine job interview. But she could be the devil in disguise, for all he cared, as long as she kept the wolves at bay and his professional life in order.

Like clockwork, a soft knock came from the large imposing door to his study, and in a brief instant, Ms. Brown was standing several respectful paces from his desk. She would stand there patiently until he was able to make eye contact. It was understood that this gesture would give her as close to his full attention as he was capable of giving anyone at that moment in time. Eye contact with Ms. Brown, however, was usually accompanied by such a pleasing smile from her that whatever self-indulgent mood he happened to be in would evaporate as quickly as the morning dew gave way to the afternoon sunshine. It also gave her permission to be seated and begin the recitation of an almost perfectly organized day, as well as highlight some of the more important events occurring sometime in the future that might require his attention now. With that, she began reading from the smartphone she carried with her at all times.

"Good morning, Professor," she greeted warmly. "I have purposely kept your schedule clear today to allow you some breathing room and to help you catch up on some of your overdue commitments. Please don't forget your meeting with Dr. Stansbury tomorrow at 8:00 a.m. sharp. He has generously set aside one hour to discuss your schedule for this semester. I have sent him a spreadsheet of everything that has been confirmed, but if I may, I would like to read to you his message from this morning."

It used to be that only outside business correspondence was channeled through Ms. Brown. Now virtually all correspondence, including both university and personal matters, went through her, unless specifically excluded by Hitch. Without hesitation, she began reading Dr. Stansbury's e-mail:

> [expletive] Hitch, it's three weeks before classes begin and we have every [expletive] freshman and their relative registered for your [expletive] intro lecture, and they don't have any [expletive] idea what it's about because we don't have any [expletive] idea what it's about. We made some [expletive] up for the roster, but can you please help us out here? See you at eight, tomorrow. Peter.

The censorship was Ms. Brown's undertaking, and unless it was absolutely necessary to the true meaning of the narrative, she never transcribed the gratuitous use of indecent language, regardless of who spoke it.

"He certainly has a way with words, doesn't he?" Hitch said with a smile.

Ms. Brown was not amused.

"I would like that syllabus by this afternoon so that it can be proofed and sent prior to your meeting," she replied. "Or would you like me to copy last year's outline?"

She knew this little slight would more than likely jar him out of his inaction. The effect was instantaneous; her boss's amusement became irritation, and his smile a growl.

"You shall have your syllabus by noon, Ms. Brown," Hitch responded coldly.

"Thank you," she replied sweetly (she read him like a book).

"You have once again committed yourself to four speaking engagements this year: one abroad and three here in the States," she continued. "I will, of course, be traveling with you to Vienna and New York City. I will make arrangements for the other two. Once you board those two planes, you are on your own."

"What's this now?" Hitch said, feigning disappointment. "Think I can't take care of myself?"

"Don't be silly," was her equally disingenuous response.

They both knew, of course, that beyond the walls of the university, Hitch was a fish out of water. Until very recently, she had gone on all his lectures, book-signing tours, and television appearances. Without her directing his every movement outside the realm of physics, he would have imploded long ago. With all her power and influence, however, Ms. Brown was extremely careful not to overshadow her boss or admonish him for his gruffness in public. In fact, the diligence applied to maintaining a low profile was so effective that many believed she was simply a menial gofer… or his mistress. All preparation and correction occurred behind the scenes.

Not only was Ms. Brown good at softening Hitch's haughty intellectual image, but she was also his greatest encourager. Her admiration for him as a person was genuine, and her uplifting comments were always helpful and sincere. To this point, whenever they were on the road together, she would make certain he rested, ate well, and exercised. As Hitch became more and more comfortable with traveling and all its rigors, she slowly backed off going on all his trips. This was difficult on him at first, except that the arrangements and itinerary were so perfectly tuned to his personality and behavior patterns that it was almost as if she were there beside him. In cases of emergency, she was always a text or e-mail away. Her response time to his inquiries was almost always immediate, and she usually had the exact answer he was looking for; that is, of course, unless the inquiries were trivial or too late in the evening, whereupon she would text back "Figure it out yourself" or "Go to sleep."

After a time, Hitch's concentration began to slip involuntarily from what Ms. Brown had to say about his comings and goings for the semester and onto his invitation to visit Vienna, Austria, for a symposium of some sort. The symposium meant nothing to him, and he would normally have had Ms. Brown RSVP his regrets, but he could not resist this one. It was, after all, being hosted in the hometown of one of the greatest minds in human history, Dr. Sigmund Freud. He had very little in common with the founder of psychoanalysis, other than their similar passionate worldviews: they both hated God and denied His existence.

Unfortunately for both Hitch and Sigmund, these seemingly incompatible feelings about God presented two very problematic dilemmas: First, logically a person cannot prove a negative; you cannot prove God does not exist. Second, hating something you do not believe exists is blatantly incongruent. Apparently, this made little difference to either one of them. Instead of letting it go, they spent an inordinate amount of their valuable time with an almost pathological preoccupation to destroy God. Freud described this whole idea of religion as the "universal obsessional neurosis of humanity."

Freud's thoughts on religion were made abundantly clear in his extensive writings on such matters. Hitch's desire to rid humanity of religion was far less obvious than Freud's, but no less dogmatic. He certainly did not hide the fact that he was an avowed atheist, and he took great pleasure in shredding the absurdities of ignorant believers, both publicly and privately, when antagonized; but he was extremely mindful not to let this worldview come through in his books or writings, lest he be classified a kook and his work dismissed or called into question. But it had been his dream since Harvard that he would someday develop the "Theory of Irrefutability," as he liked to call it. It would be the theory that would finally and irrevocably displace the plethora of other theories attempting to answer the question of how the universe came into being, and that theory, whether mathematical or otherwise, would be expressible in easily understandable terms similar to that of Einstein's general theory of relativity, $E = mc^2$.

In any case, he was looking forward to visiting Vienna and paying homage to the man he would proudly credit as being one of the major influences in his decision to discard his family's Christian beliefs and replace these mass delusions with the clearer, more trustworthy scientific worldview.

His innocuous little daydream was summarily shortened when he sensed Ms. Brown's tone of voice change.

"Well, it is easy to see that I have lost your attention, Professor," she admonished. "So I will leave you to your thoughts, but please, if you remember anything, remember this: your classes will begin in three weeks, and this year has the potential to be one of your busiest. Text me if you need anything; otherwise, I will see you again this afternoon at one o'clock."

With that, she left the room.

Busted again, he thought with a sigh.

He stood up and walked slowly to the large windows, seeking out the understanding of the gently rolling courtyard beyond. The act of being caught in these semiconscious interludes would normally refocus his attention back to the task at hand, but his thoughts were too far along and needed resolution. They now gravitated painfully toward his disappointment at not having fully captured that one elusive theory. He was as certain that the explanation existed and was definable, just as he knew night followed day, but he felt it slipping away.

I must have the answer, he thought wistfully.

"Think, you damned fool," he muttered to himself, "before you end up with nothing but words... like Freud."

"You shall have an answer if you want it," a voice offered from behind him.

Shocked by the unexpected realization that he was not alone, Hitch spun around excitedly only to find a tall, younger man standing perfectly still in the middle of his study, gazing back at him harmlessly. The stranger was well groomed and wore a finely tailored suit. His hands were clasped casually in front of him. His soft blue eyes and sheepish smile gave Hitch a strange assurance there was no malice in him.

"Who are you, and how did you get in here?" Hitch screeched at the intruder.

Frantically he scrolled through his smartphone, looking for the message from Ms. Brown that would explain how a person had made it all the way to his study unannounced. Finding nothing from Ms. Brown, he attempted an alert to get her in here as fast as she could, but it would not send.

That has never happened before, he thought.

"Do not be afraid, Professor," the stranger said. "You have been granted a wonderful opportunity."

"First, I am not afraid of you, because I detect no weapon on you—and I have a loaded 38 in my desk drawer for just such an emergency," Hitch lied while still fumbling with his phone.

Smartphone, my ass, he grumbled internally.

"Secondly, I'm sure I don't know what opportunity you are referring to, and thirdly, I'm still waiting for the answers to my questions. So, if you will be so kind, who are you, and how did you get in?" Hitch asked, finally lobbing the useless phone onto the desk in frustration.

"Time will not allow me to explain those last two questions to your satisfaction," the man spoke kindly. With a slight grin to his expression, he continued. "And we both know the only object resembling a weapon in your desk is the letter opener your 'personal secretary' gave you last year because of the haphazard way you open your mail... or should I say your 'executive administrative director' gave it to you?"

How could he possibly know any of that? Hitch thought

"Then perhaps you can explain this wonderful opportunity of yours... quickly," Hitch shot back. "Since you seem to know a little more about me than I know about you, you must know I am a busy man."

"Why the answer to your irrefutable theory, of course!" the stranger said enthusiastically.

There, he did it again, Hitch thought.

He was starting to become annoyed with the stranger for knowing about a theory he had not divulged to anyone since Harvard.

"Why now?" Hitch responded with some irritation. "Why did you not present your opportunity thirty years ago?"

"You would not have listened then," the stranger mused. "Perhaps it is your loneliness, as you call it, rather than your intellect that has brought me to your door. Now, don't be a fool and waste this opportunity, or if you prefer... research."

"How are you doing that?" Hitch said angrily.

"Doing what?" the stranger asked. "Reading your mind?"

"Yes."

"I do not read minds, Professor. I know only what is revealed to me—nothing more."

"Revealed to you by whom?"

"Again you ask a question you would not readily understand, even with your great intellect, but it will all be made clear to you shortly," the stranger answered, using his kind voice again.

"Amuse me," Hitch taunted.

"Quiet!" the stranger commanded.

Hitch could do nothing but comply.

"Tomorrow, in the courtyard, there will appear a large stone-like object, pure white and without blemish. Go to it at sunset. Once there, you and your travel partner will be given an understanding of what to do."

Hitch drifted back to the window as if these words were moving him in that direction. He surveyed the pristine beauty and serenity of the Yard. His eyes came to rest on the lone bronze statue of Colonel Hillary holding a book in the distance.

A terrible battle raged here, he recalled.

With his back still to the stranger, Hitch spoke. "Please, whoever you are, I have suddenly become weary of our conversation. If you could stop being so vague and evasive for a moment and tell me plainly, what it is you want from me?"

"I told you, a syllabus is all I need right now, Professor," came the response.

Hitch turned to see Ms. Brown in the very spot the stranger had been standing. Momentarily stunned by this transfiguration, he slowly began to extend his focus beyond her and then into a quick sweep of the room. The stranger was gone.

"I'm sorry, Professor," Ms. Brown continued, a bit troubled by her boss's confused behavior. "Your message seemed urgent, and I came as quickly as I could."

3

Jack's Visitor

Jack could not believe his good fortune. No longer would he have to conduct business in a cramped, windowless dungeon. Not only was his new office on the second floor more spacious than his previous office below ground, but it also had several wonderfully large windows that over-looked the scenic Grand Courtyard. Jack was very familiar with the Yard, especially its vast system of foot trails. That was because whenever he annoyed his wife too much, she would tell him to "go run it off." The fact that he had been running a lot lately was not a good sign.

This reminded him: *Stop with the moaning and com-plaining all the time about how bad things are at work while MJ is left to educate two lovable, but hyper boys at home all day. Think she might want some considerate, non-irritating adult conversation from time to time, Romeo?*

The miles of foot trails that meandered through and around the massive open field of the Yard and surrounding wooded countryside reminded Jack of the battlefield at Gettysburg, only on a smaller scale. Since Gettysburg was literally up the road from Hillary, he and MJ took the boys there regularly. They discovered there was nothing that could discharge youthful energy faster than a long line of cannons to climb on, or some tall observation towers to hike up and down. It was unfortunate that Hillary University's battlefield did not have any of these useful amenities. Almost everyone knew that a battle had taken place in the courtyard during the Civil War, but it was hard to tell. There were no towers, cannons, or monuments of any kind here, only the one statue of Colonel Benjamin Hillary. And one statue could not possibly hold the interest of a six and an eight-year-old boy.

Jack found the lone statue interesting, nonetheless, because it was unlike the many monuments at Gettysburg. It had always been Jack's understanding that when a Civil War hero was memorialized for having fought in battle, his statue would have him on horseback with one or more of the horse's hooves raised, depending on whether the rider had lived or died. Although Colonel Hillary was a cav-alry commander and an expert horseman, his statue was of him standing alone. The other thing that caught Jack's attention was that even though the colonel was in full mili-tary uniform with a saber by his side, it was a book he held prominently out in front of him. It was rumored that the book was a Bible, although Jack had never felt inclined to climb the statue to confirm this.

Jack also discovered from his conversations with Charlie, the university's preeminent groundskeeper, that even though the courtyard and surrounding forest were college property, the founders had legally established it as protected land, even from the university itself. In a com-plicated arrangement of trusts and deeds, other than the buildings necessary to house and educate the students, there were to be no man-made structures built within its ten-thousand-acre boundary, except for this one statue and the miles of pedestrian trails. It was Charlie's contention that these astute forefathers knew back then that the hearts of men were inherently selfish and greedy. In fact, prior to the Grand Courtyard being registered as a historic battlefield and thus federally protected, several unsuccessful attempts had been made to invalidate the original documents and sell off property—mostly for the personal gain of a few unscrupulous trustees.

With the help of MJ and the boys, Jake and Joey, it took Jack most of the weekend to move his belongings up to his new office. Of course, without the boys it probably would have taken him and MJ only a day, but it was fun pretending that they were a family of trolls moving out from under the dank bridge to a new country upstairs with fresh air, sunshine, and pizza. It was now time to get down to the business of opening young hearts and minds to great literature. He had three weeks before classes were to begin, and he needed most of that time to prepare for a new class of his entitled "Poetry: Mnemonic Strategies for Memorization and Comprehension."

Since coming on board at Hillary, Jack had received some modest recognition after his last two collections of short poems were published. Although it was not written anywhere, the university strongly urged its faculty members to have some work published within the first five years on staff. This new course would conveniently require the use of his most recent book, which had been published early last year. It was Jack's first attempt at writing an instructional manual for classroom use, and its main emphasis was on the understanding of poetry as the author intended it to be understood.

The origin of the book was mostly a response to the offensive way in which many humanist professors were throwing some of the greatest authors the world had ever known under the bus with impunity. This was especially true if their work had a moral or Christian underpinning, as most did. With his book having such a politically incorrect theme, Jack was more than a little surprised when his course application was approved for inclusion into this year's curriculum, but he felt his book was well written, well referenced, and edgy enough to find favor with the university's board of directors. He had, after all, been writing this book in his mind since he was a kid. It was explained to Jack later, however, that if not for the school's president throwing his weight behind his book and the course, it would have languished in scholastic obscurity forever—at least on this campus.

But why would Dr. Stansbury want to help me? Jack thought. He had met the man only a few times and found his overuse of foul language embarrassing and intolerable.

For the purposes of this new class, however, Jack would concentrate on that part of his book which made the case that all poetry was, by its very nature, meant to be memorized. Before Microsoft and Macintosh, before the Gutenberg printing press, before the simplest writing tools and paper were invented, poetry was the primary language used to retain and recall great amounts of wisdom literature for future generations. Jack also made the case in the book that poetry might be the best chance our Western culture had to reverse the diminishing memory capabilities of its youth.

Hey, a little hyperbole never hurt an argument... or book sales, Jack reasoned.

Then, on a truly personal level, the act of making memorization mandatory was another attempt to inject something fresh into the unsatisfying process of simply passing those who had become experts at taking a test, but gave that "deer in the headlights" look when asked what the author might have been feeling when he used *this* word instead of *that* word, *here* and not *there*.

Who am I kidding? If the students don't care, why should I? Jack thought as his grace-challenged alter ego kicked in.

Jack knew that this sentiment had a lot to do with being one of a few conscientious professors in a school unapologetically consumed with attracting shallow rich kids and increasing the school's bloated endowments. But it was simply another petty frustration he would add to his not-quite-bad-enough-to-act-upon-yet pile of gripes. It was kind of like the stray pebble that found its way into his running shoe in the middle of an afternoon jog: it was not irritating enough for him to stop his momentum and remove it.

For the next few minutes, Jack struggled with this dilemma of who should be the one to care first: the teacher or the student.

Which also begged the question, *Isn't that what you get paid for?*

He was indeed being paid well, and his future looked even more profitable. But if that was all his teaching career (his calling) had become, he wanted nothing to do with it. Ironically, it had been only a few short years ago that Jack was wrapping his arms around these apathetic yet mostly pleasant students and lavishing them with praise and encouragement. He even went as far as sitting in his gopher-hole of an office and faithfully praying for each and every one of them. But now, not only had this grace-centered kindness toward his pupils waned, but he had almost forgotten that he had once prayed for anyone in the first place.

Why do I even try anymore? he conceded. *I'll give this teaching business one more year, and if things don't turn around, I'll go back to seminary. MJ will understand.*

Fortunately, this downward spiraling train of thought was interrupted by the Christian rock ringtone of his cell phone. It was MJ.

"Hey, babe," Jack said softly.

"Good morning, sweetie," MJ offered back. "How's the view?"

"Spectacular!" Jack barked with renewed energy as he walked over to the windows.

"Charlie and his crew have the Yard looking like Wrigley Field in the middle of an arboretum. I never realized how beautiful it was until now. Hey, thanks for helping me move, by the way."

"The boys and I were happy to help. In fact, I can't get them to stop talking in that nonsensical troll language of yours... gross."

"Me not know what mom-wife listen-talk mean," Jack belched. "You snort more your silly human word-stuff... then Jack hear good."

"Yeah... that," MJ replied.

"Sorry," Jack laughed. "So what's up?"

"Well, could you keep a lookout for Joey's Angry Bird stuffed animal?" She asked. "He may have left it there yesterday and I think there is some kind of 'Calvin and Hobbes' codependency thing going on with it."

This relationship was in reference to the popular, but now retired, newspaper comic strip with a precocious six-year-old boy (Calvin) and his stuffed tiger (Hobbes) that would come alive whenever no one else was around.

"Sure thing," Jack said. "Hey listen, I'm sorry to keep grinding on you lately with my unfulfilled expectation issues. Can we meet tonight and talk about you for a while?"

After a prolonged pause, MJ answered. "Um, who is this and what have you done with my husband?" she inquired in mock seriousness. "He can be a self-absorbed brat sometimes, but I love him and want him back!"

"I'm serious," Jack groaned.

"I'm sorry," MJ's playfulness turned to sincerity. "Pamela next door owes me some sitter time. I'll see if she can give us a couple of hours tonight, but I gotta go—the boys are being way too quiet. Love you."

"Love you too," Jack replied affectionately, and after hearing MJ's phone go silent, he reluctantly hung up. He could not imagine life without his two boys, but oh how he wished that he could dwell a bit longer in these random chats with his wife again... before kids.

Okay. So where was I before I was so wonderfully interrupted? Jack sighed.

In an attempt to rise above his latest self-induced funk, he found himself debating whether to prepare for classes or attempt to answer the question *Why do I even try anymore?* for the hundredth time.

With the full intention of beginning the former rather than wasting time on the latter, Jack walked over to the door and locked it so as not to be so easily distracted, but it mattered not. His unsettled mind beckoned him back to his precious new windows. So, instead of a diligent search for the box containing the notes and materials on his new class, he focused what he could of his wayward attention onto the peaceful courtyard below. There was not a soul in sight as far as the eye could see. It was a little too early in the school year for much foot traffic on this side of campus anyway, but still, he thought it odd not to see a single person out there.

The solitude of the empty courtyard and the freshly mowed field in which every blade of grass glistened and swayed gently in the soft morning breeze only encouraged Jack's mind to wander further and further off task. His thoughts began with the childlike confession that he would never be able to keep up his workload with this kind of distraction available to him every moment of every day. After a while, his train of thought turned to some anxiety about the new school year, and then, once again, to another frustrating argument with himself as to why he was here in the first place.

I don't see the purpose for my being here, Lord, Jack professed earnestly while lifting his eyes beyond the open field and to the heavens.

This was no petty frustration. In fact, it was the most relentless theme of his recurring frustrations because it went all the way back to his decision to attend Stanford rather than Dallas Seminary. This internal wrestling match with his circumstances had come earlier than usual this year, however. It was normally triggered sometime after the semester began and his interaction with the more contentious student-atheists turned to their poetic preferences. He could always count on having at least two or three of these mostly antagonizing morons in his class every semester. The only poem they had ever chosen to memorize was "Invictus," by the otherwise fine English poet William Ernest Henley. Or rather, they were capable of recalling only the last stanza:

It matters not how strait the gait,
How charged with punishments the scroll.
I am the master of my fate:
I am the captain of my soul.

It was understandably hard to see God when you had been struggling with a terrible childhood disease your whole life as Henley had, but these bright yet so easily deceived neo-Marxists had hijacked his poem, and his suffering, to advance their humanist agenda to glorify man instead of God. Of course, when offered an equally beautiful poem that lifted God up to his rightful position, they couldn't handle it.

The Present Crisis, written by the American poet James Russell Lowell, was one of Jack's favorite poems in this regard. Lowell was a Harvard professor and several years older than Henley. In the body of this wonderful poem, he wrote:

Truth forever on the scaffold,
Wrong forever on the throne,
Yet that scaffold sways the future, and,
behind the dim unknown,
Standeth God within the shadow,
keeping watch above his own.

God the Father and creator of all things tells us repeatedly in his book that he loves us and desires a healthy relationship with us. He watches over us, wants what's best for us, and pursues us like a good father should, Jack pondered in amazement. *So why would someone reject that kind of love?*

C. S. Lewis, before his extraordinary conversion to Christianity, believed God was the great "transcendental Interferer." In Surprised by Joy, he wrote, "No word in my vocabulary expressed deeper hatred than the word *Interference*." Lewis used his atheism to satisfy his desire to be left alone.

Jack could not help but notice this same need to be free from any interference in virtually all of his shortsighted, self-centered, worldly students. In effect, they were willing to reject God's love in order to satisfy their own twisted, unhealthy lifestyles.

Whenever Jack found himself in the midst of developing many of his Christian responses to modern-day criticisms of faith in the God of the Bible, he would almost always reference C. S. Lewis. It was Lewis's knack for supplying natural, commonsense answers to some difficult doctrinal questions by combining brilliantly reasoned logic with poetic tenderness that appealed to Jack's sensibilities.

In Mere Christianity, C. S. Lewis encapsulated Jack's heart beautifully when he wrote:

> If I find in myself a desire which no experience in this world can satisfy, the most probable explanation, is that I was made for another world. If none of my earthly pleasures satisfy it... that does not prove the universe is a fraud. Probably, earthly pleasures were never meant to satisfy it, but only to arouse it... to suggest the real thing.

> If that is so, I must take care, on the one hand, never to despise, or be unthankful for these earthly blessings, and on the other hand, never mistake them for the something else of which they are only a copy, or echo, or mirage.

Bam! *Kapow*! Like the childish verbs in the little star-burst word bubble of Jack's old Batman comic books, this hit him as making perfect sense. The fallen nature of a man would always be disappointed with the circumstances in his life, regardless of whether he experienced great things or extreme emptiness, because they were never intended to be the source of fulfillment. It always fascinated Jack to observe how the most fortunate among us suffered the hardest from this phenomenon and would, therefore, benefit the most from the tender mercies of a loving God. Of course, this could not be more true than right here at Hillary.

Again, C. S. Lewis concluded his thoughts this way:

> I must keep alive in myself the desire for my true country, which I shall not find till after death. I must never let it get snowed under or turned aside. I must make it the main object of life to press on to that country and help others do the same.

It was this final instruction to "help others do the same" that had caused most of Jack's distress since coming to Hillary. Since accepting Jesus Christ as his Savior at the age of sixteen, Jack had felt a longing to be personally welcomed into his true country (heaven) by the one true God himself. That desire also made the imperative to "help others do the same" a primary goal of his in life. But how could an infinitely wise and infallible God possibly think that any of this could be accomplished here at Hillary, when Jack found himself being "snowed under" with each passing day? Jack could not contain his deep anguish and long-suffering regrets any longer.

"God speak to me. Reveal my purpose!" Jack cried out, more loudly than he anticipated.

"It will all be revealed to you if you want it," a voice offered from behind.

Jack spun around excitedly to find an older gentleman sitting motionless in the guest chair in front of his desk. Even though the man was seated, Jack could tell that he was a tall, powerfully built man. His graying, well-trimmed beard; soft, penetrating eyes; and casual dress reminded Jack of a few sage professors he had come to know and respect through the years. This image had a calming effect that almost immediately put him at ease with this stranger.

"Whoa... hey... well, I didn't hear you come in... through the door I distinctly remember locking a few minutes ago," Jack spoke, slightly embarrassed by his effusive "reveal my purpose" comment.

"It is still locked," the stranger answered matter-of-factly, and then continued warmly. "Do not be afraid, Jack. You have been granted a wonderful opportunity."

"More startled than afraid... if you want to know," Jack responded after a brief moment to collect himself.

"You seem to be serious about your purpose in life and what the one true God thinks about it, Jack," the stranger continued amicably.

"I absolutely do take it seriously," Jack answered with a hint of self-righteousness.

Slowly Jack began to move away from the windows and toward the door. He casually walked past his uninvited guest and was now standing behind him. The stranger was generally disinterested in where Jack was going and remained seated, content with looking out the windows. As inconspicuously as he could manage, Jack tested to see if the door was indeed locked. It was. Not wishing to get into a confrontation with someone who could apparently walk through locked doors, yet not quite ready to over-react to it, Jack continued his walk around the room and back to his desk.

"Why do you ask?" Jack inquired as he plopped down into his seat, not wanting to come off as being rude to this kindly old locksmith... and maybe see another trick or two.

"Well, I wonder why you think you do not belong here and that God's true purpose for your life could be satis-fied only by pastoring a church," the stranger inquired. "Even if that unfortunate church might lie in Appalachia somewhere."

"Wow, do you know that I used that same imagery to illustrate a frustration of mine just a few days ago?" Jack admitted.

"Yes, I do," the stranger again answered matter-of-factly, and then added sadly, "I also know you once had a won-derful passion for the lost and broken right here, even going so far as praying for them."

Okay, now things are getting a little weird, Jack thought. *First this guy walks through a locked door, and now he's rolling out stuff about me like some kind of accountability partner. What's next—pulling a rabbit out of his hat?*

"Did MJ send you over here to freak me out?" Jack asked in an attempt to get his brain wrapped around this peculiar conversation. "Because if she did, I have already apologized to her for being an inconsiderate jerk."

Jack felt no compelling reason for continuing to talk to the man other than the guy appeared to have some basic understanding and apparently genuine concern for the direction Jack's life was now headed. Jack had to admit that he had not felt this kind of paternal interest since he was a kid.

"No, Jack, she did not. Although Joy's commitment to you and your walk with the Lord has not wavered since you were sixteen," the stranger remarked. "And I think she would approve of the opportunity being offered to you now."

There it is, Jack thought. *He pulled the rabbit out of the hat. How would he know about MJ and my acceptance of Jesus Christ when I was sixteen? It's impossible—impossible.*

"I have to be honest," Jack began. "I have enjoyed meeting you—I have. You seem like a nice fellow with... um... wow... some unusually familiar insight into my life. But I'm not quite sure I know what's going on here, so forgive me if I seem rushed. You must understand, with less than three weeks to go before classes begin, I am pressed for time. So if it is all right with you, I promise to give you my absolute fullest attention for the next five or ten minutes to allow you to make your presentation, but then I must get back to work. Please tell me, what is this wonderful opportunity of yours?" Jack asked politely as he glanced at his watch.

"To reveal God's purpose for your life, Jack," the stranger answered with absolute authority.

The words that came forth from the stranger's lips carried with them such supernatural power that they alone caused Jack to fall weakly into the back of his chair and rendered him incapable of speech. The stranger did not move a muscle, and neither did his eyes leave their comforting watchfulness over him. After a brief pause, he continued as Jack sat comfortably incapacitated.

"Tomorrow, in the courtyard, there will appear a large stone-like object, pure white and without blemish. Go to it at sunset. Once there, you and your travel partner will be given an understanding of what to do."

The stranger said no more but maintained a caring vigil over Jack. Several minutes passed after this odd instruction, and still Jack could not speak or properly address the stranger's offer, although his mobility gradually returned to him. Needing a little more time to contemplate his response, Jack rose carefully from his chair and drifted over to the windows. The complexion of the courtyard two stories below had not changed much since he moved away from this spot only moments ago, except now there was one lone person standing with his back to him several hundred feet down the Yard's center trail. Jack was somewhat relieved to have something, or someone, to occupy the thoughts that overwhelmed him.

The longer Jack watched the man outside, however, the more fascinated with him he became. The man stood stone still and hunched forward slightly as if absorbed in something directly in front of him. He wore a long herringbone overcoat and had both hands buried deep into its pockets. The collar was turned up around his ears so that only the top of his head was visible from Jack's viewpoint. This would not have been so unusual or interesting except that the mild autumn temperatures outside did not justify such a heavy coat and most certainly did not warrant a posture that suggested the man was stalled in the middle of a windstorm. Jack continued watching and waiting for the man to move.

Finally, with his full attention still on the stone figure outside, Jack asked the sagacious stranger seated behind him the only thing that made sense.

"Are you an angel?"

The improbable question was addressed to the one seated inside, but without Jack's turning, it gave the impression he was actually talking to the one standing outside.

What was that? Jack thought almost immediately after releasing the question.

"You twitched," Jack whispered softly to the man in the herringbone overcoat standing outside. "Yes, I saw you. You definitely twitched."

The movement was almost imperceptible, but Jack had been focused long enough that nothing about the man would have escaped his attention. By this time, Jack had completely forgotten about the old man seated behind him. All that mattered now was whether or not the human statue in the center trail had come to life.

There it is again, Jack noticed with a satisfying grin, his persistence paying off.

It was unmistakable now: the outdoor figure in the overcoat was indeed alive. His motions were agonizingly slow, but the man finally straightened his back and was now standing fully erect. Then both hands exited the pockets together at a more natural speed, reached up, turned down the collar of the overcoat with a slight jerk, and returned to his side. The man now stood motionless once again but still faced away from Jack.

"You can turn around now," Jack pleaded, but the man did not budge.

"Who are you?" Jack finally asked impatiently.

As if finally responding to Jack's requests, the man in the courtyard slowly rotated both head and shoulders around from the torso and stared back directly into Jack's eyes. It was the stranger!

Jack spun around only to find seated in the guest chair a large box marked "Important/Mnemonic Strategies Class Material—Crush, Misplace, or Discard and Death Awaits You!"

Perched on top of the box was a small stuffed animal, a red bird with a large black uni-brow. Jack stood there astonished at what had happened. He spun around again and returned his attention to the Yard—nothing. No one as far as the eye could see—the stranger had vanished.

"Wow, MJ is not going to believe this," Jack sighed.

4

Hitch's Dream

"**D**id you pass anyone on your way in here?" Hitch grumbled in Ms. Brown's direction as he continued casing the room for the missing intruder.

"I did not, Professor," Ms. Brown replied calmly. "That would imply I allowed someone to enter, which I did not."

"Well, I am just as certain that I have been in conversation with someone for the last half an hour, Ms. Brown!" Hitch spoke sharply. "How he got in here does not concern me right now."

"Would you like for me to contact security?" Ms. Brown offered.

She would have already made the call to campus security personnel immediately after receiving the professor's frantic text messages except that she knew how intensely protective he was of his privacy. Hitch had obstinately rejected all her pleas for the installation of security cameras inside their offices, or at least in the labyrinth of hallways. He had only begrudgingly accepted the use of these devices outside the building because police and fire rescue services dictated it. Ms. Brown had always felt it was only a matter of time before some lunatic attempted to prove a point by doing harm to a vulnerable celebrity like the professor. This was one of the many reasons she had trained for, and received, a concealed-carry license. A loaded revolver, aptly called the "Judge," was in her purse at all times. This was exactly the reason she carried her purse with her now.

"You may contact security to see if our cunning trespasser has gotten himself lost inside the building, but I do not wish to discuss this with anyone or pursue the matter further even if he is caught!" Hitch stated emphatically. "Is that understood?"

"I understand perfectly. Would you like to provide a description of the person you were in conversation with?" she asked politely.

"How many intruders do you think they will find, Ms. Brown?" he replied curtly.

When Ms. Brown returned this unwarranted sarcasm with frigid silence and a bone-chilling look, Hitch knew he had gone too far. He had seen that face before, and no number of mind-reading necromancers could cause more havoc to his way of life than to have Ms. Brown angry with him, especially when her irritation could be perceived as justifiable. He had to acknowledge that without any supporting evidence, his story of a mysterious intruder did lack some credibility. To restore peace and avoid certain retribution later, he quickly sought to diffuse the present situation.

"I'm sorry, Ms. Brown," Hitch stated apologetically. "I do not mean to suggest that any of this was your fault. This experience has been rather disconcerting, as you can imagine. As a consequence, I have even less time to accomplish all of what you have rightfully requested of me today."

That should do the trick, he thought shrewdly.

"I will have security investigate without mentioning your name," she stated flatly and turned to leave.

Yes, another masterful extrication from a pile of crap of my own creation, he thought with some sense of pride.

"I still need that syllabus... without the excuses, if you please," she added without looking back and left.

Satisfied with conjuring up as much remorse as was necessary, Hitch began to remove himself mentally from this latest episode so that he barely heard Ms. Brown's closing petition. Instead, he found himself at a crossroads once again. Should he get back to the many important things (that had now become urgent) or waste even more precious time attempting to resolve this new mystery put before him?

He determined swiftly and prudently not to make the same mistake that had produced his mysterious guest—real or imagined—in the first place. Whatever event was to take place as a result of his meeting with the *mind-reading necromancer* would not occur until tomorrow evening, as he recalled. This gave him over a day to contemplate the preposterous yet irresistibly intriguing, wonderful opportunity presented to him. The syllabus, on the other hand, was promised by noon today, giving him only a few short hours to conceive it and then complete it.

Admittedly, Hitch actually enjoyed these annual one-day lectures for the university and the excitement it generated. Having over two thousand people jam themselves into an ancient lecture hall to listen to what was on his mind was, to the best of his understanding of the term, *humbling*. It made little difference to him that most of them were no more than rich, peevish little brats with pathetically indulgent parents, since boosting his own ego

61

was an aspect that had become less and less important to him anyway. He could have easily filled any of the new ten-thousand-seat auditoriums across campus, if he had wanted. All that mattered to him now was that he was being listened to. In fact, the only thing that bothered him more than his unwelcome sense of loneliness was irrelevance.

However, Hitch was currently hotter and more in demand than ever. Through the years, he had developed an uncanny ability to choose such compelling topics and deliver such entertaining discourses for these intimate little get-togethers that many other campuses around the country joined in the online webinar discussions that ensued. He was quoted often enough by *Rolling Stone* and *Time* magazines soon after these annual performances that it would not surprise him if they had a reporter embedded in his audience, and that Dr. Stansbury had provided the tickets. The attention given him and his lectures would in turn strike a chord with the general public and initiate a slew of invitations to appear on the national cable networks to get his perspective on the topic he originated weeks earlier. It energized him to know that the world was changing rapidly in his favor.

The question now was, what would the country want to talk about over the next three to six months?

Quantum mechanics and mathematics were, of course, Hitch's bread and butter, but the necessity to dummy down these dynamic subjects for general consumption was never enjoyable to him. Astrophysics and astrobiology were both enjoyable, but pretty pictures from the Hubbell Space Telescope or NASA's Curiosity rover on Mars and the assorted theories attached to them didn't generate the emotional fascination the public demanded these days— unless, of course, they could capture another life-threatening comet strike like that which occurred on Jupiter in 1994.

Politics and philosophy were of great interest to him. Unfortunately, the men and women who occupied the most powerful political positions on the planet and the so-called journalists that should be impartially examining the effect they were having on its inhabitants had become so com-mingled and intertwined that any attempt to debunk their ineptitude and insufferable behaviors bordered on impos-sible for now. The empty-suited politicians and their cro-nies in media had become no better than empty-headed Hollywood celebrities, and were best left to the late-night comedians for the cheap laughs they deserved.

Oh, what I wouldn't do for another Karl Marx–like per-sonality or the devil himself to arise and shake things up, Hitch thought.

Then there was God and man—or more accurately, "man's invention" and man. This topic moved up a notch in the selection process with the promise of a resolution to his Irrefutability Theory, even though the promise may have come from a madman. Admittedly, the subject had been clearly on his mind prior to the stranger's appear-ance, though.

This was the part that actually caused so much of the delay. It wasn't the compilation of data to support the sub-ject once the subject was chosen. In fact, he could summon a dozen or more graduate students at a moment's notice, all clamoring to do his research so that they might be rec-ognized for it. The delay was more in the choosing of the topic itself. Inspiration had a lot to do with it, but inspi-ration under pressure produced the best results, so he waited. The last thing Hitch wanted to do was jump onto something that had already reached its peak of interest and, like the star running out of its own fuel, would soon go supernova and die. Summer subjects were unpredictable like that. Besides, there were few matters of global significance that Hitch had not already meticulously researched, formed an opinion on, and could discuss extemporaneously for hours.

Hitch also enjoyed the anticipation of a serious Face-to-face debate in the weeks that followed his lecture—not so much from the insipid questioning of a bubbleheaded cable news babe, but rather, from the occasional learned professional who wanted nothing more than to trip up the reigning genius. Unfortunately for these intrepid antagonists, Hitch was on top of his game, and to debate him once his current position was fully developed was a futile exercise.

There was always good reason for this. Hitch was never so arrogant or dogmatic as to ignore or attempt to hide trustworthy information to fit some preconceived conclusion. He often referred to this deficiency as the "Gore principle." This was a man he had voted for, but unfortunately, the man had conveniently succumbed to his love of power and money at the expense of truth. As a result of Hitch's commitment to the truth, whenever the steady stream of data brought to his attention was determined by him to be more reliable than what was currently being used, Hitch found no fault in altering a previously held belief to reflect this new information, and to do so without hesitation. This was true even if it contradicted his current position. He firmly believed it was incumbent on him to do so because of his perceived authority as a leader. Ms. Brown considered this personal integrity to be the professor's finest quality.

Therefore, the best others could hope to accomplish when questioning or debating Hitch was to portray these corrections as flip-flopping. Should this insult occur during the course of a debate, rather than argue, he calmly borrowed a technique from Muhammad Ali's playbook, known to all boxing fans as "rope-a-dope." He would allow his overzealous opponents to throw yesterday's data and blind ideology at him until they exhausted themselves. When the flailing of these bygone ideas came to an end, Hitch would pause briefly, as if to give his opponent's viewpoint consideration. This was used only for effect, because Hitch knew almost immediately after his opponent opened his mouth exactly which strategy was going to be presented and whose data they had based their opinions on; their weakness was almost always in the data. In a few of these cases, Hitch might have even used the same information to support his work for a time. When this coincidence occurred in the course of a debate, Hitch would begin his countering remarks with the mocking phrase, "I believed that... once."

He may have used this prefatory statement only once or twice before it became his signature catchphrase, much like the late astrophysicist Carl Sagan was caricaturized for having once uttered "billions and billions." In any case, Hitch's rebuttal was swift, merciless, and complete. Still, he made an extraordinary effort to dismantle the evidence and not the person. Ms. Brown could not help but notice how challenging this struggle with arrogance within in the professor's DNA makeup was and appreciated these efforts to be "nice."

It did not take long before Hitch had his topic. As a tribute to the great Professor Freud, he would make *"the opium of the people,"* the world's infinite number of religions, his subject. With the ever-evolving insanity in the Middle East and the Christian chatter of mankind being in the end times, a reasoned discussion on the absurdity of all religions should liven things up. In fact, all he needed was a murderous bombing of innocent bystanders, or better yet, a missile attack on Israel and the subsequent bloody retaliation to occur while he was in Austria as a guest of the University of Vienna, for his choice to become a perfect storm. What could be more predictable than man's insanity towards man?

Unfortunately, this choice would also limit the opportunities to use his "I believed that... once" signature catchphrase, because his unbelief in God was a position he had not yet found any justification to alter.

It took less than an hour to outline his thoughts and shoot them off to Ms. Brown for editing, with a side note that he did not want to be disturbed prior to their meeting in the afternoon. This left him with an hour and a strong urge for a power nap. He found the only administrative meetings worth paying attention to at all were those he had with Ms. Brown, and he needed a clear mind to keep up with her. A quick check of his smartphone confirmed Ms. Brown's promise to keep his schedule open for the day. Once again, with all the knowledge he possessed, Hitch could not fathom what would become of him without Ms. Brown. If forced to admit it, to him she would be the only evidence of a merciful God. And damn to the darkest regions of hell the man who should cause her to fall in love and leave him.

The brief rest accomplished its desired effect, and Hitch's meeting with Ms. Brown went flawlessly, even though he thought he heard her sigh when given the topic. Regardless, her thoughtfulness in having his favorite dish of eggplant Parmesan over angel hair pasta with a bowl of cream-of-crab soup delivered shortly after the beginning of their meeting only reinforced his opinion of her as being an angel sent from heaven, if there were such a thing.

Except for the occasional feeling of being watched, so went the remainder of his day: busy and productive. By nightfall he was exhausted. Nothing mattered to him now but a good night's sleep; not even his meeting with Dr. Stansbury in the morning bothered him. The intensity of the day may have been intended for the mind to receive and resolve, but the stress had filtered down into every bone in his body instead, and his bed never looked more inviting.

This soreness did not come as a surprise. He had taken the summer off, and he was rusty. Much like Major League Baseball's use of spring training in Florida (aka the Grapefruit League) to recondition the players after a winter's break, Hitch knew it would take several days of cerebral practicing for this problem to go away. So for now, the best remedy from this preseason discomfort was to allow his head to sink deep into his thick down pillow and his body to maneuver into its most favorable position in his spacious bed. This would allow the "grapefruit between the ears" to shut down all systems except those essential for sustaining life and to begin to relax his stress-induced muscles.

Hitch could not tell when sleep finally overtook him, but when next his eyes were open, he was immersed in a blinding white light and utter silence. So intense was this light that it took several seconds of consciousness to see an outline of the hand he had positioned only a few inches from his face in a vain attempt to shield his eyes from the brilliance. The whiteness soon gained color and form, and from the silence came sound. It did not take long, however, for his senses to go from nothingness to being bombarded with a tapestry of dazzling color and the melding of every kind of noise that, when combined suddenly, produced a momentary state of confusion.

Fortunately, Hitch had the presence of mind to surmise two details of his current predicament that relieved some of this anxiety. The most obvious detail was his location: he was thankfully on solid ground and standing inside an ancient outdoor stadium of some sort, perhaps in Italy or Greece. The most important detail, however, was his circumstance: he was most certainly dreaming this.

This was no phony reenactment being performed in the ruins of some historic building. Hitch had indeed been transported into a well-maintained, beautifully marbled coliseum that bustled with thousands of people in ancient clothing going about their lives in ancient fashion. Even though he maintained all the working knowledge of a twenty-first-century physics professor, it was difficult to know exactly which one of the great coliseums it was, because he had arrived inside the belly of the massive structure.

All around him, Hitch could see vendors hawking their goods and services from wooden stalls as far as the eye could see. Next to each of these stalls were portals leading inside to the spectator seating, similar to modern-day football stadiums. The area behind him was wide open and sloped gently uphill. There were no boundary walls, no gates, and no ticket counters or manned turnstiles to prevent anyone, rich or poor, from attending the events inside the stadium.

If only I could find a coin, a mosaic, or even a child's toy, I might be able to make out the place and time, Hitch thought as he looked about more purposefully.

Almost immediately in his search for a clue, Hitch noticed a towering figure standing near one of the portals some distance away who appeared to be staring directly at him. The giant man stood there motionless, head and shoulders above the crowd. The constantly moving stream of people prevented Hitch from standing in one spot for very long without being picked up and deposited a few feet in one direction or another by the human tide. Apparently, a soldier, the frighteningly large and ominous creature, was now obviously tracking Hitch's every movement.

Hitch tried to avert direct eye contact in the event he was somehow in trouble with the law. However, from a series of indirect glances at the soldier, Hitch was able to put together his first clue as to where he might be. The man wore on his head a helmet, but not any helmet. It was made of bronze with a line of distinctive feathering running along its crest from front to back. The shell had a long, sloping iron trim to protect the neck. A short, narrower piece of iron followed the ridge of the nose, and there were large cheek plates hinged at the top to protect the face. The helmet and that part of the body armor covering the top of the shoulders were all that Hitch could make out from his vantage point, but it was enough. He was in Rome, and this huge brute was a Roman legionary.

Well then, that narrows this place down to the Circus Maximus or the Roman Colosseum, Hitch surmised, not having been in either one before now—at least not while he was awake.

Impatient with the separation between them, the soldier was now calling out to Hitch and waving him towards himself and the portals. Unfortunately, even if Hitch's relaxed, twenty-first-century efforts to move in Goliath's direction were successful, it would still take some time to close the gap against the flow of the crowd. Eventually the soldier came to the same conclusion and proceeded to assert his authority. With a few "out of my way(s)," he was standing in front of Hitch in seconds. Hitch's guess proved accurate; the apron of metal plates riveted to thick leather straps of various lengths draped over a tunic, the leather sandals woven halfway up the shin, and of course the long double-edged sword on the right and the short dagger on the left, in addition to the helmet, were all standard legionary attire.

"My lord, it might please you to know the emperor does not like to be kept waiting!" the soldier barked forcefully.

Now that Hitch knew he wasn't going to be flogged for some mishap that he was not aware of, he had to smile to himself when he imagined this gorilla looking at his forearm for a watch that would prove how late they were going to be, but the missing thing would not be invented for another couple of thousand years. His lightheartedness faded when he suddenly realized that this killing machine was his escort to see the emperor of Rome, whoever that was.

Great, I answer one question only to be given another that requires an even more immediate solution, Hitch thought. *Let's see... how many of these lunatics do I have to choose from?*

He was quickly becoming annoyed with the direction of this dream.

What does the start of another school year and a few aching muscles have to do with Rome anyway? he asked himself. *Well, two can play at this game.*

"And which emperor do you serve, mule?" Hitch inquired in a calm, slightly pompous voice. He didn't intend to say *mule*, but in his irritation, it came out.

What's the difference? It's only a dream, he reasoned.

"My life, and that of all Rome, belongs to Emperor Nero Claudius Caesar Augustus Germanicus," the soldier replied boldly and without hesitation.

The legionary wasn't quite sure what this little philosopher and new advisor to his emperor meant by *mule*, but he didn't like the sound of it. His right hand slipped unconsciously to the hilt of his sword.

Nero! Hitch thought. *Okay, he ascended to the throne as a teenager, a popular guy until he went crazy and had his mother whacked for nothing more than meddling; during the fire in AD 64, he was said to have played the fiddle, which, of course, wasn't invented yet; he ordered the only sane person left in town, Seneca, to commit suicide on trumped-up conspiracy charges... just my luck.*

"And what year is it, soldier?" Hitch asked in a much kinder voice.

"The tenth year of the reign of Emperor Nero," came the angry response. "My lord, we do not have time for these simple games. This theatrical rot will soon be over, and the event you were commanded to attend is next. We must hurry!"

What the soldier didn't say was that, emperor's advisor or not, they would be on time if he had to strap Hitch to his back and carry him the rest of the way.

Tenth year, Hitch grimaced. *Okay, he ascended to the throne in AD 54 after his mother poisoned her husband, Claudius, who happened to be the emperor of Rome at the time; Mom is now dead; the great fire of '64 occurred last year; Seneca is probably dead as well. So who am I to Nero?*

He was about to ask his obviously distressed escort just that, but decided not to push his luck.

"Take me to Nero!" Hitch commanded.

As soon as they had breached the portal to the seating area, Hitch knew he was standing in the astonishingly beautiful Circus Maximus. Its long oval shape and marvelous center spina with its seven large sculpted eggs on one end, seven large bronze dolphin-shaped lap counters on the other, and Augustus's obelisk in the middle were as unique as any structure in antiquity and perfectly suited for the great Roman pastime of chariot racing.

Nero did a nice job of cleaning up after himself. Hard to tell this place burned down along with half the city last year, Hitch thought.

I wonder... would it change the course of history if I were to explain to Mr. Nero that I come from the future and murdering Christians isn't going to be enough to shift all this responsibility?

Hitch chuckled again.

This is the second time this spineless aristocrat has laughed at me, the legionary thought. *When Nero decides to rid himself of this insolent fool, I hope it will be by my sword and not a coward's poison, like with Seneca.*

It was the legionary's turn to chuckle.

The Circus had the capacity to seat 150,000 spectators, and today every seat in the house was taken. Dream or not, it took Hitch's breath away to be among so many people assembled in one massive arena built by an artisan's hand, not by gas-powered machines. The crowd appeared in a frenzied mood over what they had seen or in anticipation of what was to come... the event he was commanded to watch with Nero. The last of the musicians, dancers, jesters, and jugglers were exiting by the grand arch to his left, which caused the crowd to become even more animated. To his right, built into the first-tier terrace so as to be closest to the action, was the imperial box and the impressively ornate Pulvinar, or shrine to the gods. This is where Nero would be enjoying the show and was to be Hitch's destination. After a few more twists and turns, he came to a halt at its rear opening.

"Well, my clever administrator has finally arrived," a voice spoke from in front of one of the two oversized, high-backed chairs at the front of the room. "The Circus does not meet with your mythically high standards that I must order you to partake in its pleasures?"

Okay, Seneca must be dead, and I am now the emperor's new puppet, Hitch thought.

"If you have seen one chariot race, you have seen them all, my glorious emperor," Hitch responded, assuming he was speaking to Nero and not knowing exactly what else to say.

"Oh no, my dear Hitch, there are no races today." Nero laughed and patted the arm of the empty seat next to him. "Come now, sit beside me and speak more words of wisdom while we wait for the far superior entertainment to begin."

Hitch was given a final, unfriendly nudge by his soldier companion to begin moving forward. As he approached the plush chairs, he could hear the soft, pleasant sound of a tenor's voice, accompanied by the skillful strumming of a stringed instrument. It was a little disconcerting that in a room that could easily accommodate a hundred or more people, there were only the two chairs, each positioned inches from the other, centered and pushed as far forward as they could go.

I appear to be Nero's only guest for the evening, Hitch thought. *And he brought his fiddle—how delightful.*

In this same brief moment of levity, Hitch became intensely curious to see if the face of Nero was the same as those he remembered on the old marble statues, or if his dream would transform it into the face of someone else more contemporary to him, like maybe Elton John, weird glasses and all. He rounded the right-side chair and sat down, but his moment of amusement and curiosity instantly vanished from his mind when the great multitude of people that surrounded him became so vivid and so real that he found it impossible to take his eyes off them. He could literally look into any one of the 150,000 faces and see the person in astonishing detail and without duplication. To test this new acute ability to recall so many different faces, Hitch would look away and come back moments later without having any of the person's features change or blur, over and over and over again.

How is it possible for my mind to create so much singularity? Hitch mused. *This is almost too real.*

It was then that Hitch noticed possibly another fifty thousand or more who had gathered on the slopes of the adjacent hill outside the stadium.

"Gladiators, then?" Hitch asked, still in awe and without even fully intending to ask anything at all.

At this inquiry, Nero amended his perpetual serenade on the lyre and came to a more natural and pleasing conclusion.

"Better," Nero answered with sinister delight. "Christians!"

"What about them?" Hitch asked nervously.

"For an acclaimed scholar of stately matters, you can be utterly dense sometimes," Nero puffed with some irritation. "You are about to witness a perfect and worthy punishment. It will be justly imposed upon those who have destroyed Roman property, who continue to corrupt the minds of many innocent people of Rome, and, greatest of all treasons, dare to worship someone other than their benevolent emperor!"

As Nero spoke these words, trumpets sounded and a large number of forlorn-looking people began streaming aimlessly into the arena through the giant arch to the left. Many were bent over and having a difficult time walking a straight line, but they were prodded along to one side of the center spina or the other by the tip of a legionary's spear. All of them were filthy dirty and dressed in ragged sackcloth tunics. Some appeared to be cloaked in the hides of various types of animals, with heads still attached that flopped back and forth across their shoulders as they struggled to walk.

As the ill-treated creatures on the right drew closer to the imperial box, Hitch thought he heard singing, or at least an almost joyful noise rising up from their direction, but it was difficult to be sure because of the crowd noise. As he strained to hear what they were saying, he believed he heard the words *forgive them* or something like that several times as they passed him on their way to the flat end of the Circus where the chariots would normally enter the arena. Surprisingly, Hitch found himself feeling a profound sense of compassion for these dream people. Then a sudden and pronounced gasp came from the crowd, and even a few trumpeters noticeably missed a beat.

"Children!" Hitch exhaled as a long, violent shiver coursed through his entire body. Unable to move a muscle, he watched while as many as a dozen families all huddled together slowly entered the arena.

The adults in this forsaken group clung tightly to their littlest ones but could not prevent them from looking about in ignorant fascination, oblivious to what was to be their fate. Once inside the arena, the one large group was forcibly divided into two smaller groups, half going to the left and the other to the right of the spina. Apparently, this abrupt split caused several children to become separated from their parents, and in their panic, they became hysterical. They were quickly ushered to the center of their new smaller group before a soldier could get to them. As these families shuffled down both sides of the Circus, Hitch observed many women in the stands faint into the arms of those next to them, incapable of processing the horror of this unimaginable cruelty to a mother and her child. The small family group driven to the right side of the arena settled in a spot below the imperial box.

When the last of these desperate Christians were inside the arena and evenly dispersed around the raceway, the soldiers moved quickly to exit through the arch, and its large gates were closed and locked. Understanding completely what was about to occur, and sickened by it, Hitch decided he had seen enough. He was about to excuse himself and finish out this dream in a Roman bathhouse somewhere when Nero stood up and the whole world hushed.

"Citizens of Rome," Nero addressed the now subdued crowd with arms open wide. With mock sadness in his voice, he continued. "There comes a time when we all must choose whom we will serve. The answer will ultimately determine our happiness or suffering, riches or poverty, kinship or isolation, life or death. That time has arrived for the malcontented you see before you."

He paused to allow that thought to simmer with the crowd. Leaning forward slightly allowed him to direct his gaze down into the arena. The Christians, most of whom were kneeling and could now be heard praying, seemed disinterested in what Nero had to say. This infuriated Nero.

"Rome has fed them and clothed them!" Nero's voice boomed angrily into the pit, momentarily interrupting many of those praying, yet his words were intended more for the crowd above than the Christians below.

"She has sheltered them and protected them." His voice grew louder, causing the crowds in the stadium to become more and more restless and agitated.

"She has embraced them and even loved them." Nero's voice grew louder still.

"And for this, they repay her with fire and ruin!" Nero boomed.

This, of course, was a lie, but it had been his mantra for the last year, and for the most part, the citizens of Rome had swallowed it hook, line, and sinker. The crowds, including those on the hillsides, were all on their feet now and cheering their beloved emperor. He had them.

"Will Rome die so easily?" Nero shouted over the renewed pandemonium.

The response was immediate and deafening.

"Long live Rome! Long live Nero!" the crowd chanted over and over.

Nero looked back at Hitch and smiled. Hitch returned his look in utter amazement and contempt. After a minute or so, Nero raised his hands to the crowd and allowed the chanting to subside. Patiently he waited. Finally, when he felt not even the gods could restrain themselves any longer, Nero cried out boldly.

"Rome will endure forever!"

With this the crowd erupted. Nero tossed the linen flag he held in his hand into the arena, signaling the beginning of the ultimate punishment for his Christian scapegoats. He calmly picked up his lyre and sat down. Before the cloth had even touched the ground, the stadium began filling with lions, lionesses, and their cubs. They poured in through the starting gates on the flat side of the Circus to Hitch's right. They all appeared so much larger than Hitch had remembered seeing in a zoo as a kid; even the cubs were exceptionally big. Once inside, the animals trotted around their human prey, sometimes crouching and staring, sometimes scuffling with each other over territory as they quickly moved around the raceway, but not yet attacking anyone.

This was all too much and much too real for Hitch. He was not going to watch anyone, especially children, being mauled, even in a dream. As he started from his seat, Nero gently laid a hand on his arm as if he knew what Hitch was thinking.

"Sit… and watch with me," Nero said softly. "After all, this was your idea."

"What did you say?" Hitch shot back, horrified by the accusation.

"Come now. It wasn't that long ago," Nero said. "You were quite persuasive."

"I would never order the slaughter of hundreds of innocent people!" Hitch cried out indignantly.

"Hundreds?" Nero laughed. "My dear counselor, you underestimate this Christian menace. While you dallied, we have put to death over a thousand already, in one form or another, and we have a thousand more where they came from. Their membership seems inexhaustible, and your remedy is the only reason you are here and Seneca is not."

Nero's chilling humor quickly turned serious.

"But you worry me when you talk of innocence. You are beginning to remind me too much of poor Seneca,"

Nero said with a disingenuous concern. "Will you follow too closely in his footsteps, Hitch?"

"This is murder!" Hitch shouted.

He attempted to stand once again, only this time he was met with the tip of a sword at his throat and instantly felt a searing pain. He was driven as far back into the seat as he could go, yet the sword continued a slow forward progress even further into his neck until he thought it would soon decapitate him. Out of the corner of his eye, he could see the sword's master. The sneer in the smile, the disdain in the eyes—it was the legionary.

This trained killer would know from experience exactly how much pressure it would take for his weapon to produce the greatest amount of pain before it severed an artery or performed a tracheotomy on demand, Hitch thought as the sweat escaped from every pore in his body. *And he would not think twice about quartering me if only his emperor would allow it.*

But this isn't real, he told himself. *Resist, wake up: do something you pathetic coward. It's nothing but an invention… a dream!*

"Why are they not attacking?" Nero screamed furiously.

It had been several minutes, yet not one person had been harmed by the lions. The Christians remained bowed in prayer.

Without warning, the lions appeared to double in size and in unison began leaping the ten-foot walls and into the crowd. Terror spread among those spectators not instantly crushed in the path of the surging lions. The lions apparently had no interest in anything but taking out as many people in the stands as quickly as they could. Not even those spectators outside the Circus Maximus were safe, as several of these deadly beasts did not slow their ascent to the uppermost terrace and then without hesitation leapt onto the adjacent hills beyond to continue their brutal assault. Spears shattered, swords cracked in half, and arrows splintered whenever they made contact with the animal's impenetrable bodies. Still, the Christians prayed—unharmed.

In an instant, several of these ferocious mutations were inside the imperial box, where the emperor's guards crumpled like rag dolls in the lions' powerful jaws, including the mighty legionary holding Hitch hostage. The largest of these gigantic lions now stood fixed only a foot or two away from Hitch's face, panting and snarling heavily. Nero was curled in a fetal position in his seat, untouched.

"Kill them, kill them!" Nero began to screech repeatedly, not realizing there was no one left alive within earshot. The giant lion stationed directly in front of Hitch turned his terrifying head toward Nero and let out such a thunderous roar that it rattled the stadium's terrace seating, collapsed the Pulvinar shrine, and forced Nero's chair backward several feet before it toppled over with Nero still in it. Upon impact, Nero tumbled head over heels right into the side of an immense lioness that still had the limp neck of a guard in her mouth. She instantly laid one of her massive paws on his chest, pinning him securely to the ground.

Satisfied with Nero's abrupt dethronement, the great lion shook his magnificent mane and returned his steely gaze to Hitch. There was not much Hitch could do but sit and wait for death. His whole body trembled uncontrollably, but for some strange reason, he did not feel the need to cower like Nero. In some respects, he was too angry for that—angry he had gotten caught up in this dream; angry that something inside of him could even birth such a heinous dream; angry that he was made to feel powerless; angry that his life had become such a lonely, unfulfilled mess.

He was so angry by now that he was ready to sock the big cat right in the kisser to end this charade, but instead, the two stared at each other. The lion was no longer huffing and puffing or even trying to be scary, for that matter. He stood there looking at Hitch. After a minute or so, Hitch broke the silence.

"What do you want, lion?" Hitch asked rhetorically.

"I want you, Edmond," the giant lion replied after a short pause.

With that, the giant lion turned and leapt back onto the raceway, as did the rest of the pride. Hitch stood up and watched as they all returned to their normal size and walked contentedly back toward the starting gates from which they had come in. The Christians were now on their feet, but the lions disregarded them and were gone. Hitch looked up to see the carnage left behind in the stands, then back down to the raceway.

"Christians, listen to me," Hitch yelled as loudly as he could, discovering the acoustics to be so good that his voice could have been heard throughout the Circus Maximus with only half the effort. When he noticed that every eye was on him, he continued. "Go home. Nero cannot hurt you anymore!"

"So, this is your doing, is it?" Nero labored to breathe but spoke bitterly. "I swear I will crucify every one of them—and you as their prophet."

Hitch turned and glared at Nero's crippled body still lying on the floor. Without any conscious effort, Hitch began a steady pace toward Nero until he was standing directly above him. There was no sign on his face that betrayed the hatred he had for the monster now lying incapacitated at his feet. Nero peered up at him spitefully, and in between the intermittent coughing and wheezing caused by his injuries, he emitted a low, snarling laughter.

To Nero's left lay the lifeless body of the legionary who had tormented Hitch from the beginning of this nightmare, and in his cold dead hand, the sword. Hitch bent over and with some effort relieved the heavy weapon from the grip of its cruel master. Standing upright once again and with both hands on the hilt, he raised it above his head so that the sharpened tip was pointed down in Nero's direction. Hitch could see his own distorted face in the hardened steel blade, and it awakened in him feelings of strength and courage he had never known before. He had never thought of himself as being a hero, but today, at this moment in time, he was going to set things right.

"You don't have the guts, Edmond," Nero hissed.

5

Flowers!

There came a knock at the door.

"Once upon a midnight dreary, while I pondered weak and weary," Jack called out. "Tis some visitor tapping at my chamber door, only this, and nothing more!"

Perhaps it was his son's stuffed Angry Bird, now safely relocated to the shelf overhead, that caused Jack to respond to the knock with a passage from "The Raven" by Edgar Allan Poe. He had been working diligently on his class work for a few hours since the mysterious visitation and was glad to have a little diversion.

"Nevertheless," a squawking reply came.

"Nevertheless?" Jack screamed in mocking outrage. "*Nevermore*, you rogue, the raven replies, 'Nevermore!'"

"Nevertheless," came the same reply.

Oh, you're good, Jack thought, knowing he was now being taunted just as the raven had taunted Lenore's spurned lover.

"Let my heart be still a moment and this mystery explore," Jack said. "Tis the wind and nothing more!"

"Nevertheless," came the anticipated reply.

"Okay, okay, you win," Jack surrendered. "Enter, and let's have a look at you, good raven."

Jack was hoping it was a returning student to tell him how they had fallen in love with great literature.

"It's locked," the unexpected reply came in a more natural tone. Jack now recognized the voice.

"Hold on, Charlie," Jack called out.

Just the man I wanted to see too, Jack thought.

Their relationship went back to the first day Jack set foot on Hillary soil. Charlie was officially the director of horticulture and the curator for the university. Unofficially, he was the lone ambassador for the kingdom of Christ on campus. He took both positions seriously.

As director, Charlie was not without considerable power and influence. His office had complete control over the care and maintenance of the ten-thousand-acre property, including the Grand Courtyard and the various rare collections located in and around the historic buildings. Although he was part of the university system, his directorship had total autonomy from the school's board of directors and its president. This position, and its sovereignty, had been established as yet another safeguard by the university's founding fathers. It provided the same checks and balances as the original documents that had saved the property from its own unscrupulous trustees in the past. The remainder of the school's property, including all buildings and infrastructure, was managed separately by the university's Facilities Maintenance Department.

According to the wishes of the founders, this directorship was to be a position for life, unless vacated voluntarily or as a result of blatant malfeasance. Charlie had been hand-picked by his predecessor, who had occupied the position for over fifty years. He was hired right out of the University of Colorado Boulder after earning doctorate degrees in both environmental engineering and law. It could be said that CU Boulder was considered by many to be one of a few "public" Ivy League schools in the country. Charlie had occupied this eclectic position of groundskeeper and historian for almost thirty years, though many had tried to have him removed.

As ambassador for Christ, Charlie took it upon himself to personally greet each new employee on their first day. He had performed this personally rewarding yet exhaustive act continuously for the past twenty-six of his thirty years at Hillary. With less than a handful of exceptions (all of which were out of his control), he had met them all. It did not matter to him whether the newcomer was hired to be a professor, a president, or a janitor.

On the day Jack arrived four years ago, Charlie showed up at his bottom-of-the-food-chain office door located in the basement of Turner Hall. He politely introduced himself with the understated title of "chief groundskeeper" and welcomed him to Hillary cheerfully and sincerely. At first, Jack thought it strange that the fabulously posh Hillary University would send out the lawn guys for the purpose of greeting its newcomers, only to discover later that Charlie was the only one greeting anyone, and no one had asked him to do it in the first place.

In fact, if the university could have stopped him, they would have done so. When the brief salutations were over and all of Jack's lingering questions were answered, Charlie cordially asked him if he would like to join him and a group of guys on Wednesday evenings in the Sanctuary for a Bible study, or if he might be interested in going to the upcoming Promise Keepers conference later in the year. It was, of course, this last piece of business that sent many a recently hired humanist scrambling to the university president or on occasion the Americans United for Separation of Church and State group, demanding Charlie be censored or fired, only to be told that it was out of their hands.

What Jack didn't know was that four years after being hired, Charlie had also been ready to quit. Much like Jack, Charlie felt a calling from God and questioned why he had ever come to Hillary in the first place. That's when God laid on Charlie's heart this modest greeting ministry, but only after Charlie finally yielded his intellectual need to be in control back over to God. You would think that should have been humbling enough for a man with two doctorate degrees, but then God, in his infinite wisdom and humor, gifted Charlie with the newly acquired Harvard phenomenon, Dr. Edmond Hitchinson, to be his first greeting.

"You stayed?" Charlie asked when Jack opened the door.

"I prefer charm over sterility any day," Jack replied.

Charlie's question was in reference to Jack's opting to stay where he was in the old historic buildings versus moving into the new facilities across campus.

"I hope you prefer a longer walk to your first class as well," Charlie pointed out.

"It will keep me in shape," Jack quipped. "I didn't know you were a fan of Poe."

"Grew up on him," Charlie said. "In Boy Scouts, some of us patrol leaders would recite 'The Tell-Tale Heart' at campfire and wait to see which of the new kids would wet themselves that night. The scoutmasters gave us extra latrine duty, should that occur and they found out, but it was worth it."

"Let me guess—Eagle Scout too?" Jack guessed again.

"Yes, I am an Eagle Scout," Charlie responded with pride, then chided, "Please let me know if you have trouble finding your way to your first class."

"Not sure I need your help there, but I did have something come up this morning that you might be able to help me with, if you have time?" Jack asked.

"Is this an emergency, Jack?" Charlie asked with some concern.

"No, no, nothing like that," Jack replied.

"Okay, let's get together later in the week then," Charlie answered as he started for the door. "I only dropped by to say welcome back. Looks like you lost some weight this summer."

"Been running more," Jack mused, reminding him of his latest bout of selfishness and his resolute intention to get flowers for MJ tonight.

"By the way," Jack continued, "did you have anything to do with getting my new class approved for this school year? I know you and Dr. Stansbury are pretty tight, and well, call me Sherlock, but shortly after I gave you my new book to look over... *poof!*... I got a class."

It always amazed Jack how Charlie could tolerate, let alone befriend, their foul-mouthed president.

"Not sure what you mean, Jack," Charlie said with a big grin. "Well, must run myself. Have ten new people to greet today."

Now there goes a man's man, boys, Jack thought in admiration.

By the end of the workday, Jack felt mentally drained but comfortable that his new class would make a difference somehow. Driving home, all he could think about was spending some time loving on his wife over dinner and then hopefully making love to her when they returned home, if she was in the mood. It put a smile on his face thinking of the possibilities, when a sudden chill went down his back.

"Flowers!" Jack shouted as he immediately pulled the car over and came to a screeching halt. There were at least two upscale flower shops between school and home, but it wasn't until Jack rounded the last corner from the house that he remembered them.

Flowers are a game changer, Jack hypothesized anxiously.

Jack was no mathematician, but he knew this equation well, and it went something like this: no flowers + no mood = no romance. There were many more variables to this problem, but the main idea was to remove as many of the negatives as possible and replace them with as many positives as possible. He looked quickly at his watch.

There's still time, Jack thought thankfully.

He jammed his car into reverse and attempted one of those Hollywood 180-degree-stunt-car moves. He was able to pull off about half of it, but it was enough to get him in a direction that did not require him to put the car in reverse again.

Please, Lord, you knew this was going to happen, Jack prayed flippantly, yet continued with the prayer anyway. *Heck, I knew this was going to happen. Lord Jesus, please let the supermarket up the street have already received their weekly supply of fresh flowers today. Please let them last longer than a day. I pray this in Jesus' name. Amen.*

The supermarket did have a better than usual selection, except the roses he was after dropped petals like leaves off a tree in autumn. As he stood there contemplating the risk factor of being late just to drive to the closest flower boutique for fresh roses, he was approached by a store employee. After his brief "general admission" version of his reasons for wanting roses, the lady asked him what color he was looking for and disappeared into the back. She returned shortly thereafter, holding twelve short-stemmed roses sold as a bundle and twelve long-stemmed roses sold individually in the color he had requested.

"These came in today, and I haven't had time to put 'em out," she said apologetically. "Wasn't sure if you wanted the long stem or short, so I got both."

Jack was about to break into a Snoopy dance and explain to the nice lady the whole prayer-story thing, but decided a simple "thank you" for her kindness was adequate. He gave an internal shout-out to God for being who He always was, bought the long-stemmed roses, and headed home.

He was greeted in the driveway by his two boys, who immediately tried to pick their dad up by the legs and pile drive him to the ground. Unfortunately for them, that would have to wait a few more years, as Dad simply peeled them off and tossed them backward a few feet. After several minutes of this "cling, peel, toss, repeat" horseplay, Jack asked them if they would do a "g-eye-normous" favor for Dad. At this point, he noticed his youngest son looking back at him with a deep sadness in his eyes.

"What's the matter, slugger?" he asked gently.

"He lost his Angry Bird, Dad," Jake answered for his brother.

"Oh really," Jack responded as he reached into the backseat of the car and pulled out his son's stuffed toy. "Well, guess who flew into my car at the stop sign back there?"

Joey grabbed his capricious friend out of Dad's hand and dashed back into the house, screaming for his mother.

"Okay then... you're welcome," Jack said to the thin air that formerly surrounded his youngest son.

"He can't fly, Dad," Jake said matter-of-factly about the stuffed toy.

"I know, but if I told your brother that I found his bird begging for change at the main intersection in town, it would have broken his heart," Jack said in all seriousness.

"Dad!" Jake said, not buying any of it.

"Okay, it looks like it's you and me, sport," Jack continued. "Let's huddle up."

He bent over at the waist and rested his hands on his knees as if he were the quarterback calling the next play. Knowing this game, Jake did likewise.

"I got Mom some flowers because girls like flowers from time to time," Jack began, raising his head and looking from side to side to see if anyone from the imaginary opposing team might be listening. "You with me so far?"

"Yup," Jake confirmed while looking from side to side.

"I want you to take these flowers in to Mom and say"— Jack paused to look from side to side again—"say, 'Dad wants to know if you will go out to dinner with him tonight.' Can you do that for me?"

"Yup." Jake grabbed the flowers and bolted into the house, screaming for his mother.

"Okay then... careful of any stickers," Jack said to the thin air that formerly surrounded his oldest son.

Jack would have preferred some rehearsal of the lines but figured it would be much more entertaining this way. He gathered the remainder of his stuff from the car and went inside. Once inside he followed the sound of pots and pans to the kitchen, where MJ was preparing dinner for the boys.

"Hey, sweetness," Jack whispered in her ear, and kissed her softly on the back of the neck.

"Hi, sweetheart," MJ replied, and then inquired, "So, if I understand this correctly, we are having these flowers for dinner, and you like girls. Is that about right?"

"Well, pretty much, unless you have something else in mind for dinner," Jack replied straight-faced while noticing the flowers already in a glass container on the counter. "I see my messenger has performed his task most expeditiously."

"Expeditiously, maybe; flawlessly, not so much," MJ spoke softly so as not to be overheard by the messenger. "If there was supposed to be a dozen, only eleven made it in."

"Yase, I knaw," Jack said in his best Antonio Banderas Spanish accent. He pulled the twelfth rose from behind his back and stuck it in his mouth sideways.

"Now we daunce," he spoke between clenched teeth.

He grabbed MJ's hand and waist and began to swing her around the kitchen in an exaggerated dance combination of waltzing and a Texas two-step, intentionally knocking an empty plastic cup and a wooden spoon from the countertop in the process. This freedom of motion and carefree silliness soon began to feel as though they were captive riders on a high- speed roller coaster. They giggled and swayed about the room for several minutes until, like all good coaster rides, the pace began to slow and signal the end of the ride was approaching.

He let the rose he was still holding between his teeth fall to the ground and brought MJ in closer to himself until they could feel each other's heart now beating more rapidly from the short but intense workout. Both of his arms were now wrapped around MJ's waist, and her head now rested comfortably on his chest as they continued their dance, barely moving. Jack released his hold on MJ enough to allow his head to drop and their lips to meet gently. He would have picked her up and carried her upstairs right then and there except for one little problem.

"Mom, I'm hungry," Jake interrupted.

Make that two little problems.

"I'm hungry too," Joey added.

To Jack's amazement, he watched MJ go from wife and lover to mom and nurturer instantaneously. For Jack, however, this process was going to take some time and would probably necessitate a shower... perhaps a cold one. To save precious time, they agreed that Jack would shower first while MJ completed the feeding frenzy, and then MJ would shower while Jack got the boys bathed and ready for bed. This initial phase to the evening's plan proceeded like clockwork, and they were on their way to dinner as soon as the neighbor arrived.

The Mediterranean café Jack chose was perfectly suited for the evening he imagined: unpretentious atmosphere, delightful food, and solitude. His intention to listen to whatever MJ wanted to talk about and thus enhance the romance equation began well—that is, until he decided to open his mouth.

"You're not going to believe...," Jack began, then hesitated.

What he was going to say next was "... what happened to me this morning."

After all, it was not every day you had someone in your room one minute only to have them reappear outside the next. But that would have made the conversation about him—again. This insignificant indiscretion would have most likely undone all that had been accomplished thus far in making MJ feel she was going to be the focus of all his attention tonight. Fortunately, he caught himself in time and was able to alter this critical opening statement without any trace of stupidity.

"... how much I have been looking forward to talking about you for a change," Jack continued honestly. "Without two extra pairs of eyes looking back at me, that is."

"Yeah, sometimes it seems there are more than two of them," MJ added.

It did not take long before Jack found himself immersed in the ups and downs of an extremely intelligent and highly motivated stay-at-home mom. If they had gone the route of most of their friends from Stanford, MJ would have earned her master's in business instead of a bachelor's, started a career, and trusted the public school system to raise the boys. After a lot of prayer, they decided the homeschool track suited their family best, with the understanding that they were sacrificing his-and-her Lexus convertibles every three or four years.

Although their time together was refreshing and relaxed, it soon became clear to Jack that the natural yet admittedly archaic ecosystem in which they decided to raise their kids had its own set of problems. MJ would have never demanded it; however, by the end of dinner, Jack had to acknowledge one thing. If he truly loved and appreciated the woman that God had blessed him with, he need only demonstrate that love by becoming a much better listener. She was capable of the rest.

The easy, uninterrupted conversation in which Jack encouraged MJ to do most of the talking had him almost forgetting about his fatigue and physical desire for his wife... well, maybe his fatigue, anyway. It was actually his wife who tenderly reminded him it was okay to head home. This suggestion was closely followed up with an "I am now yours" glance from her soft brown eyes and then punctuated with an "understand what I'm saying, big guy?" look from a slow-appearing, seductive half smile. Jack, now in total sync with everything his wife said and did, immediately requested the check to no one in particular and without ever taking his eyes off the face of the one who would forever be the cherished love of his life.

To help increase the odds that this final phase of their evening went according to plan, Jack actually turned off the engine and coasted the car into the driveway. He then took MJ by the hand, and they quietly slipped back into the house as stealthily as a couple of teenagers who had long since exceeded their curfew. It was encouraging to Jack to have MJ playing along with this whole cloak-and-dagger, boy-risks-all-for-girl, Romeo-and-Juliet performance of his. So soundlessly did they advance that it even startled their babysitting neighbor who had taken advantage of the peace and quiet of a house that was not her own and dozed off in the easy chair. After a few pleasantries, Jack politely ushered his neighbor home with many thanks and a jumbo piece of baklava from the café. A quick peek into the boys' room gave him some confidence that there was a low probability for interruption and that the fruits of the evening were his for the taking.

When Jack arrived at their bedroom, MJ was in the master bathroom, humming softly and doing whatever women do in preparation for bed.

"What exactly do they do in there that takes so long anyway?" Jack grumbled under his breath. "Use the toilet and brush your teeth—what else is there?"

6

Jack's Dream

R esigned to the fact that MJ could still take a while, Jack stripped down to his skivvies and made himself comfortable on the bed. A bit too comfortable it would seem, for the latent fatigue he had held in check so well for so long awoke inside him, and its fiendish accomplice, sleep, ensnared him. At some point, the dark emptiness of sleep relaxed its grip, and the artificial consciousness of a dream took over.

All too suddenly Jack found himself standing alone and off to the side of an enormous stage behind a magnificent set of long curtains that climbed upward into the darkness of the rafters without end. The air was filled with loud music and the exuberant voices of a large crowd, although he could not yet see the people in the audience from where he stood. The screaming guitars and pounding bass line had the feel of being at a rock concert except for one thing: there was no band. The stage was darkened slightly, and there was a dazzling light show of many colors in progress, but wherever the music was coming from, whether live or recorded, it was not being produced from anyone onstage.

In fact, there were only two objects that Jack could see on the massive stage. Front and center and standing on a raised platform stood a physically fit and handsomely dressed young man. His arms were outstretched as he directed and sang along with the crowd. Apparently, this raised platform was a pulpit of some sort because behind the man stood a tall cross, a geometrically confusing post-modern cross. Jack couldn't put his finger on it, because he had seen many designs for Calvary's cross before, but there was something about this one that made him uncomfortable. It was extravagant and undignified... unholy.

The cross rotated slowly on an invisible axis, giving the illusion it was perhaps a hologram, and it imperceptibly changed colors from gold to silver. For some reason, this moment reminded him of an early childhood memory when he had watched the old, scratchy version of *The Wizard of Oz* with Judy Garland. From the security of his father's lap, he remembered how incredibly in awe he was of the wonderful wizard's smoke-filled workshop at the end of the long hallway, before it was discovered that the man behind the curtain, as well as the production, was fake.

"What just happened?" Jack asked himself.

He looked around for someone to answer that very question. He knew he was dreaming—he was sure of that—but was he still Jack Lewis, or some other character created for this dream? Because of the whole *Wizard of Oz* flashback thing, maybe there was some self-psychoanalysis going on, but why now?

I was so close to getting naked with my wife, Jack lamented. *Couldn't this wait?*

Behind the fellow on the platform and the tasteless cross, and encompassing the entire height and width of the viewable stage, was a screen projecting the words to the song currently being sung by the as yet unseen congregation. It took a few seconds of following the words on the screen for Jack's eyes to begin focusing on the faded background images of many happy people at play or in leisurely repose. They were almost always accompanied by glamorous homes, cars, and yachts. If he didn't know better, Jack would have thought there was a subliminal message at work here.

No matter, Jack thought. *The sooner I'm out of here and in MJ's arms, the better.*

When the song ended, the fashionable young man on the platform continued to pump his fists into the air to keep the hands clapping and the voices chanting praises to God. It appeared to Jack that this frenetic jubilation could have gone on forever if not prompted to do otherwise. After taking several minutes to end what he had begun, the young man bowed his head, commending the crowd to do the same, and said, "Let us pray." As far as Jack could tell, the young man's prayer had something to do with God's desire for his people to be prosperous in every aspect of their lives, and how that could somehow be accomplished by the amount of their giving to the forthcoming offering plate. With that said, the fellow began to lead the congregation in yet another song. This time, however, the melody was much slower, softly contemplative, a much easier song to sing while writing a big fat check at the same time.

This was enough for Jack. It sounded more like a shakedown than Sunday worship, and what was he doing here in the first place? He was about to leave his spot when two children came flying out from behind the multiple layers of curtains and nearly ran him over. They all looked at one another in stunned silence for several seconds, and then the taller and presumably wiser of the two kids spoke up.

"Oh, hi, Pastor Jack," she said without any thought to apologizing for nearly steamrolling her pastor.

"Yeah, hi, Pastor Jack," added the shorter, younger boy.

So, a pastor am I… not bad. He viewed his surroundings with a little less criticism.

"Well, hello. How—" he began without being allowed to finish his sentence.

"Welcome back," said the girl.

"Yeah, welcome back," parroted the boy.

So, I've been away… a mission trip to the real world perhaps, Jack thought, and smiled at his own humor.

"Well, thanks. What—" Again he was interrupted by the taller girl.

"So, I guess you want to know why we were behind the stage, huh?" she asked.

The boy did not bother to repeat this last remark, possibly sensing that it was a little too self-incriminating.

"No, I don't need to know where you were. It is where you two are headed that concerns me… and God," Jack said in his best pastor-speak.

The kids seemed to get their pastor's spiritual point and nodded their heads in agreement and relief.

"I'll tell you what, though," Jack continued. "I could use some of that speed of yours."

"Sure, Pastor Jack," said the girl excitedly.

"Yeah, sure, Pastor Jack," said the boy, happy to be back in rhythm again.

"As fast as you can, go out front and grab me this morning's service bulletin, and…," Jack began his request, but without the opportunity to add his parting admonition.

"Okay," they said in unison and took off.

"Okay then, and try not to knock anyone over," Jack said to the thin air that formerly surrounded his two young congregants.

Even in my dreams, these kids are in second gear, waiting to pop the clutch, Jack thought.

Jack had every reason to believe these two figments of his imagination knew every shortcut in this imaginary building, so he didn't expect it would take them long to accomplish their mission. In the few minutes he had before their return, Jack turned his attention back toward the stage. At that moment, the hip young man still directing the music from the pulpit turned his head toward Jack and smiled generously. Without missing a beat, he casually turned his attention back to the audience, but discreetly lowered the arm closest to Jack down to his side and began opening and closing the lowered hand, spreading all five fingers in the process. There was a slight pause between the opening and closing of the hand, indicating to Jack that he was being given a sign to be ready in five minutes.

Ready for what? Jack thought.

Just then the two young speedsters pulled up fast in front of him, each clutching a bulletin. He gratefully took them both and quickly glanced at the front covers.

My God—this is my church! he thought as a broad smile came unconsciously to his face. He was looking at his picture and a caption that read: "Good News Christian Church Welcomes Back Founder and Senior Pastor, Dr. Jack Lewis."

"All right, you two, nice job," Jack said, looking up from the bulletins. "Before you go back to your seats... uh, you are going back to your seats, right?"

"Yes, sir," promised the girl and repeated by the boy.

"Okay, I forgot my glasses, so can you tell me who that is out there on the stage?" Jack lied.

"That's Pastor Mark," answered the girl and repeated by the boy.

"Okay, that's what I thought. Well, I guess it's time to scoot," Jack said affectionately. "Remember, I'll be looking for you out there, so no detours. Got it?"

"Got it!" they answered gleefully, and disappeared into the maze of curtains.

I'll be looking for you… Why would I say that? Jack thought.

Once again Jack stood there behind the tall curtains alone, only this time he wasn't so anxious to leave this dream of his. Jack knew MJ was most certainly out of the bathroom by now and willing to love and be loved, so what was he waiting for? He looked down at the bulletin with his face plastered on its front page and then to the stage. How could he be the senior pastor of a church he knew nothing about? In every other dream (and there had been more than a few of these dreams when his subconscious mind appointed him pastor), everything was familiar to him. There were always bits and pieces of his past, but the dreams were never as grand as this one—or as real.

He looked down at the bulletin once again, wanting desperately to open it and find out more about "his" church and "his" people. He intentionally felt the texture of the paper between his thumb and finger and then the soft vibration of the music on the hardwood floors beneath his feet. He raised his head and willfully breathed in the variety of perfumes and colognes that permeated the air. There was not a sight, sound, smell, or feel that suggested the state he was in could be anything but a fresh, new, and awakened experience—except Jack's resistant memory of his real life.

This is crazy. It's a dream, Jack thought in challenging his senses.

How could he take any of this seriously when he knew it was a fantasy created in his own mind and based solely on an unfulfilled desire? Yet the longer Jack stood there, the more conflicted and immobilized he became.

Yes, this dream was an intrusion and could not have come at a worse time. Maybe the longing in his heart to "follow the Lord and help others do the same" had become so intense lately that a part of him was willing to delay the greatest of all God's gifts to his gender (sexual gratification with the woman you married) to experience it. For all he knew, this dream could have been God sent, like Joseph experienced in Genesis or Solomon in 1 Kings.

Hopefully, if time in real life did not stand still until his return, MJ would understand. She must have known how tired he was before disappearing into the bathroom like that. In any case, he would make it up to her somehow.

And yes, this dream was a fake, but it was not much different from acting out a character in a Shakespearian play. This was not a minor role for an amateur summer theater group, however. From the flood of sound produced by the music and unseen congregation, to the vast dimensions of the stage and its fine drapery, to the professional audio-visual production, he was now the alpha dog in what was apparently a church of considerable size and wealth.

And yes, this dream was an attractive adventure to him, but if his true desire was to leave this fantasy world, exactly how was that to be accomplished? Would ripping the bulletin in half launch him back into bed, or would he have to wait for MJ to give his physical body a good nudge? There was little Jack could do about his predicament other than let it run its course. Or could it be that his desire to leave was only halfhearted?

What are you thinking? Jack thought while looking down at the bulletins. *Rip this up and get back to reality. Get back to MJ.*

"There you are!" shouted an unfamiliar voice. "Damn it, Jack, we've been looking all over for you. Mark's been out there ten minutes longer than he should have been already. Where's your ear gear?"

The well-dressed man of about Jack's age appeared agitated about something and approached Jack with great intensity. Without a word, Jack's hand slid involuntarily into his pants pocket and pulled out an earbud. This made the agitated man even more agitated so that by the time he had moved into Jack's personal space, it looked as if he might need duct tape to keep his head from exploding.

"Please don't start this up again, Jack," the distressed man pleaded, "or you'll have us all drinking this time."

As soon as these words were delivered, the man's demeanor instantly changed from anger to regret.

"Oh God, Jack. I'm sorry, man," the man said apologetically. "I shouldn't have said that, dude."

So I'm a pastor and a drunk, Jack thought. *And I take it that my leave of absence was for rehab.*

"It's okay, Pete," Jack responded with kindness and understanding. "I'm sober."

Jack was able to answer him by name because it was imprinted on the name tag he was wearing. Jack also recognized his face from the bulletin as being second-in-command at Good News, which meant he would have been the one who kept this ship afloat while its captain was drying out. This poor guy had every right to be concerned.

"Fortunately, the place is jammed and the collection is taking longer. That reminds me, you probably haven't heard this yet because your earpiece was in your pocket," Pete said with a smirk, "but we did two hundred in the first service—two hundred thousand, man!"

"And it was all you, Jack," Pete beamed in admiration. "That second collection was pure genius. Where do you come up with this stuff? With the numbers we have in the house now, we could easily pull a quarter-mill from this service—two hundred and fifty thou, Jack!"

How is that even possible? Jack thought as he stood dumbfounded by such an unbelievably large number. *How big is this place*?

"All right. Ready for round two, monsta?" Pete asked rhetorically as he tightened the knot on Jack's tie and straightened his jacket. "No time for makeup, dude. They'll have to watch you sweat."

"Wait!" Jack blurted out as the realization of what he was being asked to do finally hit home. "What did I say?"

"I mean, what do I say?" Jack corrected himself.

Without saying a word, Pete stopped what he was doing and gave Jack another anxious look. The adjustments to Jack's apparel were only the means by which Pete could get close enough to detect alcohol on Jack's breath. After concluding that time away from the pulpit and nerves (not drunkenness) were the probable causes of Jack's odd behavior, Pete began tapping his pointing finger on Jack's chest.

"From my heart?" Jack asked nervously, misinterpreting his associate pastor's gesturing.

Again without a word, but now with a look of frustration, Pete reached into the inside breast pocket of Jack's suit and pulled out a set of sermon notes.

"Listen to me, bro. We can't do this much longer without you. Understand me?" Pete stated unashamedly and unapologetically, then handed the sermon notes back to Jack.

"We all have families and lifestyles now. Don't forget that," Pete added sternly. "And maybe you can get your wife to smile once in a while."

MJ's here, Jack thought excitedly without grasping the less than positive inflection in Pete's voice when mentioning her name.

Neither man had noticed that Pastor Mark had concluded his portion of the second service or that he was now in the process of introducing their beloved pastor—that is, until both Pete and Jack heard a soft voice in their earbuds saying, "Pastor Jack on in ten; stage right, please." This caused them both to turn their heads in unison back toward the stage in time to hear Pastor Mark's closing statement.

"And now join me in welcoming back to 'the house that Jack built...'"

At this point, it would have made little difference if he had named Santa Claus, because everything that came afterward would have been drowned out when the crowd of faithful believers erupted in applause. Without saying another word, the young pastor simply smiled, turned to face stage right, and joined in the electrifying, welcoming celebration. Their good shepherd had returned to them.

Jack was now pumping adrenaline like an F-16 pumps jet fuel on a flattop, and he was ready to take off. This was exactly what he longed for, a hundredfold. He finally had his church, his beautiful wife and boys out in the audience somewhere, and his sermon notes. What else was there to life... or dream?

He was about to charge out onto the stage when Pete moved in front of him, grabbed him by the shoulders, and looked him square in the eyes. Pastor Mark had already stepped down from the pulpit and was now walking off stage in their direction. The voice in the earbud was calmly advising Pastor Jack to begin his advancement onto the stage. There was little time, and if Pete wanted to share a brief prayer, Jack thought he had better do so quickly.

"Two hundred and fifty thousand," Pete said loudly so as to be heard by Jack over the crowd noise, and released him.

Jack had no time to reflect on the appropriateness of Pete's comment. His responsibility right now was to feed his flock God's Word and nothing else. He was so amped up anyway that he had to consciously rein in his desire to make the pulpit the finish line in a hundred-yard dash. Once he cleared the first set of curtains and then Pastor Mark, his pace slowed automatically when he finally caught his first glimpse of the magnitude of the church. There must have been over two thousand people on their feet and cheering wildly, but there might as well have been ten thousand.

So overwhelming was this initial wave of sight and sound that the voice in the earbud calmly prompted, "Pastor Jack, please smile and continue to the pulpit. That's better, thank you."

Jack eventually made it to the raised platform and carefully laid his sermon notes on the lectern. The house lights were on but slightly dimmed so that he could see faces, yet the spotlights that roamed onto the audience were still effective at highlighting them. The room sparkled brightly as if pictures were being taken from every direction, but it wasn't the featureless white light of a camera flash. Instead, each refracted gleam of light emitted a brilliant color that could be attributable only to a large diamond or some other precious jewel.

From what Jack could see, the design of this massive structure was similar to most prestigious concert halls, whereby once the patrons entered the building, they would either enter the theater and descend to get to their seats or ascend by elevator or stairway to get to one of two balcony seating areas. The music was, in fact, being produced live, and its musicians were located in an orchestra pit at the foot of the stage. On each side of the stage were wide semicircular marble staircases, and many elegant chandeliers and candelabra sconces adorned the ceiling and walls.

The clapping and chanting went on even though Jack did nothing to encourage it. With so many people to create and then choose from, Jack thought his subconscious mind would have had to borrow at least some attributes of those familiar to him, but he recognized no one. His eyes purposely went to section GG toward the middle of the room and focused on seats 124 and 125. There he found the two kids he had met in the back moments ago. They had made it back to their seats and were clapping along with the rest of the congregation. Jack smiled, pointed in their direction, and waved as if to say, "See, I told you I would look for you." They began to jump up and down and waved furiously to the amazement of their parents and those around them.

How did I know where they were seated? Jack thought as his eyes performed another deliberate shift to section A and seats 1, 2, and 3.

There stood MJ and the boys. The boys were clapping joyfully, but MJ just stood there, looking sad and out of place. To Jack, she was still the most beautiful created being in the room, even though she dressed more modestly and wore less makeup and jewelry than all the women surrounding her. He smiled to her when their eyes finally did meet, but this did not have any effect on her, and she soon turned her eyes away.

Immediately following this troubling reaction from his wife, Jack's attention was uncontrollably drawn to seat 111 in the last row of the section nearest the lobby doors. There stood a tall muscular man. Much like MJ, he was standing but displaying no emotion. There was nothing unusual about him, nor was he familiar to Jack. The man stood stoically with his head bowed while those around him clapped and carried on as if he were not even there. Initially, Jack was curious as to why, of all the thousands of jubilant people in the audience, he would single out this guy.

As he was about to withdraw his gaze, Jack thought he saw something that sent a shiver coursing throughout his body. As the man slowly lifted his head, Jack thought he saw the man's eyes burn red as with fire and then suddenly extinguish into a soft, penetrating blue. The man smiled and began to clap respectfully when their eyes finally did meet, and Jack, still a bit shaken, responded with a reserved grin.

Without warning, he heard Pete's voice in the earbud: "Hey, Jack, my tee time's at two. Let's get this show moving, dude."

As soon as this show is over, you're fired, dude, Jack thought. *Dream or no dream...*

He smiled brightly once more, raised his hands with humility, and patiently asked for quiet. As the assembly slowly began to respond to his plea, Jack spoke lightheartedly.

"Well, I think I know how Don Henley and the gang must have felt when the Eagles began touring again," Jack said to the delight of everyone in the room, except for MJ. "It will be a great day when hell freezes over, amen?"

He allowed a brief moment for some laughter and clapping, then began again. The tall man in seat 111 was now gone.

"I think Pastor Mark may have been a bit too generous. I believe this is the house the Lord has built, not me, but the King of Kings and Lord of Lords." Jack spoke in humility and boldness. "Let us never forget from whom all blessings flow, amen?"

The congregation immediately responded with more clapping and cries of "Amen!" and "Hallelujah!"

"It is good to be back, and I do appreciate your warm welcome," Jack began in a sullen, repentant voice as he dropped his head in remorseful fashion. This theatrical maneuver also gave him an opportunity to glance down at his sermon notes.

After an appropriate pause, he raised his head and spoke again. "While I was away," Jack said coyly and flashed the universal sign for quotation marks, "I had a lot of time to meditate on God's Word. Of course, I *don't* recommend anyone doing what I did just to get a little R & R," Jack said with some self-depreciating humor. "I want to be *clear* about that, all right?" He emphasized the words *don't* and *clear* by nearly shouting them out.

"Yeah, I couldn't wait to get back and ask you a couple of questions. You know all about my struggles out there in disobedience-land, and I wondered if you were struggling with these things too," Jack said in an obvious attempt to involve his flock.

"Okay, here's one. Anyone listening to me now without sin?" Jack asked the question in a way that his listeners could not immediately determine if he was being funny or was serious. "Come on. You're being humble again." Jack was now playfully taunting his fellow believers. "Anyone without sin? No? No one?

"You're right, of course. We all sin." Jack exhaled as he spoke. "Romans 3:23: 'All have sinned and fall short of the glory of God'; and 1 John 1:10: 'If we claim to be without sin, we deceive ourselves.'

"This is not some back door way of excusing my behavior. It's not." Jack's voice strained with emotion.

He was more than willing to act his way through his dream character's humanity if it brought someone in unrepentant sin to their knees, even if that someone was simply a character in his dream. At the same time, however, Jack wondered if MJ knew it was all an act. If not, and she too was simply a character in his dream, then it must be dreadfully painful and embarrassing to her, knowing how low her pastor husband had fallen.

He had seen firsthand how drugs and alcohol devastated the lives of many of his classmates that could not handle the inexhaustible pressure at Stanford. These things now weighed heavily on Jack, and without the help of his character's sermon notes, they allowed him to weave an emotionally charged, heartbreaking tale of sin and redemption that even had MJ looking up at him with tears in her eyes. When he had finished his unscripted story, he transitioned back into the sermon notes.

"I'm going to be talking more about forgiveness in the coming weeks, so you don't want to miss that," Jack said cheerfully to lighten things up a bit. "We can compare notes on that one if you want."

This brought laughter back to the somber house.

"Here's another one. Why are the wealthy constantly being trashed and raked over the coals, especially within our own Christian community?" Jack began reading from the notes. This was apparently a source of irritation among his church body, because he sensed from the chatter that was now going on, he had every ear dialed onto this frequency.

"Did you know that we are one of the highest net-worth-per-capita congregations in the country?" Jack boasted. "Don't ask me how I know this, all right? That's what's written down here. I'm sure it's all public information, so I don't need a bunch of angry mail on this one, okay?"

This brought unreserved laughter and applause from his affluent but often misunderstood and maligned congregation.

"Did you know that God loves you as much as he loves that beggar out on the street corner?" Jack continued candidly. "You wouldn't know that in some houses of worship. Perhaps that is why you come here to Good News and not the half-empty church down the street. God loves you, I love you, we love you. Let this house be your refuge."

Jack could feel a corporate sigh of relief come from the audience, along with even more grateful applause. He was still unclear as to where these sermon notes were leading him, but so far there was nothing doctrinally wrong with them, and they had certainly put him firmly in control of this body of believers.

"So let me ask you, is being wealthy a bad thing?" Jack continued reading from the notes. "After all, wasn't it Jesus himself who said in Matthew 19:24, 'It will be easier for a camel to go through the eye of a needle than for a rich man to enter the kingdom of God'?

"Yes... yes, he did say that," Jack acknowledged softly, "but did you know that Abraham was one of the wealthiest persons to walk this planet, Genesis 13:2, and was God's friend, Isaiah 41:8 and James 2:23? Anyone care to guess why this uber-rich guy from Haran became God's friend?" Jack asked as he purposely looked out into the darkened spaces of the auditorium for a response—and got it.

"It's the love of money that is the root of all kinds of evil, 1 Timothy 6:10. It's a heart issue—not a wealth issue." Jack was in a preacher's zone now, and peaking. "Abraham was willing to give God everything he had: money, donkeys, even his son Isaac, Genesis 22:12.

"So why are you bringing this up now, Pastor Jack?" Jack asked, referring to himself in the third person. "Great question—let's talk about it.

"Where's your heart today?" Jack asked in a subdued, respectful voice. "I came back this week and was told that we had closed down some of our ministries from lack of funds.

"Lack of funds!" Jack's voice came back to life again. "This can't be right. I'm running around asking my people, who died? Please, someone tell me who died so that I might go and comfort their grieving families. Half our congregation must have died for this to be true!

"And yet here you all are." Jack's voice once again became subdued and now sorrowful.

"Where's your heart today?" Jack repeated the loaded question once again.

"I am going to test your faith today. Abraham understood it. Those of you who have already made it to the top of your profession understand it. For the benefit of those who are still making their way up that ladder, listen carefully so you too will understand.

"The angel of the Lord said to Abraham, 'I will surely bless you and make your descendants as numerous as the stars in the sky... and they will take possession of the cities of their enemies... because you have obeyed me,' Genesis 22:17."

Jack did not like the direction this sermon was headed, but it was too late to abandon ship now. In order that he might feel better about himself once this whole dream business was over (and hopefully reconcile himself with God), Jack imperceptibly switched his motivation from being a preacher to a shallow actor. He continued with the script.

"Who among you wants more blessings, not less?" Jack began to ramp up his rhetoric.

This softball question generated some hearty applause from the upper middle class that always wanted a better life for their families and made up about a third of the church's membership.

"Of course you do. Who's going to say no to that?" Jack employed another theatrical pause to allow the indisputability of the question to settle in before continuing.

"But who among you wants Abraham-size blessings?" Jack's voice became more excited and his body a bit more animated as he continued to perfect his acting skills.

This new and improved inquiry generated a thousand more takers because it attracted the comfortable but somewhat complacent six-figure-income family that easily made up the majority of the church body, and the applause spiked. As Jack looked out into the shadowy darkness of the massive auditorium, he sensed the sea of people begin to churn and ripple, like a container of water before boiling. The house was stirring—it was time.

"No, I still don't think you quite get it yet," Jack proclaimed with great conviction as he stepped down from the podium and walked toward the edge of the stage.

A soft voice came on the earbud and calmly said, "Lights, stay with him please."

"I mean *take-possession-of-your-enemies'-cities* kind of blessings!" Jack cried out with authority that even he did not know he possessed.

This was aimed at the self-made millionaire, and it hit the mark. He now had every person from every income group on their feet and in rapacious lust for blessings.

"You got 'em, Jack. You did it again, man." Jack could hear Pete's voice in the earbud. Jack continued.

"I believe Good News Christian Church is a beacon shining the prosperity of a life in Jesus Christ!" Jack shouted over the spellbound crowd as he moved from one side of the stage to the other. "Say *amen!*"

The whole room shook with the sound of a thousand or more supercharged believers shouting *amen* simultaneously, and the applause continued without waning.

"As your senior pastor here at Good News, I have asked that a second offering be taken at this time." Jack again had to shout to allow his words to be heard. "And as our Lord washed the feet of His disciples in the upper room the night before He was to be given up for us, I also ask for every employee of Good News here today to walk out into the aisles, right now, and help with this offering. It is my prayer this will demonstrate to all of you, our beloved family, what it means to be a sacrificial servant."

Jack added this impromptu directive on his own, and it added to the already amplified euphoria.

"Nice touch, dude. That was worth another 10K," Jack heard Pete say in the earbud.

"And that includes Pastor Pete and myself," Jack shouted to everyone's delight, except one.

"Damn you, Jack," Pete responded harshly on the earbud. "If we don't break a quarter-mill, I'm going to kick your ass. Then again, if we do, I'll kiss it!"

After the second offering was completed, the closing songs sung, and a brief prayer delivered, Jack began a search for MJ and the boys. This process was taking much longer than he expected, for everyone wanted to shake his hand and tell him personally how much they had given between the two offerings. After a while, the boasting became so profuse and predictable that it sickened him to listen to it anymore, and he literally began running through the crowd of sycophants for the door and fresh air. Once outside, he noticed MJ not too far off and talking to what appeared to be a police officer or sheriff's deputy. Another terrible feeling began to well up inside of him as he started across the parking lot without acknowledging anyone or anything in his path.

"MJ, what's going on?" Jack asked as he approached.

"I have asked you not to call me that," she said angrily as the officer placed himself between Jack and his wife.

"Are you Jonathan Lewis?" the officer inquired with an official tone of voice.

"Yes, I am," Jack replied without taking his eyes off MJ. "Could someone please tell me what's going on?"

"Sign here please," the officer stated matter-of-factly.

"What is this?" Jack asked, now looking down at the clipboard being held out in front of him.

"This is to acknowledge receipt of this petition for divorce from a Ms. Joy Lewis," the officer stated without emotion. "Please sign here."

"I will not!" Jack countered. "MJ, please tell me what's going on."

"Stop calling me MJ!" she cried out, and turned to walk away. Jack attempted to follow but was quickly cut off by the large and well-armed lawman.

"I am sorry, but I cannot allow you to pursue or in any way harass Ms. Lewis," the officer declared. "And if you do not sign for this petition, then I must take you into custody for contempt of court. Please sign here, Mr. Lewis."

Jack signed the document as tears started to form in the corners of his eyes. The officer handed Jack an envelope and turned to leave as soon as he saw the car MJ was driving pull away.

"MJ... my sweet MJ... please don't leave me like this," Jack whispered through the tears that now flowed down his cheeks. "It's only a dream, my love... Please come back... It's only a horrible dream."

"Let her go, Jack," a voice said from behind him. "She is with him who is our enemy."

Jack, still in a confused state of shock from what had occurred, did not move. Even though MJ's car had disappeared from sight, he could not turn away. *She only needs a little time, and she will be back.* His heart was crying out to her. She would be back, and she would see that he had not lost hope. He would never give up hope!

"She is not coming back, Jack," said the voice.

So slow and reluctant were his movements to turn around that he was not even sure why he was turning in the first place. Was there a voice? Who would tempt him to turn away from the one he loved? When he finally did make it all the way around, he recognized the man from seat 111.

"What did you say?" Jack uttered vacantly.

"She was never with us, Jack," the man said coldly. "She was always trying to tear down what you have built here.

And now that you know alcohol isn't going to change any of that, it's time to get back to the business of taking your church to a whole new level."

Jack was still a little fuzzy on the specifics, but he was catching on to the central theme of what this fellow was trying to say. Did MJ really lose her faith in Jesus Christ and was now attempting to destroy the church? Well, if there was anything that could bring clarity of thought and purpose back to Jack's mind, it was an attack on his wife, and the more he thought about it, the more he wanted to damage this guy for suggesting anything remotely close to this.

"Listen, friend," Jack said calmly so as not to rattle his own cage, "there are two things I know for sure. First, this church is dead because Jesus Christ does not reign here. And as far as my wife is concerned, 'My sheep listen to my voice. I know them and they follow me. My Father, who has given them to me, is greater than all. No one can snatch them out of my Father's hand.'"

The Scripture verse caused the man to rock back on his heels and let out a soft but tormented hissing noise. It took a second or two for the stranger to compose himself and respond.

"Who said anything about Joy's faith in the enemy above, Jack?" the man replied, and smiled. "It is you we seek."

The man coughed up a low hideous laugh and shook his head in delight at the sight of Jack's weak human body begin to tremble in distress. Then he laughed again with more piercing venom as Jack watched the man's face darken and his eyes flash red with fire.

"Our lord below is not pleased with your wavering, Jack, but he is patient." The man, now taking on an evil form, hissed as he belched a caustic fume that overshadowed Jack. "Yes, he is very patient."

This was more than Jack could handle, and he dropped to his knees and prayed out loud to God for help. He soon began reciting Scripture, but the foul stench from the man caused Jack to choke and forget words to verses he had committed to memory as a teenager; however, he did not stop praying.

The battle of the wills began. The louder the evil one laughed and mocked him, the louder Jack prayed, but he was tiring quickly. When Jack thought he could hold out no longer, he remembered how the Philippian church had brought relief in times of suffering to the ever besieged apostle Paul, and then these words came to his mind:

"Your attitude should be the same as that of Christ Jesus."

With that, Jack closed his eyes and began to pray aloud with renewed strength:

"Jesus, being in the nature of God, did not consider equality with God something to be grasped, but made himself nothing."

With eyes closed, Jack did not notice how this caused the demon to flinch and momentarily interrupted its hideous laughter. He continued:

"Taking on the very nature of a servant, being made in human likeness and being found in appearance as a man, he humbled himself and became obedient to death—even death on a cross."

So comforting were these words that Jack spoke, he did not notice a fresh breeze had cleared away the devilish vapor that had engulfed him, or that the evil creature had stopped laughing altogether and its body heaved and wrenched and contorted as if burning itself from the inside. Jack continued:

"Therefore, God exalted him to the highest place and gave him the name that is above all names. At the name of Jesus every knee shall bow in heaven and on earth and under the earth."

Again Jack was oblivious to how overpowering these words were or the toll it was taking on his adversary. The demon shook violently as the clothes it was wearing melted away, exposing nothing more than a skeleton wrapped tightly beneath a smoldering skin of dark red.

"Damn you to heaven!" the creature gasped, spitting fire as it spoke, until at last the flame within consumed it.

"Every tongue shall confess that Jesus Christ is Lord, to the glory of God the Father, amen."

Jack concluded and opened his eyes. Only a large pile of ash in front of him remained, and that was quickly swept away with a sudden gust of wind. Still on his knees, he searched the horizon and whispered, "MJ... it's only a dream, my love."

7

Great Awakenings

"I'm afraid you overestimate your circumstance and underestimate my tolerance for murderous tyrants, Emperor," Hitch heard himself say before waking.

He no longer held a sword in his hands, and his new surroundings were dark and peaceful. The pillow beneath his head was damp with sweat, as was the tee shirt he wore to bed. He sat up as quickly as his aching body would allow, and as soon as it was no longer necessary for propping himself up, his free hand went immediately to the area of the neck where the soldier from his dream had embedded his sword. It still hurt, but there was no bleeding as far as he could tell in the darkness. He felt around for any sharp instrument that he might have used on himself in his dream, but could find nothing.

"Damn dream," he muttered.

He was still somewhat agitated that throughout the dream, he had reacted to his plight with timidity and cowardice, until the very end when he truly believed he could have slapped that giant lion silly, even before it uttered his name. He could have driven that sword straight through Nero's heartless chest as well. This thought made him feel a little better about himself, but unfortunately, this postulation would forever remain unproven. A quick glance at the faint glow from on top of the nightstand let him know it was 1:19 a.m., and he felt worse off now than when he first went to bed three hours ago. His meeting with Peter was in less than seven hours, and he was cold, wet, achy, and now wide awake.

Without expending the effort to turn on a light, he took every stitch of clothing off his body and tossed them onto the bed. Though only one pillow suffered the considerable amount of nightmare-induced facial perspiration, he removed the cases from all four pillows and added them to the pile of clothing on the bed. He then pulled the covers off all four corners of the bed down to the mattress and rolled them into a large ball, along with the clothes and pillowcases. With one good tug, he brought the whole bundle tumbling to the floor in a heap. This should send a clear signal to his maid service that these were to be laundered that day. This service was yet another one of Ms. Brown's brilliant ideas that, like almost everything else she conceived, had become a necessity of life for him.

Finding the search for underwear another task not worthy of effort, he wandered to the wardrobe and grabbed what felt to be the heaviest set of cotton pajamas on the shelf and slipped them on. To his left, he noticed his smartphone on the bureau, blinking in the darkness that it was fully charged. He reached over, lifted it from its cradle, and let it fall into his pajama pocket.

Having taken care of his need for warmth and dryness, he drifted into the dimly lit living room, seeking relief from his assorted aches and pains. From the bar, he poured two fingers of Grand Marnier into a rocks glass and downed it without hesitation. After a brief pause to allow the drink to anesthetize every suffering nerve ending it came into contact with, he poured another generous portion of the smooth liquor into the empty glass and shuffled instinctively to his easy chair. A plush comforter was draped neatly atop the back of the chair in the event he was to spend the night here—a common practice of his, especially when reading late into the evening.

This is partially her fault, you know, he thought with little thinking.

As he settled into the chair's warm embrace, Hitch began to build a case for holding Ms. Brown somewhat accountable for his nightmare. This was in spite of the fact that the morning's clever intruder had made his startling appearance, and even more startling disappearance, before Ms. Brown entered the picture. It may have been her reaction of doubt afterward that perturbed him and had him questioning his own story. Then, in their meeting later in the day, she showed her true feelings toward his choice of topics for the upcoming lecture with a soft yet distinct groan. These two offenses, no matter how minor, must have been enough to cause his subconscious mind to create a grotesque dream clearly designed to generate sympathy for Christians and their religion, even to the point of gladly killing the madman putting them in harm's way.

I believe that entitles me to the opportunity of having her share in my misery, he reasoned boldly. *In fact, if my Latin is still reliable,* lex talionis *[the law of retaliation] seems appropriate for such a time as this.*

Hitch reached into his pocket, pulled out the phone, and in a moment of temporary insanity began typing. Fortunately, this was a slow and cumbersome process because he refused to put down his drink. Even with both hands available, he was not that proficient at texting on such a small device. After a few chaotic sentences and a host of misspelled words, he gave up and wisely put the phone down on the lamp stand.

Have you truly lost your mind, Hitchinson? he admonished himself mildly, for being so reckless... or drunk... or both.

Once composure was restored, Hitch held his half-full glass of Grand Marnier out in front of his face. With a thumb and two fingers holding onto the bottom, he slowly rotated it clockwise and then back again. As he did so, he peered at the reversed images in his bookcase through the amber liquid until one book in particular caught his eye. It was in a large collection of books that he had carried with him since he was a teenager. He remembered reading the book several times but had never studied it thoroughly. He knew it well but could not say that he had mastered all its concepts.

He took a sip from the glass and set it down on the lamp stand. Slowly but deliberately, he made his way to the bookcase and plucked the old book from its peaceful resting spot. It showed signs of being dusted hurriedly but still needed to be wiped off before being allowed to make contact with clothing intended to remain clean. Satisfied with his selection, he returned to his easy chair, spread open the comforter, and made himself comfortable beneath it. He felt much more at ease with his circumstances now. He put on the reading glasses that remained permanently on the lamp stand, and looking down at the book lying in his lap before him, he mouthed the title and author's name with anticipation: "*The Interpretation of Dreams*, Dr. Sigmund Freud."

* * * * *

Jack's head popped off the pillow so fast it took several seconds to overcome the dizziness. Everything was dark. The alarm clock on his nightstand read 2:17 a.m. Beyond the foot of the bed, he noticed the door to the bathroom open and the light off.

"Damn dream," he muttered.

He sat up slowly and turned his head to the right to confirm his fears. He gazed over at the sleek contours of MJ's body lying fast asleep under the covers on the other side of bed. There was no way he was going to initiate anything now, though the idea did cross his mind momentarily.

What was that all about? he thought as he buried his face in his hands.

A shiver coursed through his body as the memory from the dream of MJ's car driving off suddenly flashed in his mind, and he released a spontaneous moan. He lifted his head quickly so as not to be captured by another dream. Looking again at his sleeping wife, he smiled and exhaled deeply.

"I don't know what I would do without you, my Joy," he whispered to her.

He rotated himself out of bed and wobbled into the bathroom. After lifting the seat, he parked himself in front of the toilet and let it rip. There was no need to turn on a light; this was a fairly routine and mostly accurate exercise. From there he went to the sink and washed his hands and brushed his teeth in the semidarkness, but instead of immediately returning to bed, he lingered at the basin, splashing cold water onto his face and the back of his neck. He pivoted his head upward so that he was now looking at the darkened image of himself in the mirror.

"Okay, what gives, Lord?" He spoke in a soft voice as if Jesus himself were standing close by him. "This is the second killer event in less than twenty-four hours. First, some guy pins me to my chair with his words, and now I get a church and lose my wife in a dream. Is there something you want to tell me?... because if there is, you got my attention."

After allowing God an opportunity to respond if He so chose, Jack grabbed a towel, dried his face, and headed back to bed. It was only when he reached down to grab a handful of covers that he noticed a good-sized lump in the center of the bed. Carefully lifting the covers, he discovered his youngest son, Joey, asleep in a ball and clutching his stuffed bird.

He must have been there the whole time. Maybe that's why MJ didn't wake me, Jack reasoned as his mind started processing this new information.

Yes, I get a do-over, Jack concluded optimistically as a sophomoric smile replaced his frustrated scowl, and he shot both fists into the air.

Encouraged by this new development but now feeling very weary, he rolled back into bed and was out like a light. The next thing he knew, MJ was sitting on his side of the bed, playing with his hair and talking to him in gentle whispers.

"I think it's time to get up, sweetheart," he heard her say.

Jack looked up at her through narrow glazed eyes and smiled. The room lights were off, but the morning sun on the closed blinds provided enough soft radiance for him to faintly make out that she had on the dress shirt he was going to wear to work, with only the bottom half of the buttons fastened... and nothing more. He glanced at the clock, which remained a bluish- green blur, and then quickly turned his attention to the center of the bed.

"Joey okay?" he asked.

"He was complaining of an upset stomach and monsters last night, so I brought him into bed with us," she explained tenderly. "He is back in his own bed now. They are both in bed now."

She snuggled her way under the covers next to him and spoke softly in his ear: "And the door is locked."

* * * * *

As usual, Charlie was up at 5:00 a.m. and finished his daily devotions and breakfast with his wife Sarah, the love of his life and an early riser like himself. Yesterday had been a long day, but a good day for him. He had met all ten new hires and was harshly asked to leave only three times. What those three newcomers didn't realize was that their hostile reaction to his cordial greeting and polite invitations only caused them to be entered into a journal of those deserving a little more grace and kindness. They were "John 15:18 haters," after all, and it was to be expected.

Charlie took solace in knowing that in time he would develop a close relationship with at least one and a half of those unrepentant sinners—that is to say, although it might not end up being one of those three individuals specifically, the probability of a person warming up after displaying such caustic responses at their initial meeting was close to 50 percent. He had been doing this a long time, and the numbers didn't lie. It might even border on miraculous, but several of these irascible unbelievers would credit him with ultimately leading them to the cross and to a relationship with Jesus Christ. Although there were not as many of these who would come to know the love of the Savior through him as he would like, there were certainly more than if he had waited for them to knock on his door. What mattered most was that each one was precious to God.

It was now six, and there was still much left to be done at the college before students started arriving in the coming weeks. His top priority right now was the condition of the Grand Courtyard. Two thousand people would jam themselves into the historic Walker Auditorium to hear Professor Hitchinson's address to the incoming class, and another thousand people without invitations would be milling around outside waiting for its conclusion. The Yard would then become the scene of many gatherings and provide the backdrop for both personal and business-related photo opportunities. To emphasize how significant this occasion was to the university, Dr. Stansbury had requested a meeting with Charlie immediately following his meeting with Dr. Hitchinson this morning.

Charlie had his work crew out mowing all week, and they had completed this critical task yesterday. This would also be the last cut of the year for the Yard, and they had done a magnificent job with nearly perfect lines. They would be back out today working on any trail- maintenance issues. The trimming and mulching of the decorative shrubbery and trees had been accomplished the week before so that the freshly cut grass of this week would not be disturbed. The more delicate greenery Charlie would tend himself. This would include the careful removal of any dead or diseased branches from the university's prized David Austin roses, whole sections of which were older and taller than he was. After watching Charlie spend so much time doting on these spectacular bushes, it was Jack who had enlightened him on the legend of Aphrodite, the Greek goddess of love. She would create the rose from a mixture of her tears and the blood of her wounded lover, Adonis. To this Charlie responded, "If that were so, then it was his blood, my sweat, and her tears that have kept these alive to this day!"

Charlie's work crew consisted of Alex and Francesca (or Frannie), two social misfits in their early twenties whom he had taken in several years ago. They both came from broken homes and most certainly had been headed for prison if he had not taken them under his wing. As a result of his kindness and guidance, they considered him more as a father figure than a boss, something they had been missing for most of their young lives.

Charlie used to take on additional part-time help this time of year, but that was before the university started opening up dorms, classrooms, and office space in the new campus complex. This had reduced the foot traffic substantially and therefore reduced the need for help to repair the damage caused by the foot traffic, especially intoxicated foot traffic. Now, if students or faculty had class or business on the historic side of campus, most took public transportation or used their own personal vehicles and traveled the five or six tedious miles around the university and through town rather than walk or bike the mile or so through the quiet solitude of a wooded hillside and rolling pastures. Charlie had every intention of starting out with Alex and Frannie this morning, but there was work still left to be done in the office in preparation for his nine o'clock meeting with Dr. Stansbury.

Whereas most of the faculty shivered at the thought of having to justify their value to the university to Dr. Stansbury each year, Charlie was actually looking forward to this meeting. Indeed, Peter could be a menacing figure. He was a powerful six-foot-four-inches tall, 230-pound combat-tested marine who took great pleasure in going nose to nose with Hillary's resource-draining malcontents. With his Ph.D. in history and philosophy of science from the University of the Fighting Irish at Notre Dame, extensive postdoctoral research in epistemology, and a marine's vocabulary to back it all up, even the most radical tenured professor cowered in his presence.

As Charlie recalled, Peter was by far the worst of those ill-tempered "John 15:18 haters" he had ever met in his twenty-five years of greeting newcomers at Hillary. Not only did he tell Charlie to get out and threaten to dismiss him as soon as he was unpacked, but he punctuated each remark with every known repugnant invective conceived by decadent man. Charlie truly believed that when the time came, Peter would be furnished a speed pass through hell's tollgate that would plunge him straight into darkness for eternity. This heartfelt concern caused him to pray even more earnestly, but not his normal prayer for the lost; rather, it was a prayer for actual engagement with him.

That was almost ten years ago. Today they considered each other a friend. Their friendship had not been an easy road, nor was it built overnight; nor was it anything anyone could have imagined or predicted. In fact, after that first night, Peter had fully intended to make good on his promise to fire Charlie, only to discover he had no authority to do so. Even after learning that this simple groundskeeper had two doctorate degrees to his one and was an extraordinarily capable administrator and well respected among his peers, Peter remained angry and indignant.

It didn't help that every summer he had to look out those giant windows of the president's study and see majestic roses blooming in every corner of the Yard. It was not well known, but as big and brutish as Peter was, he was also an avid gardener at home with a fanatical affection for this particular flower. It infuriated him to compare the roses he grew at home to those under Charlie's care... if one could actually consider his dull and lifeless blooms "growth." Year after year, he tried new pruning strategies, hydration scheduling, fertilizers, and pesticides, and year after year, the same pathetic results remained. He even crossed over to growing the bearded iris with great success, but this proved to be of little consolation. For those true to themselves, there was simply no flower more pleasing to the eye or that produced a more intoxicating scent or promoted more joy in the heart of the gardener than the inimitable rose.

This unreciprocated love for the rose came to a point where Peter finally had enough. In his desperation, he commanded his secretary, Anne, to clear his schedule and get Charlie into his office as soon as possible without explanation. Once this had been arranged and he had Charlie seated in front of him, it did not take long for Peter to dispense with any sense of civility and cut to the chase. In his typical draconian style, Peter began by impassively acknowledging that from all appearances the responsibilities for which Charlie was held accountable were in order. Of course, some aspects of his performance were more in order than others, but there was nothing necessitating corrective action at this time.

For his part, Charlie sat there patiently listening and curiously wondering why Peter would call for an emergency meeting to tell him he was doing his job... sort of. Peter continued along the same lines of parceling out indiscernible compliments with subtle irritation until the topic abruptly turned to landscaping and, more specifically, the tending of the roses. His demeanor, now grave and agitated, betrayed his superficial rhetoric. He reasoned that since these bushes were university property, the manner in which they were being cared for was also university property. If this was true, then it was also reasonable to conclude that he was entitled, as Hillary's new president, to know all the details concerning the welfare of such property.

Charlie had not been asked a single question yet and was still unclear as to whether or not this was the true purpose of their meeting. He sat quietly waiting for the point to make itself known or for Peter to lose his temper and unleash a plethora of profanity. He got both.

"God damn you, Charlie; don't give me that vacuous-lawyer-shit-face like you don't know what the hell I'm talking about!" Peter barked, no longer attempting to mask his motive. "I demand to know all your fucking little secrets for growing those perfect roses of yours. And I don't give a rat's ass if all you do is piss on them; I want to know what time of day you piss on them. Now do I make myself clear?...

"Over-priced gardener," he added under his breath.

It took a few seconds for Charlie to shake off this polluted blustering, but he soon came to understand that this was actually the answer to his prayers for this man; and the words from a sermon given by Martin Luther King Jr. suddenly came to mind: "Darkness cannot drive out darkness; only light can do that. Hate cannot drive out hate; only love can do that."

Instead of becoming righteously indignant and walking out (leaving Peter in his darkness), Charlie simply apologized to Peter for being slow to pick up on his exasperation with the rose, thanked him for the compliment of thinking he had some secret for growing them, and began questioning him on what he was doing with his garden. After receiving some preliminary background information,

Charlie went on to explain how plants use sunlight to undergo photosynthesis to convert light into food, chemically creating sugars for energy, and how roses in their hardiness zone must deal with the challenging conditions of all four seasons. Before he knew it, an otherwise predictably contentious meeting scheduled for an hour became an unforeseeably pleasant exchange of mutual experiences with a temperamental flower lasting over two hours. And from it emerged a new friendship.

Charlie had accepted the fact that Peter was still unsaved, still had a temper, and still had a vocabulary that would make most hip-hop rappers envious. Since that meeting seven years ago, however, he had noticed small changes in Peter's mannerisms whenever he was around. The most obvious evolution was how Peter restrained from, or at least modified, his use of vulgar language in Charlie's presence. To the untrained ear, this change might be imperceptible, but even Anne would give him a smile and a wink when they both observed Peter pause mid-sentence to search for a more dignified obscenity when speaking to Charlie. Unfortunately, just when he thought that the light of Jesus might be penetrating Peter's psyche, something would trigger the marine's defense mechanism, and off the deep end he would go.

They did not meet often, but when they did, it was Charlie's custom to bring Peter one or more books or articles on gardening in their zone. Of course, the majority of these resources were dedicated to the rose, with fundamental information on what to look for when coming out of one season and what to expect when going into another. Charlie enjoyed making himself available whenever Peter needed his expertise on the more complicated issues and had been to his home on many occasions to check on his progress. If they had not met for an extended period of time, Charlie would leave a stack of books with Anne. Every so often he would slip in a book on the life and ministry of Jesus Christ, which in the early years of their friendship would be returned to him, as if they had been included in the stack of books by mistake. To Charlie's great delight, Peter's roses were doing exceptionally well, and without explanation Peter now kept every book given him, including those expounding on the life of Jesus.

It was now eight o'clock and time for Charlie to make his way across campus. He was about to give his golf cart some gas (or electric in his case) when his phone began to chirp. It was Alex.

"Good morning, Chief," Alex said. "Frannie and I are up here at West Lawn and want to know what you want us to do with this big rock."

"Good morning, Alex," Charlie replied. "What rock are you referring to?"

"Um... well, the big white one sitting right in the middle of West Lawn here," Alex said.

"Alex, I'm about to go into a meeting, so I don't have much time," Charlie replied. "I was up there yesterday and would have remembered seeing a big white rock in the middle of West Lawn. Can you tell me where you think it may have come from?"

"We don't know where it came from, and Frannie mowed this spot yesterday," Alex said. "But Chief—it's big!"

"How big?"

"Big."

"Alex, how big?"

"Big as a car, Chief."

"*A car!*" Charlie shouted unintentionally. "Alex, are you telling me that we now have a rock the size of a car in the middle of West Lawn that was not there yesterday?"

"Yes, sir," Alex said apologetically.

"Okay. Okay, sorry for the outburst... not your fault," Charlie replied with more self-control.

"Are you certain it's a rock, Alex? Maybe it is a car disguised as a rock. Do you see any tire marks?"

"No, sir. We looked. We can't find any tracks going to it from the trail, and besides, Frannie and I don't see any tires on the thing," Alex said confidently. "But we haven't been up close to it yet 'cause we didn't want to mess up the grass."

"Okay, good job Alex," Charlie replied. "You and Francesca have my permission to take a cart up to it and attempt to remove it. Hopefully, it's not a rock at all, and the two of you can make it disappear. Alex, please try to run your cart parallel with your mower lines as best you can. I will be out of my meeting around ten. Let me know what you find out then, okay?"

"Roger that, Chief," Alex said, and hung up.

If it's not a car, what else can it be? Charlie thought. *One of those hot-air weather balloons maybe. No matter, I'll let the two of them figure it out.*

Charlie arrived at the offices of the president situated high atop the new administration building a half hour early so that he could spend some time chatting with Anne before his meeting. She was a delightful lady with the patience of a saint. Their chat was occasionally interrupted with what sounded like a fist pounding a desk or a loud angry voice that easily pierced the technologically advanced paper-thin walls.

"Anne, where is your defibrillator?" Charlie asked as he looked intently around the room. "You're going to need it for when Peter pops that last coronary."

"Don't you worry, Charlie. I know where it is," Anne replied with a sheepish grin. "And I might not wait for him to have a heart attack to use it."

Suddenly the door to Peter's office popped opened and out strode Professor Hitchinson. From inside his office, Peter was still screaming.

"And you can tell that damn *personal secretary* of yours, I said so!"

At this point, Hitch turned to face the open doorway and replied calmly, "You may tell her yourself, Peter… and please be sure to address her as my 'personal secretary,' will you?"

Then turning once again to exit the office, he spoke as he walked. "Anne, have a lovely day!"

"Thank you, Professor."

"Charlie, nice to see you."

"Always a pleasure to see you as well, Professor."

No sooner had Hitch closed the reception room door behind himself than Peter cried out from inside his office. "Anne, please send in the next son of a… Charlie… oh… okay then… Well, you can tell him he better have some good news because I'm ready to shoot myself this time and damn happy to take someone with me!"

"You heard him. Go on in 'son of a Charlie,'" Anne said, then smiled and winked.

"Must I?" Charlie whispered.

"You're his only hope, Charlie," Anne whispered back.

"In that case, he is in big trouble," Charlie whispered again.

"Please don't think I can't hear you two clowns whispering out there—at my expense, no doubt," Peter yelled.

"I am a busy man with a college to run. Dr. Mushnick, would it be possible to get your butt in here sometime today?"

Peter would occasionally use the moniker Dr. Mushnick when addressing Charlie. He especially enjoyed using it in public where only he and Charlie would understand its meaning. The name itself was taken from the 1960s film *The Little Shop of Horrors* and referred to the young man who created a man-eating Venus flytrap that devoured half the cast. Peter used it as an endearing term, originally meant to express his total amazement with Charlie's ability to resurrect his roses... without having to feed them humans. Of course, the character's name in the movie was actually Seymour, but Peter got a kick out of saying "Mushnick," the name of the shop owner at the place where Seymour worked, and then applying Charlie's academic credentials to it.

As usual, their meeting was a pleasant one, with business taking approximately ten minutes and the remaining time in deep conversation on how to keep the roses in optimum health going into winter. Knowing how the meetings between these two had a tendency to go far over their allotted time unless she took some corrective action, Anne would start texting her boss the time at five-minute intervals, beginning at ten minutes before the hour.

At 10:01, Charlie received a text from Alex saying, "The rock won't move."

At 10:05, Peter received his third annoying text about the time and raised his hands in surrender.

"You win, damn it!" Peter yelled at the wall that separated him from Anne. "I guess this means our time is up," he said, returning to a normal speaking voice. "I can't overemphasize what the Yard and those David Austin's mean to this university. Those roses are our face, our persona, our pride, no less than the Golden Dome is to Notre Dame. So please, Charlie, I'm begging you, no fricking surprises, okay?"

"No surprises, Peter. We had a mild summer, and the Yard and the roses are in great shape," Charlie replied as he hastened from his chair to the door.

Halfway through the doorway, Charlie could not keep from turning around and as nonchalantly as possible asking Peter if he knew anything about a large rock being delivered to the Yard yesterday. As soon as the words exited his mouth, however, he knew he had made a grievous mistake.

"What the hell is that supposed to mean?" Peter screamed. "Do I look like someone who would order rocks for your little Garden of Eden? Is this something I need to be concerned about, Charlie? Because if it is, what the hell do I need you for?"

Charlie leaned backwards through the doorway and glanced at Anne, who by now had a big grin on her face, and then he looked at a young professor he remembered greeting last year. She sat nervously erect and had a grimaced look on her face because she was evidently Peter's next victim.

"No need to be concerned, Peter," Charlie said calmly. "Forget I asked."

Then turning once again to exit the office, he spoke as he walked. "Anne, have a lovely day."

"Thank you, Charlie."

"Professor Daphne, I believe? It's very nice to see you again."

"Thanks," was all the rattled young professor could manage.

"Next!" Peter cried out from inside his office.

8

The Rock Won't Move

As soon as Charlie was clear of the administration building, he called his crew and Frannie answered.

"Hello, Francesca. So tell me what we have going on over there."

"Chief, you're not going to believe this!" Frannie said excitedly. "You gotta come over here now!"

"I'm on my way, but do you mind telling me what is so unbelievable?"

"Chief..." Frannie hesitated, apparently unsure of how to respond. "Well... we think it's floating."

"You think what is floating, Francesca?"

"The rock, sir."

"You think the rock is floating?"

"Yes, sir."

"Floating?"

"Yes, sir."

"As in not touching the ground?"

"Yes, sir."

"Okay, stay put. I'm on my way," Charlie said reassuringly so as not to provoke any unnecessary anxiety in the two, but he took off as fast as the cart would go.

Charlie stopped on the crest of the last hill before descending into the open pasture known by his crew as the West Lawn of the Grand Courtyard. He could easily make out the white object resting on the gentle slope a hundred yards from any trail or tree line. In the foreground and close to the tree line stood the statue of Colonel Hillary, and in the background was the historic section of campus, including Walker Auditorium and Turner Hall. This was the best vantage point to use the high-powered binoculars he kept in the cart to survey the area and confirm what Alex had said about not seeing any tire marks.

It was large, much larger than he expected. It was about the size of the cart that was parked alongside of it. It was also inexplicably beautiful. In the morning sunshine, it emitted a subtle array of color from within a solid body of brilliant white, much like a giant oblong pearl. But there was also something strange about the illumination that he just couldn't put his finger on.

It was true that only one set of tracks existed, and those had been made by the cart and were not entirely concealed by the mower lines. But if the mysterious thing did not have wheels of its own and could not be moved, it would seem logical that something else must have towed or hauled it in, and that something should have left a trail. From there the possibilities were endless. If it fell from the sky, there should be a massive crater. If it hovered in on its own, it should have engines. If it were transported in by helicopter, someone should have seen or heard it. None of it added up. It was just as easy to believe that it had sprouted out of the ground like a big cabbage. Satisfied with the fact that he had a large unwelcome object sitting in the middle of the courtyard without any plausible explanation, Charlie hopped back into his cart and started down the sloping trail.

That's it! he thought as he smashed the brake pedal to the floor, having traveled only a few yards.

In one smooth motion, he turned the cart off and grabbed the binoculars sitting beside him on the seat. The binoculars were in front of his eyes and ready to be focused by the time he reached full standing position outside the cart. A few quick adjustments and the object below was once again made perfectly clear.

"Where is your shadow, big guy?" he asked rhetorically.

Because of the approach of the fall equinox, the days were getting shorter. Therefore, the late-morning sun was still relatively low on the horizon, casting long shadows from everything... except the object. He continued to watch as Alex and Frannie leaned against the rock, circled the rock, put their ears to the rock, and pounded on the rock with their fists. Everywhere they went, their shadows stretched before them. Not so with the rock. Either it allowed light to pass through itself without any interference, as if it were transparent, or it was as if it did not exist.

Instead of cutting across the field from the main trail as Alex and Frannie had done, Charlie followed the tree line and came down from the back side, thinking this would be the direction they would forklift this thing out of here if necessary. He could tell the two were anxious to see him.

"So, it's not ticking, is it?" Charlie asked sarcastically as he walked over to the object and gently wiped his hand down its length.

"Very funny, Chief," Frannie answered. "We think it's a rock that someone has buffed smooth as a baby's butt."

"Definitely looks like a natural material or a very good imitation," Charlie agreed.

"Yeah, Chief, there isn't a nick or a scratch on it anywhere," Alex added. "And it must weigh a ton 'cause Frannie and I tried to move it. We even bumped it a few times with the cart. The rock won't move."

"We went back to the shed and got the heavy rope and winch," Frannie explained, "but it kept slipping off."

"Yeah, that's when it got sorta freaky," Alex said uneasily, "Cause it didn't slip off the way it went on. It slipped off the wide end—watch."

The rock itself was about twelve to fifteen feet long and had a wide side that was about five to six feet in diameter that tapered down to a narrow side of about three to four feet in diameter, similar in shape to a fuselage of a small aircraft or sports car. Alex tied a nice, tight water-bowline knot and looped it around the narrow end of the rock. The free end of the rope was then threaded into the winch. As soon as the rope became taut, it slipped easily off the wide end of the rock.

"Well, would you look at that?" Charlie said, trying very hard to suppress his own astonishment.

Charlie took the rope, inspected it, and found no defect in either the rope or the knot. He untied the knot, handed Alex one end of the rope, and motioned for him to move to the other side of the rock from where he stood. Together they walked slowly down the length of the rock so that the rope traveled underneath it. At no time did the rope pinch, bind, or resist as they both completed the exercise at the other end. Charlie nodded to himself, tossed his end of the rope in Alex's direction, hesitated for a moment, and then spoke.

"Well, guys, it looks like we got ourselves a nice little mystery, and no time to stop and figure it all out. I can tell by looking at it, it's going to take a lot of effort and some big equipment to move this thing. Agreed?"

"Agreed," the two said in unison.

"So here's the plan for today," Charlie began. "I want you to go back to the shed and get five or six large blocks to support this thing on the downhill side. We don't want it to start rolling and crush someone. Then get enough ten-foot metal-fencing posts to go around this guy, one every six to eight feet or so. Sink them into the ground about a foot with one bag of cement. It's only temporary, but I want them nice and straight. We'll pull them out and fill in the holes after school begins. Work from the inside of the fence as best you can. Any questions so far?"

"We hiding this thing, Chief?" Frannie asked.

"That is exactly what we're doing, Francesca," Charlie replied. "Tomorrow I want you to wrap it securely with eight-foot chain-link fencing—no gate, just fencing. I don't want anyone touching this thing. Then strap as many of our large camo tarps as needed to the fence. I don't want anyone peeking in on it, either. Again, I want everything nice and tight—no loose seams. Take your time. Everything you need, we should have in the shed. If not, take the business card and buy what you need. And let's use the tree line to move in and out of here. Any more questions?"

"No, sir," the two said in unison, and hopped into their cart.

"Hey, before you go," Charlie said with a tone of urgency, "I don't think I have to tell you how important it is to keep this quiet. There is an explanation for everything, just as there is an explanation for this guy right here. We don't get a whole lot of traffic down this way anymore, but if anyone should ask you what's going on or attempts to interfere in any way, call me immediately, okay?"

"Roger that, Chief," Alex replied.

"We got it, Chief," Frannie concurred.

"All right, let's make this rock disappear for a couple weeks and then get back to more pressing work," Charlie said in an attempt to downplay this extraordinary occurrence. "You two go on. I'm going to look around some."

Charlie watched the two disappear over the ridge and then carefully looked around to see if anyone might be watching him. Somewhat embarrassed, he went about the rock doing basically the very same thing he had observed Alex and Frannie do. After several minutes that added nothing to his understanding of the rock-like object, he sat down in his cart and patiently watched the rock do nothing for several more minutes.

Okay, Lord, this has got your fingerprints all over it, and I've seen your handiwork before, Charlie thought.

This would not be Charlie's first brush with the Lord's "handiwork." It happened in his fourth year at Hillary University, and the memory of it came back as if it were yesterday.

Charlie recalled standing halfway down the center aisle of the Sanctuary, in no man's land. He was responding to one of those ancient security systems developed and installed in the Sanctuary back in the mid-seventies, and it was now ten years later. In ten years, technology had advanced a hundredfold, but the Sanctuary was last on the list for upgrading to this new system because, well, who would rob a church?

If it had been up to him, Charlie would have disabled the system altogether. Its propensity to go off whenever the wind blew a little too hard or a stray cat decided to take a stroll across a windowsill was a constant intrusion on his evenings. He was in his fourth year at Hillary, and following up on every false alarm was getting old, as was everything else about Hillary.

His predecessor, a good Christian man, had promised him a challenging position that would take full advantage of his two doctorates from the University of Colorado, Boulder: law and environmental engineering. The job offer was sweetened with some vague reference to a ministry that would "most certainly present itself... in God's time." Well, he had waited patiently four years for a ministry to complement his primary responsibilities to the university, and unless responding to these annoying alarms was considered a ministry, nothing else had presented itself.

But this night would be no false alarm.

Standing in front of Charlie were two large and ominous men, who only a few seconds ago were so preoccupied with stealing everything shiny they did not notice that Charlie had entered the room. They noticed now and immediately drew large-caliber handguns from their waistbands. Charlie knew he was at point-blank range. Any movement now and he was a dead man.

"Who the hell are you?" the one asked angrily, as if Charlie had interrupted important work.

"I'm the curator of this Sanctuary," Charlie replied as calmly as he could manage, and in a brief moment of spontaneous boldness, he presented his own question. "Did you know you were stealing from God?"

"Do I look like I give a damn?" The same angry guy answered, but with a hint of uncertainty now.

"Pop him, man!" the other guy spit out without hesitation, and began pacing back and forth. "You gotta do him, man. He done seen us, man. We ain't got no masks on."

"Shut up! Let me think!"

"What you thinkin' for, man? We can't get caught. I ain't going back, man. I won't go back in them walls."

"Shut up, man!" the apparent leader of this two-man gang shouted as he turned to face his skittish accomplice. "I know what I gotta do!"

While this inimical bantering was taking place, Charlie began praying silently for family, friends, church, colleagues he had talked to on a daily basis but had not shared the love of Christ with—anything and everything, as fast and furious as his mind would go. He knew he had only until they turned their attention back to him. That's when the most unexpected thing occurred.

Having made up their minds, the would-be burglars—and soon-to- be murderers— turned back toward Charlie. Their steely gazes, however, appeared to focus on something beyond him, and the leader spoke in that direction.

"Who the hell are you?" he demanded.

This odd behavior caused even Charlie to turn his head to have a look for himself. Seeing and hearing nothing behind him, Charlie turned back to the two big angry guys with powerful guns pointed in his general direction. The leader spoke again, mockingly.

"I'll show you some truth, man!"

With that he pulled the trigger of his weapon. Charlie jerked his right arm up to his face but heard no sound and felt no pain. The weapon did not fire. The irritated thief pulled the trigger a second time—no bullet. A third time—no bullet.

"Take him out!" the leader ordered his partner.

The second thief aimed his weapon toward Charlie, but not at him. He pulled the trigger, which caused Charlie to make the same defensive motion with his arm as before—no bullet. The brute pulled the trigger a second time—no bullet.

After a brief pause, the frustrated leader spoke again to someone beyond where Charlie was standing.

"Who are you?"

Again Charlie turned his head, and again he found no one behind him, nor did he hear a sound. Without saying a word to Charlie or to each other, the two men turned suddenly and started walking hastily toward the rear of the building, presumably to leave the same way they had come in. After several steps, however, they just as suddenly stopped, dropped the dirty pillowcases full of stolen goods to the floor, gently laid their weapons on top of the sacks, and left.

Stunned by this bizarre life-or-death experience, Charlie stood motionless as he contemplated what to do next. He turned suddenly and spoke.

"Is anyone there?"

No response.

"Please. Show yourself. I want to thank you."

Nothing.

Charlie then sprinted to the back, where he found the back door, which had been jimmied open with a crowbar of some sort, flung wide open. He left the door as it was, not wanting to disturb evidence, then found the closest phone and called the police. Within minutes the exterior of the Sanctuary was awash in dazzling color from the lights of an endless stream of emergency vehicles. Other than drawing first responders, the incident did not attract much of a crowd, since the student population was home for the summer.

The detectives talking to Charlie were stupefied by his statements. In fact, they were constantly interrupting him to clarify what they thought they heard him say.

"Did you say both guns jammed?"

"And you believe they were in conversation with someone you did not see or hear?"

"Are you saying they both simply turned and left on their own accord?"

"And you can't tell us why they would leave their weapons behind?"

"Do you understand how improbable that sounds?"

Thinking shock might be the cause of these incredible responses, the detectives asked Charlie if he would be willing to have the on-site EMTs look him over. Other than showing some lingering signs of being shaken up by having his life threatened, Charlie was cleared of any immediate medical danger. At this point, the detectives thought it best to allow their only eyewitness to get some rest. They would revisit him tomorrow in hopes of extracting some useful information.

The long night of evidence gathering, picture taking, and dusting for prints was finally complete. The detectives took with them the two guns and the pillowcases, but left the university's property. Charlie returned these articles—some invaluable originals dating back to the Civil War—to their shelves. He maneuvered a heavy desk against the back door to keep it shut for the night, then enabled the antiquated but now more highly appreciated security system and left. He knew his evening was not over however. That was because his second call of the night had been to his wife, who was waiting anxiously for his return home.

Charlie remembered the detectives returning the following day to apologize. The ballistics team had found the primers within three fully charged cartridges of one gun and the primers within two charged cartridges of the other gun showing signs of being successfully struck by their firing pins. Their conclusion: There was no good reason why both weapons should not have discharged their rounds and a dead body discovered. That did not solve all the riddles presented by this case, but the detectives were clearly surprised and happy with the results so far. They promised to keep Charlie up-to-date with their investigation.

This preliminary information was forwarded to the university as well. The very next day, no less than six contractors were seen taking measurements for the installation of a more sophisticated security system for all four original buildings, starting with the Sanctuary.

The detectives returned a week later to tell Charlie that one of the suspects in his case had been identified by his fingerprints but was fatally shot by officers in another failed burglary. Charlie thanked the gentlemen for putting themselves in harm's way on a daily basis and for their visit, but this news did not bring any joy to Charlie's heart. Something else had happened that night, and it wasn't about justice—it was about mercy.

Charlie could not have ever imagined how right he was.

It had been more than two weeks since the burglary, and there was no word as to what had happened to the other thief, the leader. For some reason, this felt more like good news than bad to Charlie. This, of course, made no sense, when that dude had been more than willing to take Charlie's life. And who knows how many other lives were at risk with this angry and desperate person on the street?

But Charlie actually found himself praying for this lost soul since being made aware of his partner's death.

If the other burglar were to die, would anyone mourn? Charlie remembered thinking.

The Sanctuary had been locked up for summer break, and it was the first opportunity for Charlie to check things out—except for false alarms, of course. He was not in the downstairs mess hall for long, but when he arrived back upstairs, he noticed a man sitting in the center pews of the worship hall. It was not unusual for a person to pop in for some quiet time with the Lord, but classes would not begin for another three weeks and the campus was, for the most part, empty. As Charlie stood silently watching the man's body language, he could tell something weighed heavily on him. The man's broad shoulders drooped forward, and his head was buried deep in his large hands. Every now and again the man's head would rise slightly, as if to take a much needed breath of air, but then collapse once again.

No longer able to stand by watching as this poor man wrestled the demons inside alone, Charlie walked to the pew in which the man was seated and spoke gently. "May I pray for you?"

"I would be grateful," the man replied, and lifted his head.

It was the thief, the leader!

"You returned?" Charlie asked breathlessly.

"Yes," the man stated firmly.

"Why?"

"To ask you for forgiveness," the anguished man replied.

"My forgiveness?"

"You have the right to hate me," the man confessed, "but I was told to go and ask anyways."

"Who told you?"

"The angel of the Lord," the man answered without hesitation. "You were here."

"Where?"

"Right here," the man replied, and looked at Charlie quizzically.

"I knew it!" Charlie spoke softly to himself.

"First, I forgive you," Charlie said honestly, but hurriedly. "Now, tell me what you saw that night after you and your partner talked."

Before the man could respond, Charlie spoke again. "And I'm sorry to hear about your partner."

"He was my cousin," the man stated, "But we was both brought up by my mom. I tried to stop him from going out that night, but he wouldn't listen."

Charlie wasn't expecting this kind of news and was stunned into silence; he should be asking for this man's forgiveness for taking the loss of his relative so lightly.

"I bear witness to the truth, and the truth shall set you free," the man said.

"I'm sorry, what?" Charlie blurted out.

"That's what the angel said," the man replied. "That's when I tried to shoot him."

"But your guns didn't work," Charlie added. "Then what happened?"

"The angel said, 'Your weapons are useless in this house. Go now and sin no more.'"

"That's why you turned to leave," Charlie said softly, beginning to put the pieces together. "But why did you drop the sacks and your guns?"

"'Cause the angel said, 'Leave what does not belong to you,'" the man replied. "We stole those guns, so we left 'em."

"Did the angel say anything else?" Charlie asked.

"Why you asking me this?" the man asked. "He was standing right behind you."

"All right, I get that," Charlie said politely. "Can I ask your name?"

"Isaac," the man replied, without fear of giving himself away.

"Isaac, I didn't see or hear anything you just described," Charlie admitted. "I'm telling you the truth."

This information didn't seem to change Isaac's disposition or his purpose.

"Well, thank you for forgiving me," Isaac answered in his straight-to-the-point way of speaking. "Can I go?"

"You can go. I see no good reason to call the authorities now," Charlie replied. "But why do it this way, Isaac? Why come here at all?"

"'Cause my mom, she told me what the Lord was asking me to do," Isaac replied. "Before I can be forgiven my trespasses, I gotta ask everyone I hurt for forgiveness."

"Isaac, is it your intention to talk to everyone you hurt?" Charlie asked in disbelief.

"That's right."

"Isaac, I don't know all that you have done, but some people might not be as understanding as I have been," Charlie stated, much like any attorney would counsel a client on self-incrimination.

"I ain't afraid of no jail... or dying," Isaac replied. "I'm on the Lord's side now."

"Isaac, I'm not going to try to talk you out of this," Charlie said nervously, "but I want you to take my number and call me if things get too hot. Understand me? Keep it close to you— don't lose it."

Charlie remembered getting two calls from Isaac after their meeting: one to say he was going to jail, and the other, six months later, saying he was out. Charlie knew it was only a petty theft charge and offered Isaac a position at the university when he was released. But the second call was simply a courtesy call from Isaac telling Charlie he had found a good job and a good woman, both in his church.

As the soft translucent veil of the daydream slowly dissipated, Charlie found himself still sitting in his cart and staring at a large white rock doing what large white rocks do—nothing.

Charlie enjoyed reminiscing about that day the Lord had saved two men... Isaac and himself. He had shared the specifics of that event with his wife alone, but it played a pivotal role in his decision to stay at Hillary. Soon afterward, he began his ministry to welcome each and every new hire to the university, beginning with a young and cocky professor from Harvard named Hitchinson.

"Well, Lord, I don't get the feeling your handiwork here was intended for me," Charlie said softly. "So do your will, and I'm sure you'll let me know what to do with this thing once it's served your purpose." With that rudimentary and arguably far-reaching synopsis, Charlie started up the cart and took off.

Alex and Frannie were back in an hour with the supplies needed to begin the process of making the floating rock disappear from sight. They used the route going to and from the rock as they were asked to do and were very careful to keep their work contained inside the perimeter of the fence they were about to erect. In fact, they were much more careful about their impact on the area surrounding the rock than the impact on the rock itself. Charlie did not seem to give a hoot about the rock, and therefore, neither did they. They leaned the rock-breaking bar, posthole digger, shovel, and the ten poles against its side and stacked the bags of cement on top of it. When Alex set the blocks on the downhill side of the rock, he was sure to give each an extra kick or two to ensure a nice tight fit. He couldn't help but notice how the block's jagged edges cut huge scars into the rock's smooth surface, but what did he care?

Wait till the crane gets hold of it, he thought.

However, after kicking the third block into place, he looked back at the first two, and the scars were gone. In the few seconds it took to look away from the third block and back again, its scar was gone too.

"Frannie, come here quick!" Alex called out.

"What's up?" she asked.

"Watch this," he said as he picked up a block and heaved it at the rock.

"Are you crazy?" Frannie screamed as the block careened off the side of the rock, causing a huge gash in the flawless white shell.

"Keep watching," Alex said.

They both watched in amazement as the gash slowly disappeared before their eyes.

"You got any lipstick on you?" Alex asked.

"Do you see me wearing lipstick?" Frannie replied abruptly. "Why do you need lipstick anyway?"

Instead of answering Frannie, he walked over to the cart and returned moments later with a large black permanent marker. In the same spot he had thrown the block, Alex wrote "FRANNIE WAS HERE."

"You jerk!" Frannie screamed again. "Why'd you use my name?"

But it didn't take long for the large black letters to fade white.

"We need to tell Chief," Alex said with renewed excitement.

"I get the feeling Chief already knows what's going on and not telling us yet," Frannie answered calmly. "I say we get the poles in the ground like we were told, and then we tell him."

"Okay, you're right," Alex agreed, and then remarked, "I wonder what else it can do."

"I don't know and I don't care," Frannie snapped back. "You're not going to tell anybody about this, are you?"

"I'd never go back on my word to Chief," Alex stated unequivocally. "Not in a million years!"

"Good," Frannie replied in all seriousness. "I'd hate to have to hurt you!"

Neither of them could remember a time when they had been asked to dig a hole on university property and not have to use the rock-breaking bar or jackhammer to burrow through rock at some point. Today, however, the posthole digger was all that was necessary to dig ten perfect little holes a foot deep. This allowed them to set the poles in cement and clean up in record time. They agreed that by noon tomorrow the canvas would be put into place and this rock would be history.

"You think we should bring some No Trespassing signs out with us tomorrow?" Alex asked.

"Good question," Frannie replied. "Let's go ask Chief."

9

Traveling Partners

Hitch left Peter's office feeling renewed. He did not regret for one minute the loss of sleep for something as perceptive and rewarding as that which had come from the mind of Freud.

"Insight such as this falls to one's lot but once in a lifetime": Hitch repeated the words that Freud used, when referring to himself as being the author of Interpretation of Dreams.

He also found the university's president a worthy opponent in the vigorous exchange of differing viewpoints. Hitch quickly discovered that underneath Peter's often brutish and vulgar exterior was a first-rate intellect. Having acknowledged and accepted this seemingly incongruent idiosyncrasy in Peter, he pitied those who failed to recognize the deception. In many ways, he actually enjoyed those encounters with Peter.

But now Hitch had other problems: they had booted his car. Yes, it was parked in a space reserved for the handicapped, and the university apparently had zero tolerance for this transgression, but did they not recognize his vehicle? Was he not on someone's "Do Not Piss Off" list? In addition to this oversight, did they not realize that by incapacitating his car like this, they only prolonged the inconvenience of those they sought to help? He was livid and looked for someone... anyone... in an official-looking uniform to unleash his discontent. Finding no one who fit the description, he pulled out his smartphone and began texting Ms. Brown:

> Good morning, Ms. Brown. At your convenience, please have someone remove the boot from my car that is parked in a handicapped spot in front of Peter's little ivory tower. It is unlocked, and the keys are in the ignition. Perhaps they would be so kind as to move it to another spot once they discover who it is they booted—imbeciles! For the benefit of those who might approach me in my current frame of mind, I have decided to walk back to my office. I need not remind you that this will take some time, so please adjust my schedule accordingly. Thank you for your assistance in this matter, and thank you for not ever reminding me that the incident was, of course, my fault in the first place.

The morning chill could not be more conducive for a walk, and the natural quietude of the dense woodlands prior to reaching the open pastures of the courtyard could not have been more relaxing. Hitch soon forgot this latest annoyance and wondered to himself why he had not taken Ms. Brown's advice to walk this path more often—except for an opportunity to say no to her every now and again. Other than the occasional white-tailed deer, there was nothing that interrupted his concentration for very long, until he cleared the last hill and began the gentle slope down into the Yard. It was hard to miss the large white object and the two people attempting to drag it with a rope and a cart. By the time the trail took him to within a hundred yards of this strange affair, he had watched the two lasso the inanimate white beast three times, only to have the rope fall to the ground with the slightest tug.

Hitch felt no particular inclination to stop and explain to them that they had most likely underestimated the object's density. In other words, whatever the substance was, its mass had obviously exceeded the capability of their rope-and-cart exercise. He recognized the two young people as Charlie's employees, and that Charlie, currently in a meeting with Peter, would most likely be along shortly. As long as they were not in a position to hurt themselves, Hitch pressed on towards his office in Turner Hall. He looked back only once when he heard a loud booming sound that echoed in the field. He turned and observed the cart being used a second time as a battering ram against the object, without effect. He was not far from the building when he received a text message back from Ms. Brown:

Good morning, Professor. I would be happy to work on getting the boot removed from your car if only you would work on your indifference to those less fortunate than yourself. I have been told that you are close. I was unable to cancel your first appointment because of such short notice, and now your second appointment has arrived. Your publisher, who has been rescheduled three times, is due to arrive in half an hour. I suggest you enter your office through the back and decide who it is you want to disappoint. Please advise at your convenience.

Thankful for the warning, Hitch entered through one of the back doors that would ultimately wind its way to his office. The tablet that sat prominently on his desk instantly reminded him that his first appointment was with a representative from the University of Vienna. The second appointment was with a young Millennial with a sharp mind and in whom he had invested a lot of time. There had been others before this young man, but Hitch had high hopes for this one. Fortunately, the decision to disappoint was made easy this time. The fellow from the University of Vienna was not a member of Freud's immediate or extended family and therefore meant nothing to him. The publisher was in effect a salesman and would gladly reschedule a hundred times if it meant making a book sale. The student, on the other hand, presented another chance for him to build on his legacy, and he was rapidly running out of time... and prospects. Hitch sent his response:

Ms. Brown, I could have one of those car rear-view-mirror hangers that imply a disability tomorrow, if I chose to be dishonest about it—a trick I have observed many able-bodied liars do. Please dispatch the representative from Vienna any way you wish, with my apologies, of course. Reschedule my publisher a fourth time, with regrets, and send in the student. I had a sleepless night, so after my meeting with this young man, I wish to use the time available to discuss the remainder of my day.

Hitch eased his way over to the enormous windows to check the progress of Charlie's energetic yet ill-equipped worker bees just as Charlie pulled up. He watched Charlie exit his cart and walk up to the large, curious thing as if he too were surprised by its presence. Hitch thought it fascinating that Charlie could be unaware that such an immense object had been delivered to his proverbial doorstep.

"You should have seen his face!" A familiar voice came from behind.

"And who would that be, Ryan?" Hitch inquired dispassionately and without turning his head.

Hitch continued to watch the events going on outside. After a brief exchange with his young helpers, Charlie was given the same demonstration with the rope and cart that Hitch had seen only a short time ago, with the exact same results.

"I believe the man said he was from the University of Vienna and traveled a long way to be here today," the young genius-in-the-making replied. "When I was invited to come in by Ms. Brown and he was told you were unavailable, his face turned a bright orange-red, like the element neon will do when blasted with some serious voltage."

"Come over here, please," Hitch said, being more interested in Charlie's movements than his student's story. When the young man was by his side, he spoke again.

"Tell me, Ryan, what does that large white object out there weigh?"

Occasionally, in an effort to get his gifted yet somewhat anal-retentive star students to look outside the box (to think for themselves instead of giving textbook responses), Hitch would draw their attention to some random scientific, philosophic, economic, political, or religious conundrum and pose a seemingly obscure question that might or might not have a definitive solution. He did not equate the expression *anal retentive* as having the same meaning as being *anal* (the disparaging metaphor in today's vernacular). Being anal retentive was, in fact, a pathologic behavior first theorized by Dr. Freud. This behavior originates in childhood and manifests itself later in adulthood as an obsession to do everything by the book.

Well aware that this might be one of those obscure trial balloons Dr. Hitchinson was famous for, the young apprentice waited patiently to see whether more information was forthcoming, before he formulated an answer.

Both student and teacher watched silently as Charlie untied the knot in the rope and handed one end to Alex. The student, meanwhile, concentrated on the large white object itself and what had been asked of him. He paid little attention to Charlie and Alex pulling a rope underneath the length of an immovable object without effort.

"Can I ask what it is made of?" Ryan finally asked politely.

Hitch was astonished at what he had just witnessed in the Yard—or what he thought he had witnessed. This was the second time in two days that he had experienced an event that defied explanation. He was equally astonished that his young protégé could be so dense as to witness something so incredible and so obvious yet allow his mind to disregard it completely. These were the rare opportunities that helped Hitch identify the makings of a prospective genius. A free and unfettered mind was absolutely essential. In fact, the sole purpose of these multifarious tests had nothing to do with proving how intelligent a student was—he already knew that. These tests were given to see whether a student would observe and recognize what others observe but fail to recognize. Unfortunately, this year's brightest star had just flamed out.

Hitch said nothing but continued to watch and see how Charlie might react to this extraordinary new development.

"All right then," Ryan said matter-of-factly, taking the silence of his eccentric professor in stride, and continued to speak. "You wish to know the weight of that white object down there, and that must come with my first assumption of it being a rock."

Ryan paused momentarily to allow an opportunity for correction but got none.

"Any discussion of a rock's mass must take into account a composition of minerals and voids in various proportions that will affect its true density. This particular specimen has a finely polished white outer surface that suggests the substance could be marble. Unless I am corrected, that will be my second assumption."

Receiving nothing back from his mentor, Ryan continued with his calculations.

"If I'm not mistaken, marble has an approximate density of 2.5 grams per cubic centimeter. Fortunately, the cart parked alongside this crystalline stone is familiar to me and is similar in size. This provides me with an excellent gauge to calculate its volume, which I estimate to be just over fifteen cubic meters. Therefore, without the benefit of more detailed information, my answer is approximately thirty-eight thousand kilograms."

Even though computed without the use of a calculator, Ryan felt confident in his answer, but he received no confirmation from the professor. Undaunted, he quickly converted his answer from kilograms to pounds.

"That's eighty-four thousand pounds and some change," he quipped jovially, but still he got no response.

"Forty-two tons?" he asked quizzically, but again got nothing.

Hitch could sense his student was speaking to him, but he was not going to look away and chance missing any new information that could help explain what he had just seen. Charlie had obviously given his two employees instructions and sent them on their way. Now the man with a doctorate in law and another in earthy matters, which Hitch presumed included large white rocks, began to inspect the thing himself.

Slightly annoyed with being asked such an ill-defined question and then having his genuine attempt at some sort of reasonable answer dismissed, Ryan decided to have some fun with his distracted mentor's question.

"Then again, it could be filled with marshmallows and weigh less than a thousand pounds," he chuckled. "Since marshmallows have a density that is less than water, it would float too!"

This latest absurdity was intended to jolt his mentor out of whatever daze he was in, and yet the answer was still more or less accurate. The effort, however, fared no better in getting the professor's attention than his previous earnest attempt. The idea that he was being ignored only encouraged Ryan to continue with his baiting witticism.

"On the other hand, it might be a white dwarf star," he said in mock seriousness. "It's small, but with a density of 10^{10}, we're looking at a weight of 1.6 trillion tons."

By this time, Hitch sensed things were about to come to an unsatisfying conclusion down in the Yard. Charlie had disappeared into his cart, and the rock did nothing but glisten in the morning sunshine. There was something else about the stone's illumination that intrigued him, but the ambient chattering of his apprentice caused his concentration to waver. Hitch relaxed once more, turned slowly to face his brilliant young protégé and spoke placidly.

"That will be all for today, Ryan. I will see you in class two weeks from now."

"But I thought we were going to kick around some plasma and high-energy astrophysics modeling today?" Ryan answered indignantly. "If my attempts to be amusing while you daydreamed were offensive, I am truly sorry, Professor."

"I was not daydreaming," Hitch said calmly. "And you could have been telling me my hair was on fire and I would not have heard a word of it, so there is no need to apologize for anything you may have said."

Hitch hesitated a moment, then walked over to a massive wall of books and withdrew one from a thousand. He opened it for a second or two and closed it again. Returning to the window, he handed the book to the young man and spoke.

"See Ms. Brown to schedule another meeting. An hour will do," Hitch sighed.

What was I thinking, giving this blind neophyte another hour of my time? he thought. *I have every right to bill his parents a thousand dollars.*

"In that time, I would like you to have read chapters 3 through 23 with all the fervor you can muster. Also read and internalize Dr. Thomas's thesis that I reference in my bibliography. Do you understand what I am asking, Ryan?"

"I do, sir, and thank you," Ryan answered gratefully.

Ryan may not have caught the rope trick that occurred outside, but he did know the meaning of the professor's sigh. He took the book and left.

Hitch remained at the window. If he had not known any better, he would have believed he was soul-searching—whatever that meant. It seemed only a few minutes had passed when he noticed Ms. Brown standing patiently in front of his desk.

"You wished to discuss your schedule, Professor?" she asked politely.

"Yes, thank you," he replied wearily, suddenly feeling the effects of having very little sleep. "Were you able to relieve my car from its shackles?"

"Your car is resting peacefully in your reserved spot downstairs," Ms. Brown said, with more compassion after noticing the professor's labored demeanor. "But as far as we can tell, it was never booted."

"What do you mean?" Hitch asked incredulously.

"Before I sent anyone out to move your car, I contacted the campus police to pay any fines and was told they do not use the boot," Ms. Brown began. "So I called the local police and was told they do not patrol university property. When my associate arrived at your car, he informed me that there was no boot on it."

Hitch dropped his head, and his shoulders slumped as if a heavy weight had just been placed on them.

"Professor, are you all right? Ms. Brown asked bluntly. "I am concerned about you."

"I... I don't know," he whispered.

"That's it—I am clearing your schedule!" Ms. Brown declared with imputed authority. "I am quite certain that I will be able to convince Dr. Roberts to see you for an examination later today, or at the very latest tomorrow, once he understands the circumstances."

"Wait... please?" Hitch spoke softly, not as an imperative, but as a request, as in, *can we talk about this first?*

"I do not disagree with you that my behavior lately might be some sort of chemical imbalance or vitamin deficiency," Hitch began, "but, as you know, I have a reputation to protect. Should it be leaked that I am having conversations with ghosts and seeing large orange mechanical devices attached to my car where there are none, my goose will be cooked, as they say."

"I don't care about your reputation or your goose," Ms. Brown said gravely. "I care about you and your health."

Ms. Brown's words of concern greatly moved Hitch, but he knew he was a bit vulnerable right now. Full disclosure of these various episodes of his was dangerous, and no one was ever going to convince him they were not real... even the dream. Still, he could not help feeling he was being attacked, metaphorically speaking, and wanted nothing more than to open up these feelings to discussion with someone he could trust.

Meanwhile, thinking she was about to lose her troubled boss to another daydream— which was not that unusual—Ms. Brown spoke again.

"Professor, I can't find you help if you won't tell me what's going on," she pleaded. "Please, anyone can see how you are not yourself."

Not so, Ms. Brown. Only you care enough to see it, Hitch thought. *Oh, if only I had a son with whom you might fall in love, then remain in my life forever.*

"You are right, Ms. Brown. I do believe I need help," Hitch began. "But I'm not so sure it is Dr. Roberts's expertise that I need. If you have the time, I will try to explain."

"Give me one second... to make... a few contacts and... " She spoke and typed feverishly on her smartphone simultaneously. "There—we will not be interrupted for one hour. Will that be enough time, Professor?"

"That should do it, Ms. Brown," he said in amazement.

Without hesitation or deliberate concealment, Hitch described the three strange events of the last twenty-four hours, beginning with the intruder who appeared yesterday and offered to answer his Irrefutability Theory, then disappeared just before Ms. Brown arrived. He told her about the stranger's ability to read his mind and with a word prevent him from speaking. Hitch did not withhold anything except that for some reason, he didn't mention the stranger's parting comment about the "stone-like object without blemish." This was not willful evasion on his part; he simply forgot to include it in his storytelling.

Hitch went into even greater detail of his dream with Nero and the lions, which brought Ms. Brown to tears and in psychosomatic fashion revived the pain in his neck where the legionary had nearly buried his sword. He spoke about harboring some resentment toward her for having caused the vivid dream in the first place, most likely alcohol induced, and even admitted to his unsuccessful efforts to let her know it very, very early this morning.

Hitch finished their hour together with a brief explanation of his decision to spend the night reading instead of sleeping, his battle of wits with Dr. Stansbury this morning, and the undeniable fact there had been a boot fastened to his car's wheel, which forced him to walk the courtyard trail back to his office. He mentioned passing Charlie's crew and witnessing their inability to move a large rock that now sat in the middle of the Yard, just before receiving her text to enter Turner Hall from a back door.

"Thank you for listening, Ms. Brown," Hitch stated appreciatively when their time had expired. "I do not expect you to resolve any of these mysteries. I only ask that you understand my circumstances and keep what I have just described in confidence."

"I assure you that no one will hear a word of it from my lips, Professor," Ms. Brown promised. "But if what you have told me is true—and I don't doubt your sincerity—you must let me know how I can help you through this."

"You already have, Ms. Brown," Hitch said. "You listened perfectly."

"Well, I am still scheduling that appointment with Dr. Roberts, and you must promise me you will go," she replied. "I will tell him nothing other than you have had trouble sleeping and it was affecting your commitments to the university."

"I will go," he responded with a drawn smile. "Please try not to be too melodramatic on my behalf. Roberts is a good man and will fit me in when he can."

"Now, I believe a two-hour power nap taken right here in the comfort of my study will be all that is necessary for me to fulfill this afternoon's commitments," Hitch continued. "Can you arrange, or rearrange, that for me please, Ms. Brown?"

"I wish you would allow me to clear your day, but if you insist... yes, I will do as you ask." She smiled and left.

As soon as the comforter was thrown into the air and had come to rest over his body, Hitch was dead to the world. There would be no lions or tigers or bears to interrupt his sleep this time.

* * * * *

When Jack finally came back down to earth, he was sitting at his office desk on the second floor of Turner Hall, shuffling papers. He had very little memory of how he got there. He must have driven himself, of course, but could have easily run every light between home and Hillary. Life with MJ was like that sometimes, and not necessarily following great sex. His love for her was so much more than the perfect assembly of body parts and the way they could so easily smoke every one of his five senses when their bodies collided. In fact, the thought of experiencing these extraordinary erotic sensations most often preceded love-making, not afterwards. No, the wandering thoughts that had kept him two feet off the ground since this morning's rendezvous with his wife could more easily be explained as reliving the fun he had been having with his best friend.

Jack was looking forward to calling MJ just to ask her the name of the perfume that wouldn't allow him to concentrate on anything but her, now that he was wearing the dress shirt he had slipped off her this morning. But it was still too early. He would have to wait till around the time she and the boys broke for lunch. That gave him just enough time to kick back and read a little Frost or Dickinson or perhaps T. S. Eliot's "Prufrock." Jack let go of the meaningless papers he was holding and pushed himself away from the desk. The books of poetry and prose he had every intention of organizing were still lying across the room in teetering stacks on the floor.

Crossing the room, however, would mean walking past those large, irresistibly enticing windows—a trip he knew had the potential of robbing him of precious time if he succumbed to their enchantment. The strategy, therefore, was to keep his eyes trained on the stack of books and not stop walking until he reached them. Unfortunately, his peripheral vision was too keen, and from the corner of his eye, he couldn't help but notice Charlie's cart parked next to a large white object in the middle of the Yard.

Now what's he up to? Jack thought as his momentum began to slow precipitously.

Fortunately, Charlie's cart began to pull away from the white object or container, which did not immediately interest Jack, so there was no complete stop in front of the windows this time. He knew that whatever Charlie was up to, it most certainly had something to do with Dr. Hitchinson's highly anticipated lecture in a couple of weeks.

This idea caused Jack to begin fabricating a few ludicrous topics on which the Hillary don could lecture, like, for example, a call for the establishment of a fourth branch of government made up exclusively of mathematicians and physicists, with Einstein wigs and veto powers. On the other hand, Jack could easily envision this brilliant man surprising the world by introducing an entirely new row of elements on the periodic table that would fit nicely below the two rare earth groups. Then again, wouldn't it send a shock wave among the intellectual community worldwide if the iconic professor professed a saving faith in Jesus Christ and was baptized by immersion right there on stage?

"Wowza!" Jack said, unable to contain a chuckle. "Talk about a Damascus Road moment." He was referring to the apostle Paul's extraordinary conversion from church persecutor to church planter in the book of Acts.

While these thoughts occupied his mind, Jack crossed the room, did a 180 at the wall, pressed his back to it, and slid himself down into a sitting position on the floor between two stacks of books. He grabbed the top book from the stack on his right and laid it on his lap without looking at the title or the book itself. Still contemplating the implications of a transcendent genius like Hitchinson (much like the apostle Paul) on fire for the Lord, Jack roamed the cover of the book with his fingers until they came across a bookmark protruding from its pages, and he instinctively opened to that page. Finally glancing down, Jack noticed the book he was holding was an old King

James Bible, and the last book of the New Testament was the spot bookmarked.

Jack would have probably tossed the Bible back onto the heap except that Revelation was his favorite book of the Bible, authored by his favorite New Testament writer and written in his favorite translation whenever he was hungry for God's Word in its most poetic form. Most found the prophetic and highly symbolic book of Revelation dark and scary. Truth be told, Jack believed it should give those who were prepared for the return of Jesus Christ great hope. After all, the book began with the affirmation "Blessed is he that readeth, and they that hear the words of this prophecy," and the book ended with the Aramaic expression *maranatha*, or "Even so, come, Lord Jesus," transliterated into the Greek imperative *come*, as in, "Lord Jesus, come now!" It made no sense to him why believers would think that God would lure us with a blessing at the beginning of this book and then have us plead for Jesus' quick return at its conclusion if what happened in between would do us harm.

The man chosen by God to pen Revelation was the apostle John, the son of Zebedee and "the disciple whom Jesus loved." He was also the author of the Gospel of John, another book full of symbolism and quite unlike the other three Synoptic Gospels. Jack equated the joy of reading Revelation and the Gospel of John in the King James Version's old English language to the joy of reading Shakespeare's *Macbeth* or *The Tempest*—it just did not get any better than that. So off he went into the heavenlies, where Jesus lives.

It did not take him long to finish the unveiling of Jesus Christ and the coming of the New Jerusalem and still have time for a little more literature before giving MJ a call. Jack was feeling it now as he returned the Bible to the stack. He was in his zone. Applying the same technique that had produced the last great narrative, he closed his eyes, grabbed the top book on the left, and laid it on his lap. He allowed his fingers to search for a bookmark, but found none. It was a full-sized book, but thin; perhaps it was Shakespeare's sonnets or maybe Whitman's *Leaves of Grass*. Whatever it was, it was certainly something he could finish with the time remaining. Before opening his eyes, he promised himself that no matter what it was, he would study it carefully and attempt to learn something new from it with gratitude. He had to smile when he glanced down at his next reading assignment: *Horton Hatches the Egg*.

Really? Dr. Seuss?

He yielded to his promise of learning something new, and with gratitude.

"Well, I said what I meant and I meant what I said," he said softly. "An elephant's faithful 100 percent!"

Jack had forgotten that when Jake was old enough to understand that his dad read books for a living, his son presented him with this book along with *Horton Hears a Who*. He quickly found the other book and read them both carefully, and gratefully. This did not take long, of course; but there was nothing left in his entire collection of books that could have added to his contentment at that moment. He rose and walked back over to the windows with some time to kill.

The scene was typical: quiet surroundings with an occasional runner or a pedestrian going from point A to point B with their head down. But now there was the large white thing that Charlie had left behind. It was an odd shape and seemed to produce a rainbow of color just beneath the surface of a smooth white shell that he hadn't noticed before. If it were a container for an outdoor pavilion of some sort, Jack could not detect the seam where the lid separated from the body, but it was hard to tell from where he stood. His interest in the object below reminded him of his curiosity of the old man in the herringbone overcoat who had stood stone still for so long in the middle of the trail. This was different, of course, since the thing out in the Yard might even be a stone, for all he knew, and stones are supposed to stand still. He couldn't help thinking something might happen. Just then his phone began playing his Christian rock ringtone. It was MJ.

"Hey, babe," Jack answered cheerfully as he moved away from the windows.

"Hi, sweetheart," MJ responded in kind. "You busy?"

"Why, yes I am," Jack responded eagerly. "I'm thinking of you."

"Ah, that's sweet," MJ said softly. "Thank you for last night. I know you put a lot of thought into it, and I appreciate you doing that for me."

"MJ, I am madly in love with you and cherish our marriage. It is my responsibility as your husband to never let you forget that, and yet I have to admit that I have been slacking off in that area lately," Jack confided. "Besides, I never enjoyed a dinner more... or breakfast if you know what I mean?"

"I love you too, sweetie," MJ responded with a smile in her voice. "You know that I get so preoccupied with the boys' needs that I feel bad when I am ignoring yours sometimes. By giving me an outlet for some of the issues that get bottled up in my head, you freed up a woman who is desperately in love with her husband."

"Then, as God is my witness, you shall not want for a good listener," Jack promised.

"Then you shall not want for a loving wife, my darling," MJ promised in return.

"Then we have an accord, My Joy," Jack declared. "By the way, how is Joey feeling?"

"I let him sleep late, and he woke up as if nothing had happened," MJ said, "which means I'm getting a nice workout, so I gotta go. Remember, the boys and I will be spending the night over at my parents' house, so it's okay if you need to work late to make up for this morning... leftovers in the fridge... love you."

"Okay, love you too," Jack replied reluctantly, as if he were forgetting something. "Wait—what perfume do you wear?"

It was too late. She was gone.

Jack couldn't help feeling that wasn't the only thing he was forgetting—and the answer might be somewhere outside those windows. A lot had happened in the short period of time since Jack's encounter with the old guy who seemed to have no problem blowing off the whole concept of staying within the boundaries of a three-dimensional world, but he remembered now.

Could that thing outside be the "stone-like object" the old guy was talking about when he had me pinned to the back of my chair? Jack thought.

He walked back over to the window to give it another look and noticed that Alex and Frannie had taken Charlie's place beside the stone-like object. He knew Alex and Frannie well and had even had both over to his home a few times for weekend barbecues and dinner with the family over the holidays. It was really hard to tell if the stone was "pure white and without blemish" because of all the stuff that was leaning against and piled on top of it now. But he did know for a fact that it wasn't there yesterday, and now it was. If Alex and Frannie's job was to break the thing apart and haul it away, then Jack would know there was nothing to what the old guy had said. If their purpose was something other than that, he would know what it was before sunset, so he went back to organizing his new office.

Jack made good progress towards making his new office friendly and comfortable, without the interruptions of uninvited guests knowing things they ought not to know. The theme was simple: lots of books surrounded by lots of framed pictures of family and friends. There was no room for superfluous items such as scaled-down busts of Shakespeare or a figurine of a monkey sitting on a stack of books and contemplating a skull. He was sure to glance out the window from time to time to check on Alex and Frannie, who were also making good progress. Apparently, the stone was going to stay and be fenced in. The ten poles now sticking out of the ground were much taller than standard-sized fencing, and that kindled Jack's curiosity.

Who knows, but I might just take a stroll down there to check it out before they close it up, Jack mused. *With MJ and the boys gone, I've got nothing else to do tonight.*

By sunset there were still plenty of books left in stacks on the floor, but no shelf space left to put them on. At least everything was out of boxes and accounted for. It had been a long day, and Jack was looking forward to a quiet dinner, some time with MJ on the phone, and an early bedtime. Tomorrow he would begin a search for an abandoned shelving unit or two. It was late, and these happy thoughts easily took his mind off the half-hearted idea of taking a side trip across the Yard, just to look at a large stone... as if it had really been delivered there for him.

Jack gathered his gear, turned off the lights, and locked the door behind him. There was nothing unusual about his descent down the two flights of stairs or the walk through the large anteroom prior to exiting the front door of Turner Hall and walking to the front parking lot, except that once Jack was outside, he found himself already halfway down the Yard's center trail and heading in the general direction of the large white stone.

How was that possible? Jack thought, and with great agitation stopped in his tracks. *The stairs lead to the lobby, and the lobby leads to the front door, and the front door leads to the parking lot.*

"Can someone tell me how I got here?" Jack said out loud.

Jack looked back at Turner Hall and up to his darkened second-story window. He then looked back toward the brilliant white stone sitting peacefully in the center of ten tall fence posts without fencing. It suddenly appeared to Jack that the fence posts stood there like ten thin sentinels attempting to hold the gigantic white stone captive.

"Boys, if I were you and that prisoner of yours wanted to escape, I wouldn't stand in its way," Jack heckled the posts.

Well, I'm here now, Jack thought. *Let's have a look.*

Jack approached the stone cautiously but not fearfully. He kept a watchful eye out for anyone or anything that could be following him or what lay ahead of him. It was not so dark yet that he couldn't see some distance away. As he got closer, however, he thought he heard a sound coming from the stone itself.

"Hello!" Jack called out.

From the opposite side of the stone came a grunt, and up popped Hitch with a stick in his hand.

"Ahhhh, so you are my travel partner," Hitch replied.

"Professor Hitchinson?" Jack asked curiously.

"You wouldn't have a rope on you by any chance?" Hitch asked in all seriousness.

"No... sir... I don't," Jack replied. "But I—"

"But you thought you were going someplace else tonight and ended up here," Hitch interrupted. "Am I correct?"

"Yes... sir... you are," Jack replied. "So I—"

"So you are my travel partner then, Professor," Hitch interrupted. "My apologies—I have forgotten your name."

"Professor Lewis, English and American literature... Stanford," Jack replied. "You can call me Jack if you wish. Can I ask—"

"Well, Jack, I think I have this mostly figured out," Hitch interrupted kindly. "And please don't interrupt.

"You and I have been 'granted a wonderful opportunity' to be players, contestants, pawns—not sure which—in someone's very clever and technologically elaborate game," Hitch began. "We have both been visited by a mysterious intruder who offered to answer some deeply rooted yet unsatisfied craving of ours, and it is to begin here... at this 'stone-like object, pure white and without blemish.' It begins now, at sunset, and with you as my 'travel partner,' it implies that we must be going somewhere. You have had one or more equally bizarre occurrences, like a dream, intended to keep you off balance, and you probably couldn't leave here if you tried. How am I doing so far?" Hitch asked matter-of-factly.

"Old guy... able to walk through locked doors?" Jack asked, describing the mysterious intruder who had visited him yesterday morning.

"Young guy... but came and went as he pleased," Hitch replied, describing his visitor.

"So what's up with the stick?" Jack asked calmly, as if what the professor had just theorized was not totally unexpected.

"This morning I observed Charlie and his crew pull a rope under the entire length of this rock, which I believe is something other than what it appears to be," Hitch replied. "I thought I might try it with a stick while waiting for you to arrive."

"You think it's not touching the ground?"

"That's correct."

"Why?"

"Why is it not touching the ground?"

"No. Why this? Why you and me?"

"Don't know," Hitch replied. "But if you recall, we were to be given an 'understanding' once we got here."

"So we wait?" Jack asked.

"Do you have a better idea?"

"Maybe if we knew each other's craving, the one our visitor offered to answer, that would give us a clue," Jack suggested, but got the cold shoulder from Hitch.

"I'll go first," Jack offered. "At the age of sixteen, I gave my life to Jesus Christ. Since then, it has been my desire to bring as many people as I can to a knowledge of Him. But I'm not sure that is His purpose for my life anymore."

"That was enlightening, Jack," Hitch responded in a polite manner, "because it has been my desire to pull as many people as I can out of the Dark Ages by providing indisputable proof that omnipotent, omnipresent, omnificent gods of any kind cannot possibly exist. I'm quite certain that is one of my many purposes in life."

"So this is about God?" Jack asked rhetorically.

Without making a sound, the top portion of the stone moved back toward the rear, exposing the inside, which was hollow except for two comfortable-looking, high-backed bucket seats. There were no buttons, no knobs, no radio, no steering wheel, no floor mats—just the two seats. This occurred in the blink of an eye, and both men took a step backward when they suddenly realized they were now looking inside the stone.

"This drone, or whatever it is, does appear fairly sophisticated by human standards, but somewhat beneath that of a maker of universes, don't you think, Jack?" Hitch asked, not wishing to sound too sarcastic in making his point.

"I suppose if God can use a talking donkey to get a prophet's attention, then I suppose He can modify a drone to get ours, don't you think, Professor?" Jack answered the question with a question, then hopped into his side of the vehicle and made himself comfortable.

"Grasping at straws from the Old Testament's book of Numbers now, are we, Jack?" Hitch responded.

"I thought you were an atheist," Jack said, in amazed disbelief that the professor had any knowledge of this passage from the Bible. "How would you know about Balaam's donkey?"

"Jack, shame on you," Hitch said with a wry smile. "You make the same mistake all of my critics make when second-guessing me—and that is that I haven't carefully researched every shred of evidence on a particular subject before making up my mind... especially if there were such a thing as an actual heaven or an actual hell waiting for me when I breathe my last."

"Then you must know of Paul's warning to the Corinthians about the wise man, the scholar, and the philosopher?" Jack asked, not to pronounce judgment, but with a sense of compassion for his new travel partner.

"You are speaking, of course, of the apostle Paul's first letter to the Corinthians and his reference to Isaiah, I believe, where God will destroy the wisdom of the wise and frustrate the intelligence of the intelligent," Hitch replied, intently rather than defensively.

Jack was stunned into silence.

Hitch continued. "Yes, I know that passage, and I am sure your kindly old Christian patriarch was being quite honest about it when he wrote those words. I too believe there is truth to this saying... just not a god being its author."

"Well, I don't know about you, but I feel like I'm stuck at the corner of 'Going' and 'Nowhere,'" Jack said. "This could be a hoax, but I don't think it is. And besides, this is absolutely the most comfortable seat this butt has ever met. You coming?"

Hitch was inclined to leave, but he too was stuck at the corner of 'No More' and 'Time.' His clear and brilliant mind was desperately trying to warn him that this chicanery made no logical sense, and yet an equally determined and pragmatic voice reminded him that time would soon run out for him and his lifelong dream, if he did nothing to make better use of it. With surprising agility, he jumped into his seat and found it to be as comfortable as was advertised.

"Where do you suppose this ship will be taking us?" Jack asked.

"To the Canary Islands is my understanding and my hope," a young Charles Darwin replied. "That is, if this damnable weather would consider becoming our companion rather than our adversary."

10

Partners Traveling

J ack was no longer sitting comfortably in a hollowed-out white stone-like object and talking to a celebrated 21st century professor. Instead, he was engaged in a sour conversation with a promising young naturalist by the name of Charles Darwin on the cold, wet upper deck of the *H.M.S. Beagle*. He still went by the name of Jack Lewis, but he was not the married 21st century college professor, and to his knowledge, this was not a dream. In his mind, the date was the twenty-seventh of December, 1831.

"Perhaps today will find some distance between us and this grim harbor, Jack," Darwin pined somberly. "Any attempt to express how heavy my heart has become as a result of our endless delay in this watery prison would be inadequate."

"Spoken like a true landlubber, my restless friend," Jack replied lightheartedly. "May I remind you the *Beagle* is not a horse-drawn carriage, and the Atlantic Ocean is not an English countryside to be traveled whenever we wish."

The *Beagle* had actually been scheduled to begin its two-year mission on the twenty-fifth of September, three months ago. It was to be her second voyage to chart the coastline of South America, but the ship had been found to be so rotten that it needed to be very nearly rebuilt to have any chance of accomplishing the ambitious task it was being asked to perform.

This current mission, however, was of great importance to the British Empire. Napoleon Bonaparte was dead, and his once-mighty navy had been destroyed, as was the Spanish navy. This left the British navy in total control of the world's oceans. The French and Spanish colonies in South America were now independent, and the vast amounts of natural resources that they possessed were there for the taking. Unfortunately, British maps of the region were incomplete at best. Therefore, the Admiralty had wasted no time and spared no expense in repairing the *Beagle* and then equipping her with every known modern device for creating the most accurate charts and maps possible.

After being declared seaworthy in November, the ship's first attempt to make it out into open waters had to be abandoned because of a confluence of gale-force winds driving her back to port, and now December had produced more of the same beastly weather. Consequently, the *H.M.S. Beagle* sat—until today.

To be clear, the only reason Jack and Darwin were standing on the upper deck of the *H.M.S. Beagle* was that they had been invited to be there by the ship's commander, Captain Robert FitzRoy. Soon after his selection as commander for this second mission, FitzRoy had recommended to his superiors that invitations be sent out to a well-educated person of science and an English missionary to accompany them. He reasoned that since their voyage would take them to far-off places, this would be a rare opportunity to collect exotic specimens as well as bring Christianity to the heathens, an opportunity that would otherwise be wasted. The idea made its way quickly up the chain of command, and the order was given by the Admiralty that two positions fitting this description be added to the ship's log for provision. A letter of intent was generated and immediately sent to Cambridge University.

Word of the invitations eventually came to the attention of Reverend John Stevens Henslow, a distinguished member of the English clergy and professor of botany at Cambridge. He had been tutoring two very bright young students who demonstrated enormous potential in the two vocations described in the invitations. Those twenty-two-year-old students were Jack Lewis and Charles Darwin. This extraordinary opportunity could not have been better timed, since both Jack and Darwin had graduated in the spring. Oddly, both graduated with bachelor degrees in theology. Jack graduated with honors; Darwin graduated, barely, and without honors. Darwin did, however, develop a strong affinity for natural history and geology under Professor Henslow's tutelage and encouragement. So in September of 1831, it was agreed the two should join the expedition with the understanding that Jack would serve the Lord among the uncivilized inhabitants, and Darwin would serve the university by sending back to Professor Henslow as many plant, insect, and animal specimens as he could find.

While studying at Cambridge, Jack had befriended the aimless young man from Shrewsbury, even though they were quite the opposites. For instance, if they shared a walk beyond the townships and into the countryside, Jack's attitude toward their surroundings was more panoramic, taking in all of God's beautiful creation. Darwin, on the other hand, would spend the majority of the trip with his nose pointed to the ground in hopes of finding an unusual relic, a vulgar bug, or the trail of some four-legged creature, and he would finish the journey with a pocket full of rocks. Or, if they were caught in the midst of some leisurely reading on board ship, Jack's choices would be the contemporary poetry of Shelley, Byron, or Keats; Darwin's choices, on the other hand, would not deviate from the more serious works, such as Sir Charles Lyell's *Principles of Geology* and Rev. Thomas Malthus's *An Essay on the Principle of Population*.

Without having commonality in personalities and tastes, perhaps it was the sorrow from the loss of their mothers at a very young age that bonded them so quickly and so closely through college. They also shared great affection and mutual admiration for Professor Henslow, who had taken them both under his protective wing. For whatever reason, Jack found Darwin's company to be irresistibly entertaining and their discussions most fascinating. As fate would have its way, the last two months of idleness had also provided both of them with an opportunity to develop a close friendship with FitzRoy, who, although a decorated captain in the British navy, was only four years their elder. It was not uncommon for the three of them to dine together in the captain's cabin and converse late into the evening.

It certainly comforted Jack to learn that FitzRoy had actually been lieutenant on the *H.M.S. Beagle's* maiden voyage to South America. Then again, it was equally unsettling to learn that on that very same journey, FitzRoy had to take command of the *Beagle* after his captain succumbed to the enormous pressure and committed suicide. With all that being said, however, the *Beagle* did make it home safe and sound under Lieutenant FitzRoy's youthful (twenty-three years of age) yet capable leadership. This past experience was, most likely, the reason the young captain was chosen to command this second mission.

Suddenly the call of the boatswain's whistle pierced the cold drizzle that permeated the air about the ship, and a flurry of men rushed to their stations. Looking back toward the stern of the ship, Jack could see FitzRoy now standing tall between the ship's helmsman to his right and the first lieutenant to his left. Without acknowledging the less than ideal weather conditions, he calmly but forcefully gave commands to his lieutenant. His lieutenant then repeated the commands with much greater intensity so that all on board could hear. Whoever it was to receive the command then repeated it back to the helm. Within moments, Jack could feel the ship react in some way to the fulfillment of the command. Finally, there was a call to weigh anchor, and the sails filled with air.

"It would appear your wish to leave this place of so much misery has been granted, Charles," Jack cried out over the howling wind and creaking timbers. "But take a good look at her, for you shall not see your beloved country again for two years."

When Jack received no response to his suggestion, he reached over and with both hands on Darwin's shoulders spun him around so that they were now standing face-to-face. Darwin's eyes were rolled back into his head, and his face had an unnatural color to it. This was not homesickness; this was seasickness.

"Let's get you down below before FitzRoy sees you, lad," Jack said with a smile.

The *H.M.S Beagle* was finally away, but the foul weather continued its malevolent behavior for the next seven days, and so did Darwin's afflictions. Jack tried to make him as comfortable as possible until they could walk on solid ground once more. Unfortunately, their first port of call off the coast of northern Africa had to be scrapped because of a sudden and violent westerly squall. Bad weather was certainly nothing new to an Englishman, but when added to a week of rough seas, it caused even Jack's nerves to begin to wear thin.

"If this insufferable weather continues, my good but utterly replaceable friend," Jack began jokingly, "I shall take it as a sign from God that you are a disobedient prophet and would have no regrets in renaming you Jonah, then tossing you overboard."

"I can assure you, my fine but treacherous friend," Darwin replied in kind, "if it could be said with certainty that I would be vomited onto shore somewhere three days hence, then I should take great delight being conveyed there in the belly of a fish."

"Ah, your sense of humor has returned!" Jack exclaimed. "I will take that as a good sign."

"I am feeling better, thank you," Darwin replied. "But that could all change if you were to tell me that while I was in my stupor, we passed the Canary Islands."

"Good news then—the islands are to be our next destination," Jack said gladly. "And the weather is going to improve shortly, according to our captain—that is, if you believe as he does that you can foretell the weather by using a mercury-filled barometer."

"That is good news on both counts," Darwin said joyfully. "The more I know about our captain, the less I doubt his resourcefulness, and expect to see clear blue skies shortly."

The weather changed for the better the following day, as Captain FitzRoy had predicted, and the day after that, the *Beagle* arrived in the Canary Islands, only to be told they would have to wait out a quarantine of two weeks before coming ashore. This was unacceptable to FitzRoy, and the ship weighed anchor. Darwin was devastated.

"Jack, if I did not know better," Darwin sighed, "I would believe God had set His hand against me."

"Do not be discouraged, Charles," Jack said. "We have only been gone less than a month of a journey expected to last years, and too many variables had to be contrived for the two of us to be standing here. No, I believe otherwise. I believe God meant for us to be exactly where we are."

They reached the Cape Verde Islands off the coast of Africa in ten days and were mercifully permitted to go ashore there. Jack and Darwin were allowed three weeks to go about exploring while FitzRoy took on provisions and prepared the *Beagle* for the crossing of the Atlantic, the equator, and onward to South America. Since the islands' population was fairly well socialized, Jack found himself tagging along with Darwin, who could not be enjoying himself more. At times they could not go more than a mile without Darwin having to stop and write something in his journal, and then off he would go again. Every so often he would point out some curiosity easily overlooked by Jack and then ask what he thought of it. Occasionally, it would be something as fascinating as a fish that could change its color, but more often than not, it was a repulsive insect or rodent of some kind, which typically caused Jack to recoil. This effect on Jack always brought a satisfied smile to Darwin's face.

On the day before they were to leave, there came a place that was familiar to Jack. In fact, he was sure that they had visited this same place a number of times before, only from different vantage points. Never once in those times had Darwin revealed his thoughts or asked for Jack's opinion. It was apparent, however, that this particular spot weighed heavily on Darwin's mind.

"What is it, Charles?" Jack finally asked.

"What is what?" Darwin responded cautiously.

"We have been here before," Jack replied, "yet I do not understand why we are back here again today."

"There!" Darwin said hesitantly and then pointed to the adjacent cliff side.

"I still do not see what it is that you see, Charles."

"Bring your eyes up the side of that cliff about fifty feet. What do you see?"

"Well, if you mean the horizontal line going from one side of the rock to the other, I do see it."

"Those are shells, Jack," Darwin said softly, as if someone might be listening. "Seashells."

"Yes?" was all Jack could think to ask.

"How did a perfectly horizontal layer of seashells embed themselves in rock fifty feet above sea level," Darwin asked, "if not that the level of the sea was once that high."

"What are you suggesting?" Jack asked without accusation, but realizing that it was contrary to church doctrine to believe in the idea that the earth could change or even to suggest that it needed changing.

"I'm not quite sure," Darwin replied honestly. "Perhaps South America will provide some answers as well as provide you with many lost souls in need of redemption."

The following day, FitzRoy set sail for the northeastern corner of South America. The three-week trek across the Atlantic could not have been more pleasant for all on board, except one. Regardless of the weather conditions,

Darwin often fell ill with seasickness and spent most days in his cabin.

On the twenty-eighth of February, 1832, two months after leaving England, the *H.M.S. Beagle* arrived at Salvador, Brazil. FitzRoy began surveying almost immediately, while both Jack and Darwin wasted no time making their presence felt in Salvador by making it clear to all who would listen their contempt for this county's wide acceptance of the black man's slavery. While Darwin was more vocal and more vehement in his condemnation, especially with those in the clergy who turned a blind eye to such an un-Christian institution, Jack went about sharing the good news of God's great love and eternal salvation directly to the enslaved, which enraged the slave owners even more. Even between themselves, Jack and Darwin found it a difficult topic to discuss.

"Although we hold identical degrees in divinity, it is no secret which of us holds the better understanding of God's Word and his instructions," Darwin freely admitted. "So I yield to your explanation, Jack. How could a loving father allow one child of his to own another child of his?"

"Charles, if I were to answer that question, it would be putting words into Scripture where there are none. It causes me to tremble in fear to even think of doing such a thing," Jack replied as tears formed in the corners of his eyes. He continued. "All I know for certain, my good friend, is that if one of these poor slaves dies without first accepting Jesus as their Savior, then he will remain a slave to the one called Satan for eternity."

Jack paused for a moment to regain his composure, then continued. "And regardless of how you and I may feel about it, the same is true for the brutal slave owner. On this matter, decency and fairness torment me greatly, but Scripture does not allow me to choose for whom Jesus died—He died for both." At the conclusion of his response, Jack wept openly, and it took a long while for Darwin to console him.

After spending several weeks in Salvador, the *Beagle* continued on her survey mission down the coast to Rio de Janeiro, then to Montevideo near Buenos Aires, then to Bahia Blanco, eventually making it all the way down to Tierra del Fuego at the southernmost tip of South America. This completed the first year of their voyage, and like every other person on board ship, Jack lived each one of those days in the moment and with the expectation of someday returning to England and family.

At each of these destinations, Jack and Darwin were permitted freedom to come and go as they pleased, even if it meant staying on shore for weeks, even months, while the *Beagle* went back out to sea to take her measurements. To assist them in the performance of their commitments, FitzRoy was more than generous in providing additional equipment and manpower whenever it was requested. This arrangement, of course, suited Darwin perfectly well, since it allowed him to spend more time and travel greater distances in collecting his specimens, as well as experience some extended periods of time in relatively good health between bouts of seasickness. Jack usually stayed close to the harbor and assisted any missionaries there, unless it was suspected that there might be an untouched group of people in the same direction as one of Darwin's treks. It was on Tierra del Fuego that Darwin, back from a successful day of collecting, asked Jack to join him the next day.

"You must come tomorrow and see for yourself," Darwin stated excitedly. "I am not quite certain whether I should pack one up and deliver him back to Professor Henslow for further study or allow you to convert him."

Darwin's hyperbole was more or less true. The following day, Darwin led Jack and his team of a dozen armed sailors back through the dense forest, requiring the use of his compass, until they found themselves surrounded by a small gathering of creatures that appeared half human, half beast. They were speaking a crude language of grunts and were without shame in their attire or manner.

After his initial revulsion to these short, leathery-skinned natives, Jack attempted to communicate in English. When that failed, he tried French, Spanish, German, and even Hebrew, without success. The only reaction to his salutations was to have one or more of these grotesque beings repeat his words exactly, but no more than a parrot would do. The only thing that interested these strange anomalies of mankind was the colorful fabrics and shiny jewelry worn by Darwin and his men.

As Jack was speaking, one of the natives made his way toward him cautiously, grunting something unrecognizable and then slapping his chest twice as some sort of punctuation.

"Yes, yes... come forward, dear fellow. Let us be friends," Jack said to the foul-smelling wretch.

"You see, Charles?" Jack spoke, without turning away from the approaching native. "They do have the capability to reason, and therefore, we should embrace them as fellow human beings."

No sooner did these words leave Jack's mouth than the hideous little "human being" ripped a silver button off Jack's vest, turned, and vanished into the jungle.

"Stop, you thief!" Jack barked, causing the remaining natives to grunt loudly and move about anxiously.

"Do not bother giving chase, Jack," Darwin laughed. "The moment you move toward them now, they will all scatter and disappear as this one did. I should know—they have my favorite writing pen!"

"So, tell me, Jack," Darwin continued, "are these men or beast or some transition between the two?"

"They are vulgar little creatures," Jack said angrily. "And if they are men, to what category of man, I could not tell you."

"My thoughts exactly!" Darwin exclaimed. "Let's be off before these primitive little pickpockets start to reason that we are easily robbed and we are forced to defend ourselves."

The *H.M.S. Beagle* finished her activities on the southern tip of South America, but rather than heading west into the Pacific Ocean and closer to the end of her mission, the ship was commanded by the Admiralty to head eastward toward the Falkland Islands. From there, the *Beagle* spent all of that year and the first half of the next traveling back up the east coast of South America to Montevideo again and then down to Tierra del Fuego.

This year and a half of backtracking actually turned into an unexpected windfall for both Jack and Darwin. Jack was able to share the gospel with many others, including a receptive group of outback gauchos, with several accepting Jesus Christ as their Savior then and there. Darwin was able to ship a dozen or more barrels of fossils, plants, insects, fish, birds and animals, along with his observations, back to the attention of Professor Henslow at Cambridge. This pleased FitzRoy greatly, since Darwin's voluminous collections were beginning to clutter his ship.

It was now June of 1834, two and a half years since leaving England, when the *H.M.S Beagle* finally rounded the cape of South America and pushed into the Pacific Ocean.

"At this rate, we shall be old men before we ever see home again, Charles," Jack stated as they watched the snow-capped Mount Sarmiento fade in the distance.

When Jack received no response to his observation, he glanced over at Darwin. Jack had seen that look many times before and without a word escorted his friend down to his cabin. It wasn't until the *Beagle* sailed north and into warmer climates that Darwin began to feel better. At Valparaiso, Chile, they were able to spend several months on dry land and take many long and profitable treks into the Andes Mountains.

Then, in October of 1834, the unthinkable happened.

Captain FitzRoy succumbed to frustration and fatigue, much like the captain did before him, and resigned his command of the *H.M.S. Beagle* without warning. Fortunately, FitzRoy's deep melancholy was not allowed to reach the point of self-destruction due to Jack's gentle and persistent counsel. This brotherly intervention caused him to change his mind about resigning. It should be noted that had Jack not been able to calm the captain's nerves, naval regulations would have put the *H.M.S. Beagle* in the command of FitzRoy's lieutenant, with instructions to terminate this mission at once and return to England, just as Lieutenant FitzRoy had been required to do on the *Beagle's* first mission after his captain committed suicide.

It could be argued that the course of history was changed at that very moment—that is, had FitzRoy's resignation not been withdrawn, it would have prevented Darwin from ever reaching the Galapagos Islands, thereby perhaps forever altering his ideas on natural selection. No one involved in this current matter could have possibly known the ramifications of FitzRoy's decisions, of course, including Jack. All Jack knew was that his friend was in trouble and in dire need of his help, even though a part of him longed to return home.

As fate, or destiny, or Providence would have it, the *H.M.S. Beagle* did arrive at the Galapagos Islands on the fifteenth of September, 1835, and she stayed in the area five weeks. After taking specimens from the islands of Chatham, Charles, Albemarle, and James, Darwin could not help but notice how distinct the plants and animals were to each individual island despite their proximity to one another.

"Jack, may I have your attention for a moment?" Darwin called out.

"If you wish to see how long I might stay atop one of your giant tortoises as it fumbles its way across the beach," Jack began his response, "you shall have to find yourself some other form of amusement."

"No, that's not it at all, although I doubt you could beat my time anyway," Darwin replied. "You have heard that the locals here can tell which island a particular tortoise calls home simply by looking at its shell?"

"I have heard this," Jack agreed.

"Well, I have by now taken three different species of mockingbirds from four different islands, each island within sight of the other," Darwin stated objectively. "Yet I can, with certainty, tell you which island these birds call home simply by looking at their features."

"Charles, please," Jack pleaded, "you should know by now that if you must present me with a mystery, you must also explain it."

"Don't you see?" Darwin asked patiently. "There is no sound reason for a creator to place three species of the same bird in the very same archipelago, when he could have easily placed the original here and forced the other two to modify themselves for survival, each to its own island.

"Jack, you have seen this with your own eyes, because for the last three years, I have shown these things to you. I have come to a point where I can no longer deny the possibility that everything we look upon today has changed over unspeakable periods of time and will continue this process as a simple matter of survival.

"The seashells forty feet above sea level in the Cape Verde Islands, the fossils of animals that no longer roam the earth in Bahia Blanca, the ape-like creatures hardly resembling mankind in Tierra del Fuego, and now the birds and tortoises of the Galapagos that have adapted to fit their conditions and circumstances all point to an opposition to the notion of immutability—it's unavoidable!

"These are, of course, only preliminary observations, and we shall have to wait and see what Professor Henslow will discover from my collections," Darwin added, carefully toning down his rhetoric. "If, however, there is the slightest foundation for these claims, we should not fear what further examination might reveal.

"So come now... I value your opinion, Jack," Darwin prompted earnestly. "Do you wish to comment on these heretical remarks of mine?"

"Your positions certainly run contrary to what we have been taught to believe, Charles," Jack stated thoughtfully. "I am also quite certain that my reaction to these apostasies of yours would have been a bit more disagreeable had I not watched for myself how meticulously you have gathered and cataloged your findings. I must admit, your explanations are compelling.

"But I have not strayed from my belief that we were both set here by the Creator of the heavens and of the earth, from whom you have accumulated your evidence. And although your observations may at first seem contrary to what we think we know of God's mind, He will always and forever have the final say.

"Therefore, I encourage you to finish what you have begun. I, for one, shall look forward to reading your conclusions someday. However, I would be very careful with whom I shared these ideas—that is, until all the evidence has been diligently sifted and refined, so that you may be prepared for the battle that is to come."

The next day, the *H.M.S. Beagle* set sail for Tahiti, then traveled around the cape of Africa, then made another relatively brief trip across the Atlantic once again. Only then was there the sensation of heading home. At every portage, Darwin added more specimens to his collection and more fuel to his theories. As for Jack, he found contentment (an equal measure of satisfaction and disappointment) in spreading the gospel to those who had never heard the name *Jesus of Nazareth*.

Then, on the second day of October, 1836, they both came to experience immense joy and relief. This was the day there came a shout from those stationed in the masts, "Land ahoy!" and their two-year mission, which had turned into a four-year, nine-month, and five-day odyssey, came to an end.

"It's good to be home, wouldn't you agree, Charles?" Jack asked in excited anticipation of seeing his beloved England again.

When he did not receive the obligatory response he was seeking, Jack turned, expecting to find his friend in the grips of seasickness. Instead, Darwin was looking him straight in the eye.

"It is very good, Jack, and it is not exaggeration to say that I would not have made it without you," Darwin stated gratefully. "Now, I have been instructed to tell you this: if you are both willing, return to the stone-like object tomorrow at sunset."

"Charles, are you well?" Jack asked with some concern. "This instruction of yours makes no sense to me."

* * * * *

Hitch did not have an opportunity to respond to his 21st century travel partner's question as to where this ship might be taking them because he was no longer a part of that century. Instead, he was standing some distance away from a large crowd that had gathered on the front steps of the Wittenberg chapel. Curious as to what might have attracted such an assembly, he altered his course to get a better look. The date was the thirty-first of October, 1517, and the only life he had ever known was the one he was in the process of living now.

"There!" someone called out from the crowd, and every face turned toward Hitch.

"Someone ask the professor what it says!"

Hitch still went by the name of Edmond Hitchinson, but responded to no nickname. He was now professor of philosophy at the University of Wittenberg in the southern province of Saxony, Germany.

"A good evening to you, Professor." A tall, powerful man moved forward and spoke boldly. "Would you be so kind as to read this announcement? We are only able to make out its author, but little else, for it is written in the holy language."

Hitch advanced easily through the crowd, neither agreeing to nor denying the large man's request. Silently he began reading the expansive document written in Latin and posted next to the door of the chapel. It read:

Out of love and concern for the truth, and with the object of eliciting it, the following propositions will be the subject of a public discussion at Wittenberg under the presidency of the Reverend Father Martin Luther, Augustinian, master of arts and sacred theology, and appointed lecturer in ordinary on these subjects in that place. Wherefore he requests that whoever is unable to be present personally to debate the matter orally will do so in absence in writing.

From there, his blood boiled a little hotter with each consecutive reading of the ninety-five propositions until, when he was done, Hitch was in a panic. This reaction could not be attributed to his religiosity, because he believed in no god. He considered himself more a follower of Aristotle than of the events surrounding a Jewish messiah and the enormously rich organization built using his name. Rather, it was more a concern for the health and safety of the document's author and his good friend. Shaken, he turned to leave, but found the crowd to be less than obliging to him leaving without some explanation of the mysterious document that had the same profound effect on all who could understand it.

"Sir, you appear to know what Father Martin has written," the large man stated indignantly as he moved to block Hitch's escape. "You shall share it with us—now."

"Of course, of course, my good man," Hitch replied in a good-natured tone of voice as he attempted a slow zigzag progression through the bewildered crowd.

"Well, for those of you who know the good reverend, you also know his fondness for good food and drink. As far as I can tell, this is a very fine collection of recipes for the preparation of all manner of food, including roasted pheasant or quail with white wine, fresh herbs, cream sauces, soups, and stewed vegetables."

"But, why is His Holiness the Pope mentioned then?" another man protested.

"Yes, well... apparently this has something to do with the Feast of Corpus Christi." Hitch continued his lies without shame or remorse. "In fact, it promises for those wishing to contribute from their farms and fields to this festival that they will be given the same freedom from God's wrath as those who have given from their money purses." This fabrication didn't satisfy all those present, but it created enough of a diversion to allow Hitch to slip away unnoticed.

"Damn that irascible monk," Hitch could not help blurting out softly once he turned the corner. He was in the habit of using the term *monk* whenever Luther frustrated him or acted too piously, which was quite often.

When Hitch and Luther met in the year 1501, they were both seventeen, and Luther had just transferred into the acclaimed University of Erfurt, where Hitch was already enrolled. Although Luther was from peasant stock and Hitch from German nobility, they immediately gravitated to the other's brilliance and keen sense of humor, as well as the ability to cut through the other's defenses that had been systematically erected to help diminish the abuse that defined their childhoods. Luther earned his bachelor's degree first... and in a single year. Not to be outdone,

Hitch not only caught up and earned his master's degree the same year as Luther, but finished number one in the class of 1505, with Luther finishing number two.

As soon as it was allowed, they both enrolled into Erfurt's prestigious law school and even talked about going into law practice together. Then, in the summer of 1505, Luther was caught up in a violent thunderstorm. He confided in Hitch a promise that was made to Saint Anna, in which he vowed, should he survive, that he would become a monk. As Luther's closest friend, Hitch tried everything to convince him of the folly of such a decision, but he knew in his heart the futility of his arguments. That was because, in Luther's mind, there was no amount of reason that could offset a promise earnestly made and within the means of the one making the promise.

So, in a few short weeks, Hitch could do nothing but sit back and watch as Luther sold off his personal belongings, left Erfurt's law school, and disappeared into an Augustinian monastery. Fortunately, the monastery Luther chose to escape his troubled life was located in Erfurt, and at certain times of the year, the two were able to meet for a beer and conversation, which consisted of his friend's desperate struggle to perform more and more good works to please God.

Hitch was there when Luther became ordained into the priesthood in 1507 and when he received his bachelor's degree in biblical studies in the year that followed. Hitch was also there when Luther transferred from the Erfurt monastery to the monastery in Wittenberg in 1511 because he was already teaching at the newly founded University of Wittenberg. In October of 1512, Luther earned his doctorate in theology from the University of

Wittenberg, and two days later he joined Hitch on staff as professor of biblical studies.

This was the sum total of what Hitch knew of his life as being the close friend of the eventual great church reformer. His only concern now, however, was finding Luther and reprimanding him for being so cavalier about confronting the church so openly, and especially the pope individually. His search took him to an unwholesome part of town and to the front door of a shabby-looking tavern. Once inside, he scanned the room until his eyes eventually fell upon a heavyset man sitting alone in the back corner. There was nothing familiar about the unkempt man with long stringy hair that drooped listlessly from under a wide-brimmed hat. Undaunted, Hitch walked over to the table where the quiet man sat peacefully before two very tall beer steins, one half-full, one empty.

"So, it is martyrdom thou seeketh, heh, monk?" Hitch spoke first.

"Ahhh, Edmond, the Wise!" the man in disguise replied. "Just the person I have been waiting for."

"I fear our meeting might be too late in its necessity," Hitch responded with a sigh. "How long have you been devising these ninety-five theses on destroying your church, and where are all your coconspirators?"

"I had sixty-five as of last week. The others came to me as I was writing them down," Luther said calmly. "And it is I alone; there are no others.

"As you can see," Luther continued as he looked down at the two steins, "I expected you one full liter ago."

"Do not believe for an instant that I find any humor in this dangerous indiscretion of yours, monk!" Hitch snapped angrily. "Why, Martin? Why did you feel the need to put your life in danger like this?"

"You need only read the Word of God as it was written in the beginning to know the answer to your question, my dear friend," Luther began softly. "If you have learned nothing from our friendship it should be this: if the believer has faith, then he cannot be restrained. He betrays himself otherwise. He must confess and preach the truth to all who will listen—even at the risk of life itself."

"Martin, be reasonable—" Hitch began, but was cut off.

"Reason?" Luther shouted, causing the other patrons to momentarily stop what they were doing and look back at this strange combination: a university professor conversing with a vagabond. "Reason is the greatest enemy that faith has!"

"But must you pick your fights with a pope, Martin?" Hitch reasoned anyway. "And must you compare him to an ancient Roman politician so despised?"

"I do not recall comparing my pope to Crassus, only to his wealth, Edmond," Luther countered. "And I only use this as an illustration in hopes that His Holiness will come to see the injustice being heaped on the poor, and the immorality of indulgences.

"But there are more important matters than this," Luther continued. "Those who believe they are buying relief from their sins by purchasing these indulgences will find themselves not only penniless, but hell bound as well.

"Edmond, don't you see, Jesus Christ has already paid that price for our sin, in His death and resurrection. He alone is the Lamb of God who takes away the sins of the world. We are all sinners—the Jew and the Gentile, the rich man and the poor man, the pope and his cardinals, you and I, but we can be justified by grace through faith in Jesus Christ—in His blood alone.

"This is necessary to the believer. Forgiveness of sin cannot be acquired or grasped by any work, law, or indulgence, yet I tell you, half the citizens sitting in our churches are destined for hell because of what they have been taught by us. I would not tell you this, Edmond, if I did not believe it with my entire heart."

"I do not deny your sincerity, monk," Hitch conceded, this time using the term *monk* affectionately. I only fear what your methods may have set in motion. There must be some way to contain this matter before it reaches your superiors."

"Would now be a good time to inform you that I have already sent Bishop Albert of Mainz a copy of my disputation?" Luther admitted sheepishly.

"Damn you, monk!" Hitch exploded again, and went back to using his original intent for the use of the term *monk*. "I doubt very much that you will receive any relief from Saint Anna this time, for you have created your own firestorm."

Hitch could not have been more prophetic. Because of the advent of the printing press, translated copies of Luther's Ninety-Five Theses spread throughout Germany within weeks and throughout Europe within months. There was no stopping its circulation or its popular message— popular, that is, except with those within the hierarchy of the Holy Roman Catholic Church. To his credit, Pope Leo X did not take the bait, nor did he rush to judgment. Instead, he waited until October of 1518 to send Cardinal Thomas Cajetan to seek a resolution to Luther's grievances and the restoration of a priest in conflict. He even allowed the diet (meeting) to be held in Germany rather than in Rome. After a year of waiting for the charge of heresy to be rendered upon his friend, this meeting could not have been more pleasing to Hitch's ears.

"Martin, this is great news!" Hitch said excitedly. "You have been given another chance to be heard. You are a good man, and I do not see where you have spoken falsely—only harshly. So, if you can only control your passions and your words, I believe an amicable accord is within reach."

"We shall see, Edmond," Luther offered reluctantly. "But what about you? What holds you back from accepting this wonderful gift of life that is for all men?"

"I'm afraid I believe too much in Saint Aristotle and not enough in Saint Augustine, monk," Hitch responded kindly. "Or perhaps I'm not one of the 'elect' that you are fond of speaking about."

"Perhaps. But even the elect must respond positively to His invitation," Luther added. "Do not allow reason to convince you out of heaven; time is slipping away for all of us."

Needless to say, the hearing with Cardinal Cajetan was a disaster and ended in a shouting match, with Luther refusing to recant anything from his writings. The cardinal was well within his rights to arrest the defiant priest on the spot, but he resisted. This allowed Luther to continue lecturing, and his appeal became so strong that people traveled to Germany from France, England, and Italy to hear him speak. Several more attempts were made during this period to persuade Luther to recant, or at least remain silent, but all were rebuffed. By June of 1520, Pope Leo was left with no other choice but to begin the process to excommunicate his rogue priest. This was crushing news to Hitch, who had stood by his friend's side throughout his death-defying fame.

"So, your pope has given you sixty days to recant," Hitch said in obvious distress. "Regardless of how much

I might want to plead with you, I know you will not bend. Therefore, in all probability, I will soon lose the greatest friend I have ever known.

"So tell me, monk," Hitch asked sorrowfully, "why would I want to follow a God who would allow this to happen to one of His greatest emissaries?"

"Faith in knowing that God works for the good of those who love Him, my dear friend," Luther replied with deep compassion. "If the destruction of this human body will cause another to be saved, then my life will not be taken from me in vain."

On the eighteenth of April, 1521, Luther appeared before the Diet of Worms (meeting in the town of Worms) as ordered. He had hoped to make this final trip with his trusted friend, but Hitch was nowhere to be found before Luther's departure from Wittenberg. At the hearing, all of his writings, including the Ninety-Five Theses, were laid out before him.

Speaking on behalf of the Holy Roman Empire and as assistant to the archbishop of Trier was Johann Eck. If Hitch was Luther's truest friend, then Eck was Luther's worst enemy within the church. It was Eck who asked if they were all from his hand and if they remained his beliefs. Luther studied each one carefully to be sure that they had not been altered. When he was satisfied, Luther confirmed they were in fact his, but requested a day to respond to the second question. The next day, Luther offered this defense to Eck and the assembly:

"Unless I am convinced by the testimony of the Scriptures or by clear reason, I am bound by the Scriptures I have quoted, and my conscience is captive to the Word of God. I cannot and will not recant anything, since it is neither safe nor right to go against conscience. Here I stand. I can do no other. God help me. Amen."

Even though this statement would ultimately seal his doom, Luther was allowed to return home to await the edict ordering his arrest. While on his way back to Wittenberg, however, Luther's carriage was intercepted by a party of masked bandits and forced to stop.

"What have we here, driver?" one of the masked men called out to the man seated on top of the carriage.

"You will find nothing of value here, kind sir," the driver cried out nervously. "A priest and two servants returning home to Wittenberg from Worms, sir."

"I will be the judge of their worth, driver!" the masked man shouted back.

"Do not harm the driver," a voice called out from within the carriage. "We will do all that you ask, and then we will pray you find another line of work, robber."

"That you will—monk!" the masked man spoke into the carriage window.

Luther's head immediately popped out of the window and looked carefully into the familiar eyes of the bandit. The masked man spoke again.

"The priest will come with us quietly, and no harm will befall the rest of you."

"Yes, yes, of course. Do whatever they say, driver," Luther cried out in feigned distress.

A horse was provided for Luther, and he and the masked bandits took off in a hurry. As soon as the carriage was out of sight, the bandits threw off their masks. Shortly after that, the entire party turned off the main road and headed directly into a dense forest. They did not slow their pace until the less traveled road they were on approached a large wooden gate, which opened without a word. Once inside the gate, they were all given new horses.

The men who had accompanied Hitch in the counterfeit abduction quickly changed into uniforms that indicated they were under the command of Prince Frederick III, the elector of Saxony, a powerful man and friend of Luther's. Hitch quickly changed into his own clothing, and Luther was given a disguise. They were all back on the road within minutes and did not stop until they reached Prince Frederick's Wartburg castle in the town of Eisenach. The charade worked flawlessly, but Hitch did not lower his guard until his good friend was safely inside the castle and the doors were locked behind them.

"Welcome to your new home, monk," Hitch announced. "You will be safe here."

"Thank you, Edmond. I do not know what would have become of me without you by my side all these years," Luther said with great affection. "Now, I have been instructed to tell you this: if you are both willing, return to the stone-like object tomorrow at sunset."

"Martin... are you certain?" Hitch asked skeptically. "Your instructions baffle me."

11

Searching for Answers

Charlie was relieved to hear that Alex and Frannie had an easy time setting the poles and that they expected the thing to be all wrapped up by noon tomorrow. Their suggestion to add signs to stop people from snooping around was a good one, but Charlie had discovered long ago that signs like No Trespassing or Keep Out had only limited success in stopping a person with an inquisitive mind and little self-control, which fairly described most of Hillary's student population.

Instead, Charlie recommended they use the signs that he had designed many years ago when testing several organic herbicides and pesticides for use on or around the roses. They read: "Experimental Weed/Pest Control Project—In Progress," and "WARNING: MAY BE TOXIC— Stay Back 100 Feet." When used in tandem, these two signs were found to be enormously effective, perhaps because they provided a definitive reason not to trespass and to keep out.

After leaving the rock earlier in the day, Charlie had spent the rest of his afternoon inside Walker Auditorium, making final preparations for Dr. Hitchinson's address to the incoming class, and the inevitable media circus. Today's indoor project was to secure the stanchion posts and ropes directing guests toward information stations, seating, restrooms, and exits, and away from the many side rooms containing precious artwork and collections dating back to the Civil War. These special rooms would be off limits to all except Dr. Stansbury's honored guests—those donating one hundred thousand dollars or more to Hillary. Early on the morning of the address, Charlie would lead this magnanimous group in a wonderfully entertaining breakfast tour through time—and the four original historic buildings: Walker Hall and Auditorium, Turner Hall, Samuel Hall, and the Sanctuary.

In anticipation of the many national and international photographers, Charlie would begin the painstaking process of pruning the university's legendary roses next week in order that they might be picture perfect by game day. These tasks were hugely important and all responsibility fell to him, but still Charlie found it difficult to keep his mind from straying back to the rock and its spontaneous arrival. There was little doubt in his mind that it was heaven sent, because he had been the recipient of more than one miracle and could smell them a mile away, either in answer to his prayer or in opposition to it. But for what purpose this conspicuous, immovable object was deposited here, he couldn't imagine. It was his intention to check on it one more time this evening before going home, to see if it would give up any more clues to its supernatural existence, other than the ability to hover and repair itself.

Satisfied with the security modifications to Walker Auditorium, Charlie had just enough time before leaving for home to inspect two adjacent buildings that would be made available in the event of inclement weather. While exiting the Walker, he couldn't help but glance toward the rock in the open field some distance away. When he did, he noticed a lone person standing beside it. Without hesitation, Charlie jumped into his cart and took off in the direction of the tree line first and then down to the rock. To his surprise, there stood Dr. Stansbury—no cart, just the man. Charlie hopped out of the cart and slowly moved in so that they were both standing shoulder to shoulder and looking at the perfectly smooth, brilliant white rock.

"She's a beauty, isn't she?" Charlie quipped.

"No one has claimed her yet?" Stansbury asked calmly.

This tepid, curse-less response only added to Charlie's suspicion that there was something wrong with this picture. Not ready to jump to conclusions, he decided to give this person standing next to him another opportunity to jump down his throat for having a large white distraction sitting in the middle of the Yard less than three weeks before the university's biggest event of the school year.

Knowing full well that Peter had meetings scheduled until late this evening, Charlie looked down at his watch and spoke. "Not yet. Does Anne know where you are?"

"No, I'm positive she doesn't," Stansbury replied in the same subdued manner.

That was enough for Charlie. There was something definitely wrong, and no more baiting one-liners were going to be necessary.

"Are you all right, Peter?" Charlie asked sincerely.

"No... I'm sure I'm not," Stansbury replied despondently without turning his gaze from the stone.

"I think I may have caused Professor Daphne to quit, I am sure I threw Professor Richards out of my office, and I believe I told Anne I was leaving, but I'm not sure I told her why or when I would return. I started walking toward the roses, thinking maybe they would provide some comfort, but they did nothing and I ended up here."

Stansbury then turned to face Charlie. With a few large, heavy tears randomly escaping each eye and slowly following the same path down his cheeks until they eventually fell off his chin one by one, he let go of his heavy burden.

"Kimberly's breast cancer has come back."

Charlie's heart sank inside his chest. He had known that Peter's wife, whom he had met several times, had been diagnosed with breast cancer several years ago, but it was thought to be in complete remission. Peter was in deep, understandable pain, and he had nothing and no one giving him any significant comfort or hope, including Kim's doctors, who were suggesting he prepare for the worst.

"She goes to church, you know... has been for years," he continued. She enjoys reading the Christian books you leave for me. I regret not telling you that. The kids have been going to church and reading the Bible with her, and they pray a lot. I hear them talk to God, and they ask him to heal her. I don't mind, as long as she does everything the doctors tell her to do, but..."

There was a long pause, and Peter let his head drop slightly. Charlie wasn't sure if his friend couldn't find the exact word (or profanity)... or maybe he needed help interpreting the prayers spoken by his family... or maybe he simply needed a moment to catch a breath. Either way, he would wait patiently for Peter to continue, and he did.

"But then she would say things like, if it is 'His will' that she should die from this disease, then she 'will go' happily; that she 'was His,' after all... and that she would be 'content' with His plan for her life. They are all so damn content."

Again he paused. Peter struggled with this kind of talk because he perceived it as words of surrender and defeat.

"At first, it angered me," he sighed, and lifted his head again. "I didn't want to upset Kim, so I kept my feelings to myself. I figured they needed some kind of coping mechanism, like denial, to manage their pain, and sooner or later they would all snap out of it. But the prayers and unwavering faith in the unseen have only intensified.

"I go to church with them now to show my support," Peter admitted, "but I still don't get it, Charlie. I don't understand. Kim says she appreciates me doing this for her, but I can tell she receives no additional comfort beyond having a shoulder to lie her head on when she tires.

"I love my wife desperately and want to be her comforter, her champion," Peter said passionately."

"I'm ready to understand. Help me understand, counselor. Please," he pleaded earnestly, "before it's too late!"

"I think I can help you with that, Peter, but not here," Charlie replied gently. "Let's find some place comfortable to hash this thing out."

As they moved toward the cart, Charlie received a new text message. It was Anne. She was worried about her boss and asked if he would keep an eye out for him. Charlie immediately responded to her that Peter was with him and okay, but it would be best if she could clear his schedule for the remainder of the day as she saw fit, and he would explain later. Within seconds he received a return text simply saying, "Done, and thanks."

Before taking off in the cart, Charlie sent a quick follow-up message asking Anne for Professor Daphne's phone number and said he would explain that later as well. He would call the young professor as soon as he could to ask how she was doing and hopefully give an adequate explanation without having to go into specifics. As far as Professor Richards was concerned, Peter had thrown him out of his office many times before, so no such call was needed.

"That was Anne. She was concerned about you," Charlie said. "I asked her to clear your schedule. I hope that wasn't too presumptuous of me."

"Hell, no!" Peter replied gratefully. "Nothing else matters right now Charlie—nothing."

* * * * *

Jack could still smell the salty sea air in his nostrils, and Hitch, the musty, unconditioned air of a sixteenth-century castle. They were again sitting side by side in the white rock with the top open, which apparently was some kind of a time machine. They looked at each other, knowing that the other had experienced a similar odyssey back in time, and smiled.

"Wowza!" Jack exhaled as he looked at his watch. "I'm not sure we took any time off the clock either."

"A most unbelievable phenomenon," Hitch admitted. "To be every bit ourselves, and yet to have lived another life entirely. This would take extraordinary technology on a molecular level."

"I'm guessing you were invited back tomorrow?" Jack asked, still basking in the extreme awesomeness of his other life.

"I was," Hitch responded halfheartedly as his mind furiously attempted to fit together the elaborate pieces of this puzzle. "Even if the technology did exist, I don't see how living lives with such preeminent historical figures in complete opposition to our own modern rationalities and beliefs will bring us any closer to the answers we were promised."

"How could you have possibly known I was with Darwin?" Jack shot back.

"Please, Professor, try to keep up," Hitch huffed in annoyance. "I didn't know who it was you were with until now, but it fits the emerging pattern of our clever host. To this point, you and I have experienced similar but contrary intruders, dreams, and now, time travel.

"Let me guess. You even had something to do with Mr. Darwin's success," Hitch continued, with a similarity in his "similar but contrary" theory. "That is, your good friend might not have accomplished all those things he was quite famous for without your involvement in his life."

"The rumors are true," Jack said, playfully teasing his partner. "You are a genius!"

"Please don't work my nerves so early in this transitory relationship of ours, Jack," Hitch reprimanded his young partner for thinking this might be all fun and games.

"Sorry," Jack apologized. "So, which preeminent historical figure did you help immortalize?"

"Martin Luther… Eisleben… Germany," Hitch replied, still in deep thought, yet, for Jack's benefit, making the distinction from the more contemporary Martin Luther King Jr.

"Martin Luther! *The* Martin Luther?" Jack shouted, as if something had been taken from him. "That can't be right. He should have been my historical figure. Maybe we were sitting in the wrong seats."

Hitch decided that he needed to be alone with his thoughts and hopped out of the rock.

"Tomorrow, you may have my seat," Hitch responded, as if speaking to a needy child, and then started walking back toward Turner Hall, "unless I can solve this nonsensical yet utterly beguiling riddle by then—in which case, you can have both seats. Good night, Professor."

"Good night," Jack responded. "See you tomorrow."

"We shall see," Hitch replied, without turning to face Jack. "May I suggest you park your butt somewhere else so that thing can close up for the evening?"

Jack took the hint and jumped out. The rock sealed itself before he hit the ground.

How could he have possibly known it was going to do that? Jack thought as he too headed for Turner Hall and his car.

No matter... This can't wait any longer. I need some MJ input—stat!

The drive home allowed Jack to reflect on the close friendship he had developed with Charles Darwin and how the man's fascinating discoveries and bold observations made perfect sense to him. This caused Jack to wonder if, given enough time, Charles would have convinced him into believing one species actually could change into another, thus determining whether his faith was truly sowed on "good soil" versus "rocky places."

Then Hitchinson was right, he thought with some irritation. *What does any of this have to do with the stranger's promise?*

When Jack rounded the corner to his home, he was grateful to be able to end, or at least suspend, the direction his thoughts were leading him. The darkened windows to his house reminded him that MJ had taken the boys to her parents for the night. He was anxious to call and break this crazy story to her, but he had not forgotten about last night. This was the perfect opportunity to practice being intentional about listening to everything MJ wanted him to know first, even though it was unlikely she could say anything that would trump the many years he had just spent with Professor Henslow at Cambridge or Captain FitzRoy and Charles Darwin on the *H.M.S. Beagle*. That also reminded him that she hadn't been told about the stranger or the horrific dream yet either. She might think him insane if he were to drop all this on her at once, and over the phone would only make it sound worse. He would make the decision of how much information was too much information once he was on the phone with her.

Fortunately, MJ's dad enjoyed spending every waking moment he was given with his two grandsons, kicking the soccer ball, swinging the bat, shooting hoops, and then sneaking out for donuts or ice cream. The respite allowed MJ to wind down with her mom, and her mood was noticeably more relaxed. This visit was no different. Jack enjoyed hearing the highlights of their busy day, and when MJ asked about his, he felt comfortable launching into his story. Jack did not begin with the events of this day, however. Instead, he started at the beginning—yesterday... and the stranger. After the tale was told, MJ had some of the same questions and concerns that Jack had and then reassured him that she had nothing to do with the stranger's appearance.

In her own unique way of putting a positive spin on difficult matters, MJ suggested the stranger could have easily been an angel, because the devil would have never thought to be so helpful as to leave Jack's box full of classroom material or Joey's missing stuffed toy on the chair before leaving. They spent the next several minutes having fun coming up with things a devil might have left behind on the chair: things like snakes and roaches, rice cakes and tofu, sulfur- scented Febreze, a red costume with horns and pointy tail (pitchfork included), anything by Pink or

Bieber, cats (Jack's idea and rejected by MJ), the IRS, the 1973 Supreme Court, etc.

When their creativity ran its course and the giggling ended, Jack let MJ know there was more to the story, but it was getting late and they could talk some more tomorrow. The dream sequence would be better discussed in her presence anyway, since it involved divorce, a concept forbidden by Jesus in the New Testament unless Jack's character was an adulterer as well as an alcoholic (the two sometimes go hand-in-hand). After reassuring her that everything was fine and that he loved her like nobody's business, Jack asked if she thought her parents would mind watching Jake and Joey sometime in the morning while they talked. After a brief pause, Jack could hear his father-in-law in the background shout, "Take a week!"

With that, breakfast plans were set for the following morning, and Jack asked to say good night to the boys, if they were still up. They were, and each took a separate phone and proceeded to tell him all the cool stuff they had done with Grampa.

"And we played soccer and beat Grampa, and I had four goals, and Grampa got tired, and we stopped and had a Coke and baseball gum in a pouch..." Jake rattled on until forced to take a breath, allowing Joey to speak—quickly.

"I had two goals and a Coke," Joey squeezed in.

"Yeah, Joey had two, and I had four, and then we played baseball and I had six home runs (anything that went beyond Grampa was a home run) and Joey had one, and—"

"Grampa said I clobbered that ball, Dad," Joey interrupted.

"Yeah, but I hit one over Grampa's head—remember that?" Jake asked indignantly.

"He did, Dad. It went way over Grampa's head," Joey added. "And we had donuts."

"Yeah, I had a Boston cream and a sprinkler," Jake said, taking over. "And then we dug some holes for Gramma's plants—"

"I had a jelly donut and a sprinkler," Joey interrupted.

"Stop interrupting, Joey!" Jake scolded.

"You stop!" Joey responded.

This bantering continued for ten minutes until the ratio between activity and arguing went from 80:20 to 20:80, at which point Jack brought the energetic conversation to a close.

They'll sleep well tonight once the Grampa-induced sugar high wears off, Jack thought, and said good night with lots of troll-like snorts and belching (troll kisses) between them.

* * * * *

Most assuredly, if Hitch could have walked away from this complex machination of his without doubt or suspicion, he would have—and never look back. But it was mocking doubt and nagging suspicion that consumed him now. Apart from the natural inquisitiveness that dwelled within him, he had never lived with these two unhealthy afflictions looming over him for long, although he had to admit that he was momentarily stumped. That made this whole affair personal to him. If he wanted to, he could easily make a few phone calls and have a thousand scientists swarming over this pseudo-rock tomorrow, but that would end any chance of learning what it was this thing had to offer him. No, he would ride this horse—or rock—to its conclusion. Besides, in the back of his mind, he was certain the moment the first scientist stepped foot on Hillary soil, this thing would vanish as suddenly as it had appeared.

As a rule, Hitch knew everything had a flaw or weakness, and there was no doubt in his mind that this exercise with the rock would be no exception to that rule. He was encouraged to be given at least one more opportunity to discover what that deficiency was. It would not be an exaggeration to say the events of the past two days were on the strange side, if not vastly inconceivable, so there was no telling what details he may have missed. Tomorrow he would be more diligent in applying his own philosophy of observing and recognizing what others observe but fail to recognize.

Perhaps I was a bit too hard on Ryan this morning, Hitch thought, now more critical of himself for almost giving up on his brilliant young protégé for missing a few details.

The drive home did not produce any significant insights, but then again, his thoughts had to contend with nighttime traffic. For not having had much sleep, Hitch felt more hungry than tired and decided to pick up some Chinese food on the way home. He found Chinese to be the perfect food for prolonged meditation because unlike most other dishes, it could be reheated several times over long periods of time and the last bite would taste as good as the first bite—that is, if one could resist the temptation to eat the whole container at one sitting, which would be disastrous for clear, fervent thinking.

Hitch was careful to remove himself from the table after eating about a third of his meal. He walked directly to the bar and filled a rocks glass half full with Grand Marnier, then parked himself in his easy chair. Now that he was properly settled, it did not take long for his acutely trained mind to take all his doubts and suspicions and boil them down to two manageable questions: what of the promise of an answer to his Irrefutability Theory, and why Martin Luther?

Hitch no longer doubted that everything that had happened to him had meaning. The intruder was not just a messenger—he had meaning; the dream was not just about Nero and a talking lion—it had meaning; the rock was not just a vehicle capable of transporting his mind and body somewhere else in time—it had meaning. Even Professor Lewis meant something beyond simply being his time-traveling sidekick. Hitch might not fully comprehend what they were all supposed to represent yet, but that didn't matter right now. If only he could reasonably discern how his life spent with Martin Luther would bring him closer to the promise, he would sleep easier tonight.

Is this about God as Jack blurted out? Hitch thought.

If it was simple reverse psychology to get him to like God, then the Manufacturer (as Hitch now preferred to characterize the genius behind the "rock shuttle") of this scheme should have known that he wouldn't fall for that one. It was not that he was anti-God, as some might believe. That would be like saying he was anti-unicorn or anti-Big Foot or anti-imagination. There was nothing inherently wrong with gods, unicorns, hairy creatures with bad posture and abnormally large feet, or imagination. There were simply better explanations for them all. The Manufacturer should also have known that he was not interested in wasting time arguing the plethora of religious theories against the plethora of secular beginning-of-time theories. That would be as productive as a watching a cat chase its tail.

So why had he been thrust into Luther's life, and why at that moment in time? Why not later in life when his good friend became a raving anti-Semitic lunatic? All he could say in utmost sincerity was that the crotchety monk had become the closest and dearest friend he had ever known—in that life or in this one. This deep affection had been cultivated over many years, and never once did he feel their relationship was either contrived or manipulated by anyone or anything. Over those many years, he had seen every side of Luther and found the man to be brilliant but humble, irascible but warmhearted, dogmatic but charming, flawed as any human ever was but principled and contrite. He began as the highly favored spiritual leader of the rich and comfortable, but ended up being the maligned advocate of the poor and weak.

And for the souls of the downtrodden, this stubborn monk would risk his life pissing off a pope, Hitch thought.

And for this stubborn monk, Hitch would risk his own life in a daring highway kidnapping.

Having allowed half an hour to tick off the clock without much hope for an early bedtime, Hitch took a satisfying swallow from his rocks glass before getting up to reheat his General Tso's food in the microwave. After scanning his phone for messages while another third of his meal disappeared, he returned to his easy chair and waited patiently for his mind to refocus on his life lived in the precarious world of Martin Luther. It felt good to reminisce on those frenzied days, knowing now that his beleaguered friend lived to fall in love, have children, and continue teaching until his natural death at the age of sixty-two. He was still quite certain the information he was seeking (the information he believed he was supposed to find) had something to do with the rebellious Augustinian monk, but not something so blatantly obvious as the same old tired god-versus-science squabbling.

Hitch's mind cleared, and all extraneous thoughts were suppressed or ignored. Without being fully aware of his actions, he once again lifted his half-full glass of Grand Marnier and peered through the murky fluid at the upside-down images in the bookcase beyond. The book his eyes fell upon this time seemed different than the others, and those that surrounded it were doing their best to keep it hidden. Its faded spine had no markings to attract him, nothing in its appearance that should make him desire to actually get up, yet that's exactly what he felt compelled to do.

He still didn't recognize it until he was able to see the front cover and read the inscription inside:

To my dearest husband,

May this new book wear better than the last. Your devotion to God's Word is an inspiration to me.

My love forever, Becca

Rebecca was Hitch's mother, and this was his father's last surviving Bible (his father owned many). Oddly enough, it was the only family heirloom that Hitch had bothered keeping. He had a vast library, so what was one more book? Hitch had read the entire Bible a number of times from a variety of translations, so there was no apprehension about reading this one again. It was getting late, and since nothing else had come to his mind, he slipped the book under his arm and went back to his chair. His only dilemma was where to begin. The thing contained sixty-six books. It was not his intention to read them all, and it was laughable to think he would close his eyes and open it to some random page, as if inspired to do so.

He took another sip of the Grand Marnier, and his mind soon focused on the three years between the time Luther posted his notorious Ninety-Five Theses to the church door and his excommunication. This was an extraordinary time when thousands of students were pouring into Wittenberg from all over Europe to hear Luther speak. He lectured on many books of the Bible from both the Old and the New Testaments, but only once did the famed theologian ever extend a special invitation to Hitch to hear him speak, and that was his lecture on the book of Romans. As Hitch recalled, the conversation went something like this:

"Edmond, I implore you, come tonight," Luther pleaded. "I will begin a new series of lectures and, if I may speak truthfully, it came about as a direct result of our long-standing friendship."

"Ah, truthfully, I ask you, Martin... when will you relent?" Hitch replied with a sigh. "You have stated your case for conversion many times, and you have done so as well as any doctor of law could argue before the courts, yet I stand before you unconvinced."

"Yes, indeed, Romans has as its main thesis God's gift of redemption by faith in Jesus Christ, that one and firm rock that we call 'justification' being the chief article of the whole Christian doctrine," Luther agreed. "But, as is often the case, I have found there to be overlooked passages and underlying qualities to Paul's letter to the Romans that I believe would be of great value to you, if not now, perhaps in the future."

"As you well know, value can mean different things to different people, Martin," Hitch noted pretentiously. "Time has the most value in my opinion. Unfortunately, it is also the thing I am completely out of, I am sorry to say. I do wish you luck with your lecture tonight, of course."

Thus ended the conversation and the flashback.

The book of Romans it is, then, Hitch thought.

It took Hitch no time at all to zip through the sixteen chapters, but at the end, he found nothing but righteousness this and unrighteousness that, all very doctrinal as expected. But that didn't make sense either because Luther, being like a brother and knowing Hitch inside and out, would not have made such claims as overlooked passages, underlying qualities, and great value if he did not know them to be true. Hitch would read the book again, this time with the expectation that his dear friend, although theatrical, was not a liar.

Hitch's first glimpse of Luther's suggestion of ancillary passages, qualities, and value that weaved their way through the book came almost immediately. In chapter 1, he read, "To all... who are loved by God"; then again in chapter 5, he read, "But God demonstrated his own love for us." Then out of nowhere, like an island in the middle of an ocean or an oasis in the middle of a desert, came chapter 8 and the whole "more than conquerors" soliloquy.

The skillful apostle alluded to it again in chapter 12: "Be devoted to one another in brotherly love"; then again in chapter 13: "Let no debt remain... except the continuing debt to love one another," and "Love is the fulfillment of the law."

Is this about love? Hitch wondered with cool ambivalence. *What am I supposed to do with that?*

12

Charlie's Enlightenment

A lex and Frannie were back at it early the following morning. Chief was confident in their understanding of the project and made no demands on them as far as time, as long as the final product was neat and tight. The chain-link fencing went up first. A light weight rebar was laced through the bottom links between the posts to add rigidity at ground level and no gateway made this first barrier virtually impenetrable. The two heavy-duty canvas tarps attached to the fencing with 12-gauge wire at every grommet and its two seams overlapping by at least two feet made the interior virtually invisible. By noon they were done. Two extension ladders, one inside and one outside, were used to climb out and then removed.

"That oughta do it," Alex said proudly. "The only people I see getting in there are marines and a few Ninja."

"Maybe we should put some razor wire on top, just in case," Frannie added sarcastically.

"Couldn't hurt," Alex replied, adding more sarcasm, "except the guy going over the top."

"Wouldn't you love to see Chief's face if he saw razor wire up there?" Frannie asked.

"Oh yeah," Alex laughed out loud. "But I wouldn't wanna be the one who put it there. Let's go grab some lunch and the signs."

"Sounds good to me," Frannie replied, and hopped into the cart first. "I'll drive."

Their destination was the new multimillion-dollar food court that offered every kind of cuisine known to prosperous man. The food was authentically prepared under the careful supervision of an elite corps of chefs from New York, Seattle, Louisiana (Alex's favorite), and Rio de Janeiro (Frannie's favorite). Before making the final turn at the tree line, Frannie stopped, and the two of them looked back at their work area. There was little evidence of their construction project outside the canvas walls.

"Chief should be happy with that," Alex said contentedly.

In fact, they had done such an exceptional job in keeping the outside area pristine that the only disturbance to the lawn that Frannie could make out from her new vantage point was two sets of footprints that she had not noticed before. They led right up to the new barrier and disappeared underneath. The same two sets of tracks just as suddenly came out from under the barrier at different locations and headed back in the same direction they had come.

"Yeah... I suppose," Frannie replied hesitantly. "Okay, let's go. I hope Chef Anabella made the shrimp pastel today."

"Well, you can keep your fancy food, *mon cher*," Alex countered in his best Cajun. "Cause the wise man always starts his day with a big ol' bowl of crawfish gumbo and a fist full of oyster crackers... I gar-own-tee."

"Really? Always? Shut up!" Frannie fired back as she put the pedal to the metal, and off they flew, buzzing the tree line.

Once the two were back on the center trail again, it was not long before they were pulling over to greet their boss, who was in his cart and traveling their way. Charlie had spent a long night filling in the gaps that prevented Peter from understanding the Christian perspective on life and death. This engagement had nothing to do with evangelism or proselytism, only clarification. Any other purpose would have most likely sent Peter into a rage and ended the evening before it began. As it was, the meeting lasted until long after midnight with Peter giving Charlie permission to pray for his family. Then, early this morning, he was able to locate and convince a clearly distraught Professor Daphne to meet with him to discuss Peter's behavior, which all agreed was unacceptable, even for him.

Charlie's reasons for heading in Alex and Frannie's direction had less to do with checking up on them and more to do with meeting Jack, which he had promised to do two days ago, and then securing the Sanctuary before Professor Hitchinson's grand lecture.

"How's it going down there?" Charlie inquired.

"The walls are up," Frannie said confidently. "I think you will like it."

"I'm sure I will, Francesca," Charlie said. "I'm on my way to a meeting with Professor Lewis and then to lock up the Sanctuary, but I'll stop by to have a look on my way back."

"We're gonna drop off this gear and then grab something to eat," Alex added. "We'll be back with the signs after lunch."

"Sounds like a plan," Charlie said. "Enjoy your lunch."

"I will. Alex is having tadpole soup, though," Frannie groaned.

"Crawfish gumbo!" Alex clarified. "Breakfast of champions!"

"I thought champions ate SOS for breakfast?" Charlie answered.

"Chief!" Frannie gasped. Alex burst out laughing.

"Stuff on Shingles," Charlie responded. "You know… creamed chipped beef on toast. What did you think I meant?"

"You know I know what you meant," Frannie smiled. "Shame on you."

"What?" Charlie feigned not to understand the problem. "Okay, I'm gonna scoot. You two enjoy your lunch. And for the record, I can't tell how you how much I appreciate you both and what you do around here."

"We love it here, Chief," Frannie said gratefully.

"Yeah, Chief. It's like home to us," Alex added.

"That's great to hear," Charlie replied. "Okay, I'm off."

Charlie glanced toward the rock in passing but did not stop; there was simply too much left to be done. Besides, from the center trail, the camo looked so unobtrusive and the yard so immaculate that, had he not known better, it would appear as though the unassuming structure had been there for years.

* * * * *

Jack, however, could not take his eyes off it.

Jack had been standing at his office window for almost an hour and watched as Charlie whizzed by the rock in his cart. He knew that Charlie was on his way to see him; they had agreed this morning to meet in the afternoon.

It had been only two days ago that Charlie popped by his office to say hello and meet a friendly face before making his controversial "welcome to Hillary" tour to the newbies. So much had happened since then that it felt more like two weeks.

I wonder what he thinks about all this, other than the floating rock needed to be covered up, Jack thought.

After discussing the events of the last couple of days with MJ this morning, it was decided that this was most certainly a spiritual encounter between him and God. The events, therefore, were best kept to themselves until the promise resolved itself. Though Charlie was one of Jack's primary spiritual leaders and a trusted friend, even his thoughts and advice must remain unsolicited.

Jack's breakfast meeting with MJ had actually involved three separate venues. The first place they hit was a little hideaway café in town, where they talked leisurely about children, parents, and friends. From there they moved to a quiet little breakfast shop for a bite to eat and to discuss the dream and its possible subliminal meanings. They concluded that divorce and alcoholism were not the main issues. The dream was more likely a warning to Jack that his obsessive motivation to be a pastor might be a form of covetousness. After breakfast they relocated to an outdoor park. It was there that Jack nearly shocked MJ off the bench with his story of sailing around the world with Darwin.

A dream was one thing; a Mr. Peabody WABAC machine was another. She was referring to the old Saturday morning cartoon with an extremely intelligent talking dog (Mr. Peabody), his young curious human friend (Sherman) and their "Way Back" contraption for traveling backwards in time.

Understanding that this other life of his would be hard to swallow and would even challenge their trust in each other, Jack had offered to bring MJ along with him tonight. That most likely meant jeopardizing the promise. The rock would not open—that was for sure—but Professor Hitchinson should be there, and MJ could cross-examine her husband's first witness. If Hitchinson did not show, at least Jack could call Charlie to the stand to attest to the fact that the rock somehow had showed up overnight without explanation and was not touching the ground (according to Hitchinson's observations).

The offer to verify his claims was enough to calm MJ's fears that her husband might be going insane. However, she agreed to defer her acceptance of the offer only as long as Jack didn't begin to hide things from her or become more weird than he already was. This was quickly agreed to by Jack, who promised to end his participation if it became obvious to either one of them that something deceitful or evil was at play.

Even though Jack had seen Charlie heading his way moments ago, the knock on the door came as a surprise. The door was open and in walked Charlie, who was immediately forced to circumvent several stacks of books on the floor.

"Good afternoon, Professor," Charlie called out warmly. "So, did the office come with all these extra books, or is shelving out of style?"

"Somehow, between the basement and here, they developed the capability to reproduce like rabbits," Jack hazarded a guess. "How did your meetings go with the newest members of our Hillary family?"

"It's amazing how you can talk about Muhammad, Buddha, and an anthropomorphic Mother Earth all day long, but as soon as you mention the name *Jesus*, all hell breaks loose," Charlie observed candidly. "But there is nothing new under the sun. How about you? You had something you wanted to talk about?"

"There was, but so much has happened since then that I'm not sure how to answer that question," Jack replied cautiously.

"I am sorry to have delayed so long in getting back to you, Jack," Charlie said with great sincerity.

"Oh, hey, listen, don't apologize," Jack responded. "I know your days are crazy busier than mine, and well, it worked out better that we didn't talk back then. I can still use your advice, but differently."

"No problem then, but do you think the advice you are seeking today will be the same a couple of days from now?" Charlie said with a wry smile. "I can come back, you know."

"Not a chance!" Jack barked. "Now that I've got you, there's no way you're leaving without shedding some light on this monkey business going on in my life."

"Okay, let's go at it then," Charlie replied, "but I've only got an hour. Is that enough time, Jack?"

"I won't keep you a second longer," Jack promised, and began a shadowy summation of the last forty-eight hours.

"To be honest, I believe I am being put to the test by God," Jack said bluntly. "Two days ago, the day you dropped in, something occurred that literally took my breath away. That is what I had wanted to question you about. But then that night, I had a dream so vivid and so troubling that I will never forget it, and I believe it had something to do with the *promise*.

"Oops, sorry, I mean the event I wanted to talk about," Jack corrected himself. "Then yesterday, another sudden and mysterious event occurred that, if I told you, you would find difficult to believe, but it had a way of tying all the other events together. And I believe there is more to come.

"So, here's my question, Charlie." Jack came to the point. "I feel I'm on trial here, but not sure why."

A sudden chill shot through Charlie's body as he reflected on his conversation with Peter a few hours ago. Discussions like the one he had with Peter concerning his wife's cancer took a heavy toll on Charlie, both physically and mentally, because they never failed to question the love of God: if God is so good why does he allow pain and suffering?

"First, may I ask if this is about someone's health?" Charlie asked in desperation.

"No, Charlie, it's not," Jack replied softly, noticing his mentor's pained look.

Thank God, Charlie thought.

"Well then, you probably already know the answer to this one, but when we are in the grips of a trial, it is good to refresh our understanding of why God allows them in the first place," Charlie began. "The simple answer to your question is found in James 1. You are being taught something, Jack. It's a lesson.

"Here's what's so shocking to you, though. When God decides this would be a good time to test you, there is no asking you if it fits into your schedule, packed as it may be. The trials we tend to question are the trials that are sudden and dramatic. Are you with me so far?"

"So far, so good."

"Good. Remember also that trials are never going to be exactly the same. They are formed to be personal for each and every person chosen to be tested. So not only can you not predict when trials are going to occur, but you aren't able to study for the particular test you are given. The answers to your test are going to be inside you... or they are not. Still tracking with me, Jack?"

"Can't predict... can't prepare... got it," Jack sighed.

"Good. So here's the good news about the trials you are going through. First, God loves you and sees something in you that needs a little tweaking, and that something is called faith. So trials are actually tests of faith. That is a good thing for those of us who love the Lord because it means we don't have to study for every eventuality that could be set before us. In fact, your test, like everyone else's test, has only two questions on it. And to make it even easier on us, they are both true-or-false questions.

"Here they are," Charlie said, clearing his throat as if he were going to say something profoundly wise, but then delivering something quite simple and obvious: "Is God good, and is He in control?

"That's it. If you believe the answer to both of those questions is true in the midst of your darkest trial, you can say with assurance you have passed the test. But you must be patient to wait on the Lord and allow perseverance to finish its work.

"Does that make sense in your situation, Jack?" Charlie asked, hoping his explanation was in the ballpark.

It did, and Jack was quick to thank Charlie for putting things back into perspective. They finished their hour together in pleasant conversation. The two would soon be seeing more of each other once their Promise Keepers meetings started back up after Hitchinson's lecture. Jack did inadvertently ask about the rock twice, maybe three times, but managed to avoid revealing the true nature of his curiosity. At least, it didn't seem to Jack that Charlie was picking up on his unusual fascination with the rock.

As soon as Charlie disappeared out the door, Jack sprawled out in his cushy desk chair and relaxed. Between them, MJ and Charlie had produced more relief to his stress than he could have ever asked for. He would make good on his word to keep MJ informed and heed Charlie's final advice to wait on the Lord because He is good and He is in control.

Well, that was enlightening, Charlie thought in the hallway. *A sudden and mysterious event occurring yesterday, followed by three haphazard questions concerning the rock.*

Charlie exited Turner Hall, jumped in his cart, and headed to the Sanctuary. Because of the delicate and irreplaceable nature of some of the articles inside the building, it would be sealed off until after Professor Hitchinson's lecture, except for portions made available to Peter's special guests while on personal tour with him.

Prior to entering the Sanctuary, Charlie always changed into a clean pair of shoes that he carried with him at all times, even when he hadn't been working in manure all day. He now entered through the back door, which led to the basement where Hillary's original galley and dining hall were located. It was still a functioning kitchen, but rarely ever used to feed exceptionally large numbers of people. This is where Charlie's men's Bible study group met on Wednesdays. He had asked Alex and Frannie to clean out the small walk-in refrigerator and deliver any perishables to the local food bank last week. This task had been followed to the letter, and Charlie was locking up the basement in less than half an hour. He ascended the narrow, uneven stairs at the opposite end of the dining hall, which led to a small antechamber at the front of the Sanctuary.

The Sanctuary was typically open from 6:00 a.m. to 10:00 p.m. seven days a week, unless it was determined by the curator (Charlie) that doing so would present some physical harm to the building or its contents. There were no security cameras anywhere inside the building, only outside per fire and rescue guidelines. The "no camera" policy was to maintain intimacy with God. Every door, window, and hallway, however, had a motion sensor assigned to it. This elaborate monitoring system gave Charlie a heads-up that a single individual had entered the Sanctuary by the front door sometime before he arrived at the back door.

A sign had been placed prominently at the front door last week notifying guests of the Sanctuary's intended closure that would begin today. On the sign was also written the specific time when the doors would be locked, and that time was quickly approaching. Unless there were extenuating circumstances that would oblige Charlie into granting more time, he would gently remind this guest of the time and request they conclude their meditations. He would never have guessed who that guest would be.

"Right on time, Charlie," Hitch said, glancing at his watch.

"Excuse me if I look surprised, Professor," Charlie responded jokingly, knowing that some things are not what they sometimes appear. "Was it something I said... oh, say, twenty-five years ago that brings you here today?"

"Please don't rush me, Charlie," Hitch said with a smile. "I understand that we do not run in the same circles, and our interaction has been sporadic except around this time of year, but there is no need, nor has there ever been a need, to refer to me by title only. So please, call me Hitch, unless that makes you uncomfortable."

"Thank you, Hitch. I will do that," Charlie answered appreciatively. "Except, of course, when protocol dictates formality."

"Fair enough," Hitch exclaimed. "Now to business—"

"Excuse me once more," Charlie interrupted politely, "but it sounds as though you have anticipated our meeting."

"Well, not exactly," Hitch explained. "I arrived approximately an hour ago and read the bulletin outside the door. I figured that you would be the one to lock up and that you would also be prompt, so I waited."

"I see. May I ask, though, why you have come to the Sanctuary?" Charlie inquired, trying to make sense of this unlikely scenario before moving on.

"Fair question," Hitch replied. "Let's say research... if I may explain?"

"Of course," Charlie agreed. "Allow me to lock up first."

Hitch agreed and waited patiently for Charlie to return. He had already spent much of his 7:00 a.m. meeting with Ms. Brown discussing matters of religious faith and love rather than appointments and deadlines. It surprised him to learn that she considered herself a born-again Christian and how proficient was her understanding of the Bible. He had not detected the famously common hypocrisy demonstrated by most who claimed to be Christians. He even felt some remorse for having to lie about the rock's ability to condense half a lifetime into a blink of an eye and instead thought it best to describe his most recent event as being another curious dream, this time with Martin Luther instead of Nero. He would have preferred telling her the truth, but he still felt too vulnerable.

As usual, Ms. Brown was helpful, especially with regards to the book of Romans, chapter 8, verses 37, 38, and 39 specifically, which had been memory verses for her as a teenager. Her understanding of Luther's life, however, went only as far as a movie made over ten years ago, and her recollections from watching it made Hitch laugh out loud, even though they weren't supposed to be funny. He had spent part of his life with Martin Luther, after all!

It was only when Ms. Brown began sharing her thoughts on the perfect and natural design of the love between a man and a woman that Hitch found himself in the unusual position of being the student. Her voice was soft and romantic, her words were carefully chosen and edifying, her delivery was irresistible and captivating, and her impact was satisfying and sustaining. Love had found an eloquent spokesperson in Ms. Brown, and if there was any truth in her articulations on love, Hitch admittedly had never been loved, nor had he truly loved a woman.

But there was no time for reflection. Whether it was by coincidence or by an innate sense of timing, Ms. Brown concluded with enough time for her boss to make his ten o'clock appointment with Dr. Roberts. Still, as insightful as it was, Hitch could not shake the feeling that this lesson on love was incomplete, or at least not exactly what Luther had in mind for him. Hitch thanked Ms. Brown for sharing what had obviously been written on her heart for a long time and for once again being a perfect listener. After his doctor's appointment, which detected nothing unusual, Hitch knew he would have to seek another opinion to resolve this issue before sunset tonight.

"Sorry about that. Sometimes it would appear that my only duty is to lock and unlock doors," Charlie apologized. "Where were we?"

"Please do not understate your value to the university, Charlie, even in jest," Hitch said earnestly. "My being here is evidence that your statement could not be more untrue."

"Thank you, Hitch," Charlie replied gratefully. "So please, tell me what you can about your research."

"You have phrased that perfectly, Charlie," Hitch began. "First, let me say that I realize the more you know of my research, the more likely you will be able to help me, but I am uncertain at what point my revealing certain information might set into motion a withdrawal of the *promise*... Excuse me, I meant to say gift," Hitch corrected himself.

Promise—there's that misspoken word again, Charlie thought, recalling his conversation with Jack. *Interesting!*

"Before we go on, may I ask if you are in trouble?" Charlie asked, sensing Hitch's foreboding hesitation.

"Nothing that sinister, I'm afraid," Hitch replied calmly. "I would simply remain in the same position I was in two days ago—that's all."

"Well then, tell me what you can, and I will do my best to help as I can," Charlie said, without the foggiest idea of what that help might look like.

"Two days ago I was offered a gift, a special gift—not a material gift, but a gift like no other," Hitch began. "In the two nights since that gift was presented to me, I have had two extraordinary dreams. The first night involved Nero and the brutality he unleashed on the Christians after the fire in AD 64, and last night I was with the Augustinian monk Martin Luther on the day he posted his Ninety-Five Theses.

"You have my permission to laugh now," Hitch quipped. "I realize there is a good bit of irony in that statement."

"I would never do that," Charlie said with an exaggerated smile. "Please continue."

"I believe the three events are interrelated," Hitch stated matter-of-factly. "I also believe I am being *tested*."

"Tested?" Charlie stated, almost too loudly and too forcefully.

It's like déjà vu all over again, Charlie thought, using one of Yogi Berra's many fractured quotes. It fit perfectly with his feeling that this meeting was beginning to take on similarities to the one he had just finished with Jack.

"I'm sorry," Charlie said, returning to his normal speaking voice. "Are you able to explain why you feel tested by the offer of an intangible gift and two dreams that have included Christians?"

"I did not say this was a feeling, Charlie," Hitch answered abruptly. "I do not have time, or the inclination, to chase answers to feelings that change with the wind, but I must confess I do not have a complete answer as to why I believe this to be a test... yet."

"Understood," Charlie replied respectfully. "You say 'yet.' That suggests you are close to solving this puzzle, so to speak. Is that right?"

"Yes."

"Very good," Charlie continued. "I believe I heard you say that you arrived at the Sanctuary not knowing that I, or anyone else, for that matter, was due to arrive within the hour. You only decided to stay once you believed that it would be I who would lock the doors according to the bulletin outside. Is that right?"

"Yes, I—"

"Excellent," Charlie continued without pausing. "That suggests it was a belief you held, regardless of how foolish it sounds now, that you might find a clue to your riddle by being inside a house of worship. When that did not occur, you stayed, thinking I might be a helpful source of information, specifically in the biblical or spiritual realm. Is that right?"

"Yes, but—"

"Please hold that thought, Hitch. I believe we are almost home." Charlie assumed consent and continued. "I see you have with you an old book. I'm assuming it is a Bible, perhaps passed down from one generation to the next until it came to rest with you. By the way it is lying open and face down on the pew, it appears you have been reading from it at that spot. May I take a look?"

Charlie again assumed consent and lifted the old book carefully. It was indeed a Bible, and he opened to the book of Romans, and in the middle of chapter 8.

"Not too unpredictable," Charlie said, almost to himself. "The intangible gift you wish to remain nameless could not have been an expense paid trip to Italy, because that would have been a material thing, but Rome appears to be the subject matter of your dreams. Your dreams were of a Roman emperor and a monk who, although German, we know gave several lectures on the apostle Paul's book of Romans. Since Nero loved no one but himself, I suspect that it was something in your dream with Martin Luther that has brought you here. You may also believe this canonical letter addressed to the Christians of Rome can help you understand why it is you are being tested. Am I close?"

"Close enough, counselor," Hitch conceded. "You have saved me valuable time. Now, with the same brevity, what can you tell me about love?"

"Love?" Charlie asked quizzically. He had not seen that one coming.

"Exactly," Hitch replied. "The kind of love the apostle scatters like seed throughout his eschatological dissertation to the Romans, and without sounding ungrateful, may I have the condensed version, please? I must be somewhere at sunset."

"Hitch, my expertise has more to do with the organic seed variety than with an exposition of the Scriptures," Charlie humbly admitted. "However, I do know several capable Bible scholars who could answer these kinds of questions better than I."

"My quest is not to provide some religious talking-head with the topic for a sermon," Hitch replied candidly. "I believe the kind of answer I am looking for will need to come from a friend, so to speak, more so than from a theologian—with all due respect for your colleagues.

"Please, Charlie," Hitch added kindly. "This is important to me."

"Very well, you asked for it," Charlie warned lightheartedly. "But don't blame me if I get 1 John 2:16 all tangled up with John Lennon's 'Can't Buy Me Love.'"

"I am not here to trip you up, Charlie," Hitch grinned. "Proceed when you're ready; I will not interrupt."

"All right then, but please do not hesitate to stop me if I stray or fail to hold your interest," Charlie said, still feeling a little intimidated.

"Charlie, I have asked a favor of you. You say what you feel is necessary, and stop when you are finished," Hitch replied patiently. "I said I would not interrupt, and I do not go back on my word."

"Okay... here we go," Charlie said as he took a deep breath and silently asked the Lord for guidance. "First, some background, if I may.

"The apostle Paul had not yet visited Rome when he wrote his letter to the Christians there. The letter was clearly written from Corinth around AD 57 or 58. You mentioned having a dream about Nero. This would have been written two or three years after Nero became Rome's emperor and six or seven years before the great fire in AD

64. So Rome was somewhat quiet at this time—at least for Christians.

"I'm not surprised that you chose this epistle, or this epistle was chosen for you. Since Rome was peaceful and there was no heresy or turmoil within the Roman church itself, Paul took the opportunity to lay down some of the purest Christian truths in all of the New Testament. As you probably have already noticed, the main theme of this letter to the Roman church is God's plan for the salvation of sinful man. This is the good news of Christ Jesus, for which Paul says he was 'set apart' and 'unashamed.' You may have also noticed—perhaps only because it was already on your mind—that interwoven throughout this doctrinal work is this matter of love.

"It's amazing how masterfully we have overlooked this practical day-to-day instruction on how we are to love one another," Charlie mused with a sigh, and continued. "Paul continues to develop the power of love in his first letter to the Corinthians. It is there that Paul uses some beautiful language—perhaps so we don't realize we are being beaten over the head—to craft a warning not to be ignored. The warning is this: we can do, and we can say, and we can be all that is prescribed by Scripture, but if we have not love, we gain nothing. So love supersedes everything," Charlie concluded, setting the premise on love.

"This brings us to your question about love. You may already know there are several Greek words used to describe love, and the Bible uses them all. *Phileo* means brotherly love, *eros* means erotic love, and *storge* refers to the love between family members. However, I believe the Greek word you have in mind is *agape*. If I could emphasize one quality of agape love that separates it from all the others, it is this: it is not based on a feeling. Agape love is not romantic, sensual, kindhearted, neighborly, sympathetic, understanding, warm, or fuzzy.

"I know of a few places where Paul uses the term *agape* for 'love' in Romans," Charlie said as he picked up Hitch's Bible and opened it carefully. When he came to the right page, he handed the book back to its unbelieving owner. "Romans 5:8: 'But God commendeth his agape toward us, in that, while we were still sinners, Christ died for us.'" Charlie recited the passage, transposing the word *love* with the word *agape*, and paused briefly before continuing in order to allow Hitch time to internalize its use.

"Knowing how dependent we are on visible evidence, God demonstrated agape love by sacrificing his Son on a cross. We didn't earn it, we don't deserve it, and we are incapable of producing agape love on our own.

"May I?" Charlie asked as he reached out his hand for the Bible. Upon receiving it, he gently thumbed the pages and returned it to Hitch.

"Romans 8:35: 'Who shall separate us from the agape of Christ?' And verse 39: 'Nothing... shall be able to separate us from the agape of God, which is in Christ Jesus our Lord.'

"Our spouse or lover may leave us or betray us, our best friend may leave us or betray us, our parent or sibling may leave us or betray us, but God won't. In fact, there has been nothing we have ever said or done, and there is nothing we will ever say or do that can change his agape love for us.

"Again, please?" Charlie asked, and again extended his hand for the Bible.

As he gingerly turned the pages, Charlie began to realize that this section of Hitch's Bible appeared to be in worse shape than the rest of the book. One could conclude that the family member that originally owned the Bible had spent a lot of time meditating on the book of Romans as well. He returned the book.

"Romans 12:9: 'Let agape be without hypocrisy.' Agape love does not come naturally to us. It involves self-sacrifice without expecting anything in return, and this is where we fall down. We say we agape-love God without also agape-loving our unlovable neighbors. This is unfortunate because we as believers are without excuse.

"One more place that I can think of and I'm done," Charlie said, again reaching out his hand for the fragile book. He carefully flipped a few pages and returned it.

"Romans 5:5 makes it perfectly clear: 'The agape love of God is poured out in our hearts through the Holy Ghost which is given unto us.' If we as Christians are filled with the Holy Ghost, or Holy Spirit, then we must also be filled with agape love," Charlie stated unequivocally. "The two go together—they are inseparable.

"Hitch, can I show you one more reference to agape love, even though it's not in the book of Romans?" Charlie asked politely. "I think it will help clarify my opening statement about agape not being a feeling."

"Of course, Charlie," Hitch responded politely, and extended his Bible to Charlie. The passage was found and the book returned.

"First John 4:8: 'He that loveth not, knoweth not God; for God is agape.' Agape love is of God and from God. It is his nature and his character. God is love.

"I hope that was helpful?" Charlie asked.

"We shall see," Hitch replied honestly. "In any event, you have more than illustrated the meaning of agape in your own life, Charlie, as you have defined it. I believe Martin Luther would have been quite fond of you. I am grateful for your time, but now I must run. Have a pleasant evening."

"To you as well, Hitch," Charlie said, and escorted quite possibly the most brilliant man on the planet to the door.

Promises, dreams, tests... Is it possible that Jack and Hitch could be on the same journey and not know it? Charlie asked himself. *In any case, that was enlightening.*

After turning off all the lights and locking up, Charlie made a dash for his cart. He wanted to check out the rock enclosure before it started getting dark. This would have to be a quick side trip because he and his wife were expecting company for dinner tonight, and a shower and a shave were in order.

13

The Promise Keeper

Love matters, he thought.

Hitch had never realized how little he knew of love and how it differed greatly from Sigmund Freud's psychoanalytical model of love that cast all love as being sexual—even between siblings, children, parents, and friends. The only thing holding us back from acting on these subliminal tendencies, according to Dr. Freud, was our own self-imposed repression.

There is little wonder why these Christians have such a strong devotion to their Jesus. This self-sacrificing love is very appealing. It bestows upon the giver a much higher reward than anything carnality has to offer, Hitch surmised.

What's more, this kind of love would insult the egocentric philanthropist who must have their name on a plaque on the wall in return for their surplus. It would astonish those who find love suitable only for the lovable. Not least, it would confound the selfish "happiness seeker' who must apportion their love somehow: "I will love you if you love me, until your love no longer fulfills my ephemeral cravings for love, and we must then part." Hitch should know—he had suffered as a consequence of each one of these unsatisfying, lesser forms of love.

On the other hand, Hitch had seen this agape love many times over in the life of Martin Luther when all everyone wanted to do was to murder his good friend. He had even seen it in the eyes of those poor, ragged Christians in his dream. They would have forgiven Nero, had he asked their forgiveness. The Manufacturer had done an exemplary job of getting him to rethink his position on this matter of love, and few could say they had accomplished such a feat. Still, he could not see the correlation between it and his desire to learn the answers to the origin of the universe... yet.

As far as Hitch knew, neither he nor Professor Lewis were ever promised a time frame for a resolution to their one all-consuming obsession in life, but it would seem at least one more joy ride would be necessary to fit this confusing piece of information into the puzzle. He must assume Jack was experiencing the same sort of dilemma from his life spent with Darwin, except without as worthy a cause as his. As taxing as this had been on his mind and body, Hitch knew what inexpressible power the Manufacturer was capable of wielding. There were still over two weeks to go before his long-awaited lecture, and if he were to receive the answer he was promised before then, it would forever be known as his Nobel Prize—winning lecture. As long as that possibility remained, he was willing to live as many lifetimes with as many bygone revolutionary thinkers as needed, if that was what the Manufacturer required.

It had been over an hour since his meeting with Charlie, and the skies were darkening quickly. He sent his last text to Ms. Brown, wishing her a pleasant evening and promising his full attention at their seven o'clock meeting tomorrow morning. This type of message was not a typical ending to the day for Hitch, but these had not been typical days. Her response was immediate and cautiously optimistic: "Careful what you promise. Good night, Professor."

Hitch escaped through a back passageway of Turner Hall and headed into the Yard. If he had not already known in which direction the rock had planted itself, he would have missed it entirely. The camouflaging and darkness combined to conceal its whereabouts until he was almost upon it, and now that he was upon it, he saw no way inside the enclosure.

"I wasn't told to bring a ladder," Hitch complained softly, as he felt around the bottom of the canvas with his feet for an opening.

"There's a gate on the other side," Jack answered from within, after recognizing Hitch's voice. "I'll open it for you."

"Alex and Frannie did a great job hiding this gate," Jack continued as Hitch entered the structure, grateful not to have to crawl underneath its canvas walls. "I only found it by accident."

There was no way for Jack to know that the gate was put in place not by Alex and Frannie, but as a temporary convenience by the Manufacturer (as Hitch would say). The gate would become an impenetrable fence and tarp again once they left.

"Nothing has happened by accident, Jack," Hitch said politely as he immediately began to inspect the softly illuminating rock more thoroughly. "Have you come to any conclusions since our last time together?"

"Not a clue, as far as my purpose goes," Jack replied. "I'm guessing this was all groundwork for what is to happen next. I am encouraged by you showing up, though. Not sure this thing would open up if one of us were to bail."

"I'm fairly certain it would not," Hitch agreed. "Now, I believe you said you wanted my seat this time. Is that still your position?"

"Oh yeah—we switch!" Jack exclaimed, and started his walk to the other side of the rock where Hitch had sat the evening before and where he was standing now. "I'm hoping to be Saint Augustine of Hippo's scribe tonight."

Hitch smiled and started his short walk around the rock. He was beginning to like this amiable Stanford upstart. In the few seconds it took to make their half circle around the closed rock, it had opened unnoticed.

"I had a feeling it was going to do that," Hitch mused before his leap inside, "yet a fleeting thought or an involuntary blink of an eye caused me to miss it."

"Same here," Jack said, not hesitating to jump inside. "I even kept my hand on the place where it separated as I walked, but I still can't tell you when it happened."

Hitch had not thought of doing that and chastised himself for the oversight. No sooner had they landed in their seats that Hitch found himself standing alongside Jack in a wide clearing halfway up the side of a mountain. Their mountain was one of many densely forested mountains and valleys below. He was surprised to see that the rock had followed them into this new adventure and was resting behind them, closed and without the camo enclosure.

It appeared to be after daybreak, and the gentle breeze that swept across Hitch's face felt cool and a bit more refreshing than usual, though he couldn't say why. He could not ignore the great volume of sound being created in the surrounding trees by a vast number of birds all singing merrily and all unimpressed by their presence. There were many narrow but well-worn paths that came and went from the clearing. A few led upward to much higher, rockier elevations, and a few more led downward into the lush valley. Two slightly wider paths at opposing ends of the clearing remained somewhat parallel to their elevation, suggesting they were together as part of a main trail.

"Are you Professor Jack Lewis?" Hitch asked with all seriousness.

"Indeed I am," Jack replied. "Are you my preeminent historical figure?"

Hitch smiled again. He must be taking a liking to this witty young professor because he was beginning to find his keen sense of humor in the midst of these implausible events rather charming.

"Do you recognize this place, Jack?" Hitch asked, instead of answering the double-edged compliment.

"No, not exactly," Jack replied after a quick survey of the panoramic countryside. "It does remind me of the Appalachian Trail along Skyline Drive in Virginia. MJ and I hiked the trails many times before the boys came along."

"I was thinking more of a tropical island... without the humidity," Hitch said, attempting his own guess.

"Hard to say from here," Jack muttered as he focused his attention above. "I might be able to get a better picture from up there. Wanna come?"

"That's a good idea," Hitch replied, acknowledging the benefits to gaining such a perspective. "But I think I'll stay put for now... if you don't mind."

"And please, Jack, don't take any unnecessary risks," Hitch added with genuine concern. "I don't know how quickly I could come to your rescue."

"Understood—no going out on a limb," Jack promised, and began his ascent. "No worries."

Hitch walked back to the rock, hoping to find two backpacks full of camping gear, water, and food, or at least a map showing the directions to the nearest town. There was nothing. He carefully walked the ridgeline in hopes of catching a glimpse of civilization between the tops of trees. There were no signs of any roads or the lazy white smoke escaping the chimney of a hunter's cabin, but there were two or three rivers—or one long, meandering river—from which they could drink. From his point of view, the closest river seemed to be about a day's hike away, if they did not get lost.

Twenty or thirty minutes had passed when Hitch heard a familiar voice coming down from above. Looking up, he saw Jack standing on one of the rock formations that jutted out of the woods about four or five hundred feet above him.

"Hitch!" Jack called out, and received back several faint echoes. "So far I see one large river that splits into four smaller rivers. One is close to us. The main trail makes a few switchbacks, but I think it will take us down to the water. I'm going a little higher to check it out."

Hitch gave him a thumbs-up, and Jack disappeared into the woods. This bit of good news helped to ease the faint but undeniable tension he had been experiencing since landing in this paradise-like setting. He also reminded himself that this was nothing more and nothing less than another unpredictable test designed by the Manufacturer. His objective must be to stay alert to the data being presented to him and, at the same time, survive the test.

He was certainly no Boy Scout, but instinctively Hitch set about looking for tinder and some combination of rock that when struck together might produce a spark. He had no idea how long they would be staying or how cold it would get after the sun set. After a short period of serious concentration on finding materials that would start a fire, he heard a loud, cracking noise from the woods below, one that a heavy creature would make if it were to step on a large dead branch. Hitch had the chilling sensation he was not alone and immediately stopped everything to focus all his attention in the direction of the ominous sound. It was also the first time he noticed that the birds had stopped their chattering, and all was quiet except for the gentle breeze that rustled through the trees.

Damn it, Hitch scolded himself. *How many more times must I be surprised by my circumstance?*

When a similar sound came from behind him, an adrenaline rush caused him to come to a full upright position and begin a slow, backward movement toward the main path farthest from the two sounds. Terror coursed through his mind when two large lions leapt into the clearing from out of nowhere; as he turned to run, he found his escape route blocked by several more. In a matter of seconds, Hitch found himself in the center of the clearing, surrounded by ten or more lions, and with only a handful of rocks as weapons.

No, this cannot be the end? Hitch thought.

In the meantime, Jack had worked up a good sweat, but he was able to refresh himself at a small stream along the way. His destination was close at hand. He had spotted an immense outcrop from his last lookout position, and it should provide him with an additional five to six hundred feet of elevation and another hundred degrees laterally from which to look into the distance. When he finally came to its base and could go no farther without resting, he sat down and took in a deep satisfying breath of the cool, refreshing air. All that was visible from where he sat were the tops of a few taller mountains. Even the horizon was below his line of vision.

This ought to do it, Jack thought thankfully as he forced his tired body to begin moving onto the rock.

With each step toward the rock's edge, the view became more and more breathtaking. Cascading mountain falls and high-soaring eagles in the distance came first. Then there was the one massive source of water from the east that branched into four separate rivers and divided the mountain ranges and plains. Jack was able to make out herds of various kinds of larger animals moving about in some of the closer, open fields. It was difficult to look at such natural beauty and not want to take pleasure in it for a while, especially after a thousand-foot climb, but he knew he could not. He would take a peek over the side to see how Hitch was getting along before making his less strenuous descent.

I wish MJ and the boys were here to see this, Jack mused one more time before taking the precarious walk to the very edge of the cliff.

The task of looking over a precipice thousands of feet higher than he had ever been before took more bravery than expected, and from five feet away, Jack was on his belly, inching his way to the edge. When he finally was able to glance over the side, the scene horrified him. There in the middle of the clearing stood Hitch, alone and surrounded by lions.

"Hitch!" Jack shouted with all his strength. "I'm coming!"

Jack backed his way from the edge on all fours as quickly as he could, cutting his knees and elbows in the process. He didn't know exactly what he was going to do when he got down there, but there was no hesitation in going.

Hitch knew this was no dream. This was no following in the shadows of some famous human being in their lifetime.

This was here, this was now, this was real, this was life threatening... and yet, this didn't make any sense. Hitch did not have the time to formulate all the questions he had as to why his predicament did not make sense, but one stood out as being the most egregious:

Why would an all-powerful Manufacturer devise such an elaborate scheme to bring me here just to be torn to pieces by lions?

For a moment, he actually considered kneeling and praying for a miracle, like the dream people did when confronted with lions in the Circus Maximus or the fictional character Daniel in the lions' den. But he would rather die than grovel before a god that would set him up like this.

He heard his name being called out from above, but it was only Jack. With Jack having a wife and kids to go home to, Hitch was grateful that Jack was safe where he was and wished... hoped... yearned... prayed that the impulsive young professor would stay up there until the gruesome business down here was complete. This fatal prospect seemed imminent as a few of the larger male lions started moving his way. They were stopped short, however, when a small herd of deer loped casually into the clearing and began to mingle with the lions. This latest group to arrive was soon followed by another male lion considerably larger than all the rest.

Hitch watched in amazement as this magnificent beast attempted to make his way into the clearing, only to have his progress impeded by several young deer calves wanting to play in between his massive legs. He gently nudged them aside, much as he might his own playful cubs, and continued forward. When the great lion finally reached the rock, which appeared to be his destination, he leapt on top gracefully, let out a lengthy thunderous roar, and lay down peacefully. The herd of deer continued on their way with a little more enthusiasm after the roar. The remaining lions all began lying down one after the other until the only creature left standing was Hitch.

The giant lion, now lounging on top of the rock, paid no attention to Hitch, nor did the other, equally slothful lions that now lay all around him in various positions of repose. They did not transform into gigantic, ravenous killing machines as the lions had done in his dream. Instead, they lay there, content in their restfulness.

As Hitch's anxiety came back down to acceptable levels and his heavy breathing subsided, he thought he recognized the giant lion as the one in his dream. Hitch would know that face anywhere; he had stared into it long enough. He could even remember the smell of the lion's breath. Without being quite sure what he was doing, Hitch began walking slowly toward the rock until he was once again face-to-face with the huge beast from his dream.

"Will you be talking to me, lion?" Hitch asked politely.

The lion said nothing, but only stretched out his front legs and yawned widely.

"Same awful breath as I recall," Hitch quipped. "Well then, if you don't mind, I'm going to see if I can make a fire with these rocks and wait for my friend to arrive."

The lion said nothing, but laid down his head to sleep.

Hitch was able to get a spark from the small collection of rocks he had gathered before the lion and deer arrived, but nothing hot enough to ignite his tinder. He knew the principle behind achieving a good spark, and that it would take two rocks of different hardness, as well as extremely clean and dry tinder. He thought nothing of walking between the dozing lions to collect new rocks and fresh tinder. This constant activity by Hitch was too much for the giant cat, who was trying to enjoy a little peace and quiet as he lay on the rock. The massive lion got up, shook his great mane, leapt off the rock, and trotted anxiously toward the nearest exit, followed closely by the other, equally annoyed lions.

Moments later, Jack came bursting out of the woods. He was out of breath, sweating profusely and caked in dirt and dried blood. With hands on his knees, he had only enough strength to raise his head slightly and take a quick look to his left and right. Without a lion in sight and seeing that Hitch was still intact, he took the liberty to collapse on the ground in exhaustion. When he finally opened his eyes again, Jack saw Hitch looking down at him tentatively.

"Are you okay?" Hitch asked pleasantly.

"The lions...," Jack began with labored breath, "where are they?"

"They are gone."

"I came as quick as I could."

"And what did you think you were going to do?"

Jack had no answer to that one and quietly remained on his back.

"Are you okay, Jack?" Hitch asked once again.

"Yes, I'm okay," Jack replied. "Just need to lie here another minute or two."

Hitch went back to doing what he was doing and, after a few more minutes, watched as Jack managed to lift himself into a seated position.

"I believe I know where we are," Hitch stated matter-of-factly.

"Where?" Jack asked, somewhat disinterested because of his exhaustion.

"Eden," Hitch replied without inflection.

"Eden?" Jack asked, a little more attentive now. "As in the 'beginning of time' Eden?"

"Yes, that one," Hitch replied. "Whether this place is real or not may help bring some clarity to the mysteries of our travels, which so far have been shrouded in implications."

"What happened down here?" Jack asked after taking a moment to process what was being suggested and who was suggesting it.

"As you can see, tearing me apart never crossed the lions' minds," Hitch began. "That is because they are not yet carnivorous. That is because it is Eden, before sin."

"The four rivers!" Jack exclaimed, adding another element to Hitch's suggestion.

"I believe the verse reads, 'A river came out of Eden to water the garden and from there it became four heads,'" Hitch quoted, reciting from Genesis as best as he could recollect.

"I looked into Eden?" Jack said in disbelief.

"We shall see," Hitch replied in the same uncommitted tone of voice.

"Then look and see what is good," came a soothing voice came from the direction of the rock.

Both Hitch and Jack spun around simultaneously to see a plain-looking man appear from behind the rock, followed by a multitude of animals of all shapes and sizes that soon filled the clearing. He was dressed in the ancient garments of a shepherd, but he carried no shepherd's crook.

"For you are standing in my Father's garden," the shepherd finished his exhortation.

"My Lord, my God!" Jack exclaimed before falling to his knees.

Hitch stood silently, not yet committing himself to the idea that this ungodlike man standing before them was the

Jesus of antiquity, as Jack obviously had. Knowing Hitch's thoughts, Jesus spoke.

"You need not demonstrate your love of the Father for the Son as Jonathan has done, Edmond. As you have stated properly, it is the beginning of man—not the end. But as you have seen it written many times, there will come a day when every knee shall bow, and that day shall come as a thief."

Hitch said nothing but carefully watched the shepherd's every move, hoping to see the flaw that he supposed was in everything.

"Rise, Jonathan, and rejoice. You have seen me and recognize me," Jesus said with resounding delight. "The day will come when I will recognize you before my Father.

"Rejoice also in this: my Father knows your heart, and what has been asked of you," Jesus continued. "The harvest is great where you are, with but a few laborers. In this, you should be glad. The seed you plant there will bear much fruit. You do not yet realize it, but you will later."

"I am such a fool. I have forgotten whose harvest it is, and I am sorry," Jack said ashamedly. "Thank you for giving me this second chance, Lord."

"You are a faithful servant, Jonathan," Jesus said. "Continue your good work and your dedication to prayer. Do not give the devil a foothold.

"I tell you the truth—my Father loves you, Edmond," Jesus said tenderly. "Absolute joy will soon replace sadness, and your seed will melt away your loneliness when he is revealed to you. I tell you this now so that when it happens, you will believe and be saved."

"That is not the answer I was promised!" Hitch stated harshly.

"Hitch, no!" Jack pleaded.

"Please be quiet, Jack. You have been given your answer," Hitch replied sternly to Jack, and then returned his resolute gaze toward the shepherd. "I simply want what I was promised.

"I understand that you may vaporize me anytime you wish, but that does not frighten me," Hitch continued boldly and without equivocation. "I was promised an answer to the beginning of time, and that it would not simply be another spectacular theory, but prove all the others as imperfect garbage... unless you have lied to me."

"Hitch... please, no," Jack whispered sorrowfully, and began praying softly for his friend.

"Edmond, I have given you your answer," Jesus replied patiently. "It is perfect and true, as simple as $E = mc^2$."

It took a moment for Hitch to reconcile in his mind an ancient shepherd quoting Albert Einstein's theory of relativity. He then looked to Jack for clarification. Jack glanced back at him but did not show any sign of knowing, when Jesus' answer was delivered. Before Hitch could object, Jesus spoke again with great warmth.

"The answer you have been promised is love, Edmond. The heavens and the earth exist only because of the Father's love," Jesus continued with innate authority. "Once you begin seeing through the eyes of His love, this will be the only answer you cannot reject. I tell you the truth—there is no case that can be made against it. There is no imperfection in His love, but you must be willing to come to Him as a child would to his Abba, Father."

These words hung in the air like a warm, gentle mist. They penetrated every pore in his body and were soothing to him. Hitch soon noticed that even the animals were beginning to go about their business after having paused to listen to the shepherd speak. He also noticed that sometime during this last captivating discourse, Jack had gone back to his knees, and his eyes remained closed. It did not take long, but when Hitch returned his attention to the great orator, he had already begun a retreat around the rock with all the animals in tow.

"Wait!" Hitch called out.

Hitch moved as quickly toward the rock as the four-legged traffic would allow. In no more than a few seconds, he was behind the rock and observed Jesus casually walking down the main path jammed with animals, but now a great distance away.

"Are you the Manufacturer?" Hitch yelled down the path.

"Even though I had two good eyes and people all around me, I was once blind and alone," a comforting voice came from behind Hitch.

"Don't start with me, Jack," Hitch said in a low, discouraged voice without turning away from the shepherd.

'I'm sorry this was not the answer you hoped for," Jack replied, careful not to let his pride enter into the reply. "I suppose I would feel the same way if this place were some celestial research-and-development laboratory cranking out solar systems instead of Eden—but it's not, Hitch."

"I must concede the tide has shifted in your favor," Hitch acknowledged after a long thoughtful pause. "I detected no flaw in that man claiming to be your Jesus of Nazareth. His olive complexion and Aramaic accent, instead of the British accent and chalky-white depictions of him today, did add to this man a touch of authenticity. The scars in his hands and feet appeared to be real, although I was not allowed to stick my finger in them as Thomas, the doubter, did. That would make this Jesus a post-crucifixion apparition."

"He was not a ghost!" Jack protested.

"Pardon me, Jack. You are right... poor choice of words," Hitch replied with genuine regret. "This was a post-crucifixion visitation. However, as long as that rock over there exists, the game is not over. Are you ready to leave?"

"Are you sure you don't want to hang around a while?" Jack asked lightheartedly. "It is Eden, after all. I heard the fruit is pretty good here."

Hitch smiled, walked to the edge of the clearing, and thought back carefully.

Did I miss something? Where was the flaw? Other than man's botched interpretations of it, what was the flaw in agape love? Was Voltaire, or Marx, or Darwin, or Freud given a similar opportunity to accept God's love as I have been given?

This was a setback, but Hitch would make one more attempt at dismantling this outcome before leaving.

"You have been to the mountaintop, so to speak," Hitch replied. "Do you think we—that is, do you think I—can make it down to the river and back by nightfall?"

"I believe we can," Jack answered.

"Lead on then."

The trek down was easy and made easier by tasting from every vine and fruit tree they passed. They could not be sure from which of the four rivers they were drinking: was it the Tigris, the Euphrates, or one of the other two, of which neither could remember the names? However, it tasted like wine in their throats. The river also had some medicinal qualities to it because the cuts on Jack's elbows and knees healed dramatically after rinsing them in the water.

Unfortunately, the hills of Eden were no different from the hills of Pennsylvania, and the way back up was a struggle. At the clearing's edge, they rested. They soon discovered each other to be a passionate sports enthusiast and took the opportunity to reflect on the current baseball season and to cast their predictions on the upcoming football season and other, not so vitally important matters. When they came to the conclusion that it was time to go, they both glanced at the rock and found it open.

"I had a feeling it was going to do that," Hitch said.

"Same here," Jack replied.

No sooner had they both jumped in on their sides than they found themselves looking up at the star-filled skies over Hillary University. Jack looked at his watch, but no apparent time had gone by. Before hopping out of the rock, he couldn't help but notice Hitch rifling through his pockets in some sort of agitation.

"Damn!" Hitch barked.

"What's the problem over there?" Jack inquired.

"Well, for analysis purposes, I filled my pockets with assorted rocks, leaves, and berries and filled my shoes with as much water from the river as they could hold," Hitch exclaimed as he reached down to take off a shoe.

"I even pulled a strand or two of hair out of a lion's tail— to his extreme consternation, I might add. Now my pockets are empty, and my socks and shoes are bone dry."

"And you thought you were going to get away with that?" Jack asked, shaking his head.

"Better to be mocked by my clever travel partner," Hitch replied while slipping his shoe back on, "than to look back and regret not having tried."

"I suppose you're right," Jack agreed. "Hey, if this should be our last journey, I want you to know that I have enjoyed your company. I used to think you were an arrogant son-of-a-biscuit-eating sea turtle, but I was wrong, and I apologize. I am grateful for this opportunity to get to know you."

"Jack, we are two entirely different people with two entirely different worldviews," Hitch replied coarsely, but then softened his response. "However, I can honestly say that I have enjoyed your company as well. Given the extraordinary circumstances of our coming together, perhaps we could meet for lunch from time to time and discuss our progress."

Jack agreed, and they both exited the rock, which closed unnoticed.

14

The Lecture

T he glorious morning sun rose over Hillary University as
it had done for the past 140- plus years, but this time
of the year was the most spectacular of all. The azure-blue
sky provided the perfect backdrop for a few wistful clouds,
and there was not a warm color that yellow and red could
produce that was left out of the forest that surrounded the
two opposing campuses. Slowly human presence began
to replace the animal presence in the peaceful transition
from night to day. The dew that now covered the surface
of the Grand Courtyard gave the impression of glistening
emeralds instead of grass. If not for the chill in the air and
the thick carpet of fallen leaves, the long, thick columns of
rosebushes that were still showing colorful blooms pointed
to springtime rather than winter. Unfortunately for many,
today would be another day to take for granted, but a few
would awaken to find their whole lives had been changed.

For Hitch, nothing interested him more than getting to
work as quickly as possible. To be more specific, he wanted
to get to his study as quickly as possible. He had endured

another restless night, but for no other reason than the anticipation of coming to work. After returning home last night, Hitch had put all of his energy into the examination of the previous three days. No matter how many times he attempted to manipulate the data or rearrange the experiences he had been through, he always came to the same conclusion. It wasn't until pure exhaustion set in that he went to his bed. He needed one more piece of data and then he would have the answer he was promised, and that data was at work.

When Hitch pulled into Turner Hall's parking lot, his was the first car there. This was probably a good thing because it was evident that personal hygiene had not been on his mind when he left home. If campus security had seen him climb out of his new Audi S7, they most certainly would have asked for identification. As it was, Hitch had a clear path to his building, to his office, to his study, and finally to the windows. At this point, he breathlessly gazed into the Yard.

Damn! he thought

* * * * *

Jack slept like a log. He had spent last evening playing with his boys until bedtime and then enjoyed listening to MJ describe the events of the day while he was at work. When the conversation swung to the events of his day, MJ was awestruck.

"Eden!" she screamed, and then covered her mouth.

After taking a moment to determine whether or not the boys had been awoken by this excited response, they continued their conversation late into the evening. It appeared to them both that the promise had been fulfilled, but from what Jack described, neither could be sure it was over. There was no doubt left in Jack's mind about his purpose, and he now had a renewed outlook on what this school year had to offer. In any case, he must learn to be content, not always knowing what the full harvest had been.

Still, from what Jack was able to recall, there was no defined ending. After Jesus spoke to them, he took his animals and left. He and Hitch were not told to come back the next day, nor were they told not to come back. At that point, MJ suggested the answer to that question might be waiting for him tomorrow at work.

The curiosity from the night before caused Jack to pull into the Turner Hall parking lot early enough to be the second car there. He wasn't exactly hurdling over guardrails, but he could sense anxiousness in his stride. The previous three days had taken so many different twists and turns that he had no idea what to look for as far as a sign telling him it was over. It would be nice, for once, to get a tap on the shoulder from God, saying, "Dude, it's over," but then again, how many people got a round-trip ticket to Eden?

Jack bounded through his office door after wasting some time trying to open it with his house key. Once inside, he tripped over a stack of books, which sent him crashing into the corner of the desk before finally making it to his chair. After the pain in his leg subsided, he peered across the room, hoping to see the kindly old man who had started this whole business come walking through the door he intentionally left open this time… not that it mattered to an angel. When that didn't occur in a reasonable amount of time, Jack got up and hobbled to the windows.

Oh… sweet! he thought.

* * * * *

Charlie was about to leave his office to get an early start on the roses when he got the call; it was Alex.

"Good morning, Alex," Charlie said.

"Chief, it's gone!" Alex said excitedly.

"What's gone?" Charlie asked.

"The rock—it's gone!" Alex said even more excitedly.

"Okay, I'm heading that way now," Charlie said, as if this news had not come as a complete surprise. "Tell me what happened."

"Frannie and I came out here this morning 'cause we were missing the posthole digger and thought we could have left it leaning on the rock," Alex began breathlessly. "When Frannie looked over the top of the fence—no rock."

"Okay, can I speak to Francesca?" Charlie asked.

"Chief, it's gone!" Frannie said frantically.

"So I heard," Charlie replied calmly. "Are you all right?"

"I think so, but can you please come out here?" Frannie asked with a slight tremble to her voice.

"I will be there in five minutes, okay?" Charlie promised.

"Okay, thanks," Frannie answered anxiously.

When Charlie peered over the top of the fence, the rock was gone, all right. Not only was it gone, but the grass within the enclosure looked as pristine as the grass outside the enclosure, and the six blocks sat gently on undisturbed mower lines. Charlie felt this whole experience with the rock could be misconstrued by his two young apprentices and therefore called for an immediate suspension of all work activity while they discussed this matter over breakfast—his treat. When they had all relocated to the university's posh dining hall and relaxed a bit, Charlie broke the ice.

"There's nothing like a big ol' plate full of SOS ("Stuff" on Shingles) and a hot cup of joe to calm the nerves, I always say."

"Really? Always? Be quiet!" Frannie said with a nervous grin.

"I'll have to try that sometime," Alex offered unconvincingly.

Without mentioning any names or titles, Charlie began revealing to them both what he knew about the rock, which was about as much as they knew. He also decided not to withhold from them a broad overview of the discussions he had with two unnamed individuals (Jack and Hitch) who may have had something to do with the rock while it was here.

"I saw footprints," Frannie said shyly, "but I didn't say anything."

"Yes, I saw them too," Charlie replied. "It's all right."

He expressed to them his thoughts about the rock from when it first appeared until now, and that his Christian perspective had not changed. He gave them permission to ask any question they wished and said that they would always receive a full and truthful answer in return. He let them know that they were free to draw their own conclusions from this experience, of course, but requested they not divulge any of this to anyone, unless there was a discovery of someone having been hurt by it. Even then, it would be hard to prove anything without the evidence. He promised them that if he received any new information about the rock, he would let them know immediately; otherwise, he was going to let go of it himself.

By the time their breakfast meeting was over, Charlie felt comfortable that Alex and Francesca would weather this supernatural occurrence fine, but he would keep his eyes open for any unusual changes in their behavior for a while. He knew the devil prowls around like a roaring lion looking for someone to devour, but the devil would not have an easy time getting these two as long as he was alive.

Charlie changed the work plans for the day to allow his two favorite employees to trim the roses, a meticulous task he believed they were capable of understanding and applying anyway. He would spend the remainder of the day undoing the enclosure, filling the holes with dirt, and topping it off with fresh sod.

* * * * *

Time passed quickly, and the day of the event that officially ushered in the new school year (and would once again launch Hillary University into the national spotlight) finally arrived. Although their days were extraordinarily busy, Jack and Hitch were surprised by how often they actually did pass each other in the course of a day, and they even found time to meet for lunch once. Their relationship was now considered friendly, but the idea of inviting the other over to watch a game would not have crossed their minds. They were still two entirely different people, as Hitch had accurately described.

Jack was able to legitimately earn his way into Walker Auditorium for the lecture by agreeing to be one of Charlie's volunteer host team members who provided comfort and guidance to the lost and bewildered guests.

Jack had seen the posters around campus and the play on words: "Science: The Other Gospel" and "Physics: A Different Kind of Religious Experience." The lecture would be a great opportunity to test his reformed, forgiveness-minded, contentment-seeking demeanor if Hitch chose to harp on his Savior.

The atmosphere surrounding Walker Auditorium was electrifying. The anticipation was similar to going to hear a world-class symphony orchestra or a performing-arts megastar on opening night. At approximately an hour before the lecture was to begin, several students dressed as town criers were sent out, with bells in hand, to gain attention. Their sole purpose was to walk back and forth around the historic building, encouraging those with tickets to please enter the auditorium and take their seats.

At approximately half an hour prior to the lecture, these same criers would announce to the straggling ticket holders that the doors to the auditorium would close at fifteen minutes before the hour—without exception. In exactly fifteen minutes before the hour, the doors were closed. All effort and manpower were now expended in getting any guests still standing into their seats. Hitch was not the stereotypical, egomaniacal prima donna who got a rise out of making people wait. He would take his seat behind the lectern on time and expected others to do the same. They would not be disappointed tonight.

As soon as Hitch stepped foot on stage, he received a standing ovation that lasted several minutes. This was one of the first lessons Ms. Brown had to teach her boss: patience with his audience. Allowing admirers an opportunity to show their appreciation and affection was a sign of maturity in a genius, just as it was in a polished statesman. The time for behaving as an insufferable bulldog was over. Hitch knew how long to wait. When that time expired, however, he took his seat and motioned for his invited guests to do the same.

"Thank you... thank you all from the bottom of my heart," Hitch began modestly. "I don't believe I have received such applause since announcing to the board of directors at Harvard that I was leaving to come teach here at Hillary."

The room erupted in laughter. This was another lesson taught by Ms. Brown: a touch of humor. And when your IQ is considerably higher than the group you are speaking to, some self-deprecating humor was better yet. Hitch wasted no time using this cordial opening to transition into his lofty diatribe.

"If I may, I would like to begin with a simple observation that I believe we all can agree upon," Hitch began pacifically. "Our universe had a beginning and will have an ending, as we know it."

This opening statement was much more conciliatory than those in the past. He was not unmoved or unchanged by the extraordinary events that had transpired three weeks ago, but the lecture's premise remained virtually the same: present a case that would examine the hostile schism between science and religion. Since no one could claim to have been there when the universe was formed, both endeavors required faith. Even in their apparent trip back to Eden, neither he nor Jack could claim to have been at the absolute beginning of time, since animals were not created until the sixth day, according to the Judeo-Christian Scriptures.

But there had been no life-altering epiphany, no personal "I have seen the light" conversion, and no "perhaps I miscalculated" wavering in Hitch's mind. His faith in the big bang model and the promising new advancements in superstring theories remained solid, whereas his awareness of religion was only minimally piqued by Christianity's belief system rooted in God's agape love as expressed in three persons: Father, Son, and Spirit.

"I also happen to believe this beginning occurred 13.8 billion years ago," he continued. "And from out of that, our relatively young solar system was formed 4.6 billion years ago."

Even for those in attendance with all of life's pressures to preoccupy their frazzled lives, Hitch's account of why he believed this opening statement was a riveting presentation. It surprised many to hear that the prevailing theories of today still incorporated some part of the big bang. This was a term Hitch would not normally use because of its simplistic nature and beleaguered past, but he felt it necessary to simplify the language to fit his audience. He preferred to use the term *inflation* to describe the universe's birth from a size smaller than an electron to its observable diameter of about 93 billion light years, all of which occurred in less than a fraction of a second, with the afterglow, or cosmic microwave background (CMB), that was produced 380,000 years after this event still being visible.

Hitch described the universe after the big bang in this way: Initially, the universe was pure hot energy. The cooling process produced particles from which the light gases hydrogen and helium formed. From there, galaxies clustered and fiery stars emerged. The result was a universe made up of atomic matter, dark matter, and dark energy. And it was expanding.

The idea that the universe was never static but always expanding was first introduced to us in the 1920s by the man who would have a space telescope named after him, Edwin Hubble. By the end of the twentieth century, astronomers determined with extraordinary precision that the universe was not only expanding, but it was doing so at a much greater rate than realized. In time, all galaxies would continue to move apart until they eventually "redshifted" out of view from one another. Dark energy was thought to be the force that drives this accelerating expansion of the universe.

"We who are theoretical physicists have spent so much of our time postulating what came after the big bang that we have forgotten, or conveniently avoided, the research to answer the question, what came before it?" Hitch stated rather apologetically. "For centuries, science has allowed religion to dictate the response to this one last mystery."

This was the pivotal moment Jack was waiting for, what the audience was waiting for, what the world had come to expect—the *Hitchinson factor*, for lack of a better term, whereby Hitch would ratchet up his rhetoric and the things being said came across as being either unreserved blustering or unfathomable. Then, days and weeks later when the hyperbole had settled, the professor's suppositions were deemed not only reasonable, but also probable.

"There are good reasons for having ignored the first law of thermodynamics, which states that all energy in an isolated system, like our universe, remained constant. It can be transformed from one form to another, but it cannot be created or destroyed.

"Or, simply put, matter cannot spring into existence out of nothingness," Hitch continued. "We simply did not have the technology to assist us in proving it can—until now!"

Hitch was in his zone now, but it would take everything he had to keep from overwhelming those of modest intelligence who were sitting in the seats before him and the cable news anchors who would begin talking about this tomorrow. But this he must do in order to advance the science behind the theoretical framework of superstring theory and its potential for solving the mystery that caused the big bang (the beginning of our universe) and the beginning of time itself.

With a foundational overview of string theory being presented on an elaborate visual display behind him, Hitch began to detail the brilliant theory of an *ageless universe*. According to Einstein's theory of relativity, or $E = mc^2$, there was a relationship between energy and its mass. In string theory, subatomic string replaced the basic subatomic particles of protons, electrons, and neutrons. The vibration of the string determines the particles' size and mass, while its frequency determines its energy. The relationship between energy and mass in Einstein's $E = mc^2$ is, therefore, replaced by an object's vibrational frequency and its mass.

This is important because the number of spatial dimensions in Einstein's theory is limitless, whereas the maximum number of spatial dimensions in string theory is only ten. Mathematically, we experience life in four-dimensional space: length or x-axis, height or y-axis, depth or z-axis, and time. According to the string theory derivative *M-theory*, our four- dimensional universe is embedded in a five-dimensional universe. In addition to our own universe, there are other universes in this five-dimensional realm. They all exist on sheet-like planes referred to as *branes* (membranes) and remain parallel to each other. These branes are constrained to their own boundaries by gravity. Our visible universe of 93 billion light years being one of those boundaries.

Even with a space telescope a thousand times more powerful than the Hubble, these other universes will forever be invisible to us because light cannot pass through the intervening space that separates them. Every trillion years, however, two of these branes collide, causing the death and subsequent rebirth of each universe. Our universe was the product of one of those collisions that occurred 13.8 billion years ago—the big bang.

"It would be inaccurate to say the big bang did not occur," Hitch explained. "We know it happened. It simply was not the beginning of space and time. I firmly believe the testing currently being performed by the Large Hadron Collider (LHC) in Geneva will validate string theory and its logical conclusion that space and time have always existed.

"These answers are finally within our grasp!" Hitch stated excitedly. "And it is my sincerest hope that the short time spent here today will be the inspiration for one or more of you to come alongside of us who care about the truth, regardless of where the truth may take you or who you may shock by it.

"Thank you for your attention," he concluded.

With that, the room erupted in exuberant ovation and cheers. Hitch rose from his seat, walked to the front of the lectern, bowed graciously to the audience, and slowly made his way off stage. This modest, subdued exit was extremely un–Hitch-like and the change did not go unnoticed by Ms. Brown, who had been watching the performance from a balcony seat.

It was Hitch's original intention to conclude his lecture with some brash comment (the Hitchinson factor) about the folly of religion. He was certainly not above using a politically correct cliché or two that promoted the fashionable point of view that religion, and especially Christianity, the great Interferer (yes, he read C. S. Lewis too), was hateful and intolerant. If he were to consider himself and his lecture truly successful, this strategy would have encouraged some obscenely liberal legislature somewhere to eliminate all religious accommodation in their state.

But that was before the rock. As the days prior to the lecture came and went, this type of inflammatory rhetoric was eliminated. The words and their intent did not fit into the context any longer. Hitch was still the pragmatic scientist, but the belligerence had somehow vanished.

"How can you deny what you have seen with your own eyes and heard with your own ears?" Jack asked of Hitch, but quietly to himself, not realizing that Charlie was now standing behind him.

"The fear you might be wrong," Charlie answered Jack's question just as quietly. "None of us are immune to it."

Not being too surprised by either Charlie's undetected presence or by his astute comment, Jack turned and replied somberly, "I suppose it could have been worse."

Both smiled in a way that suggested the other knew more than they were letting on. "Don't ask, don't tell" had become the best way to describe their code of conduct since the rock's disappearance. There was no need for Jack to try to explain his experiences to Charlie. It was a personal matter between Hitch and him, and Jesus and him, and Hitch and Jesus.

Even if Jack had felt compelled to say something, Charlie didn't seem to care about the rock anymore. It had taken less than a day for the barrier that surrounded the rock to disappear without a trace, and because of Charlie's oppressive schedule leading up to the lecture, their conversations, by necessity, had been brief, harried, and lacking all substance. The end result of these abrupt meetings was always some variation of looking forward to talking more at the Wednesday night Promise Keepers meeting after the lecture.

"Thanks for your help today," Charlie said while smoothly transitioning to a topic more suitable for open conversation.

"Glad to help out," Jack replied. "Can't wait till next year."

"I can," Charlie sighed in relief.

"I know you have plenty left to do," Jack replied, acknowledging the responsibilities that never ended for his good friend. "Is there anything else I can help with?"

"I believe your obligations have been fulfilled, Jack," Charlie answered appreciatively. "Go home and play with Jake and Joey while there's some light left. It's about time to get them into Cub Scouts, huh?"

"I'll have to talk to MJ about that. See you on Wednesday."

"See you then."

For Charlie, the remainder of the afternoon was spent maintaining order from behind the scenes at the various university events. Fortunately, it could not have been a more glorious September day, and he encountered little resistance to keeping the great mass of people out of the buildings and in the charming beauty of the Yard, except for guest access to the bathroom facilities in Turner, Walker, and Samuel Halls (there were no ghastly porta-johns invited here). Things must have been running without incident, because on one of Charlie's rotations around the courtyard, Peter smiled and stealthily raised his champagne glass in Charlie's direction.

Indeed, from the initial chatter on Facebook, Twitter, and Linkedin, this was one of Professor Hitchinson's most successful lectures by far, and the parties going on in the courtyard were well attended and spirited. The backdrop of perfectly trimmed roses made every picture look even more magnificent. For this, credit would be given where credit was due. By the end of the day, Charlie would congratulate Alex and Frannie on a job well done.

In fact, the more Charlie thought about it, the more he liked the idea of grooming these two to take over operations. As much as he liked to think of himself as Superman, capable of handling anything that came his way, he knew his tenure must come to an end sometime. It would be unreasonable, even dangerous, to expect one person to successfully preside over two demanding directorships (director of horticulture and curator). The responsibility to preserve and protect ten thousand acres of prized Pennsylvania property and a trove of priceless art, literature, and artifacts in four historical buildings was too demanding. Charlie also felt an urgency to preserve what was left of Hillary's Christian heritage from its morally and ethically "progressive" (a misnomer if he ever saw one) leadership. He remembered seeing this same desire in the eyes of his predecessor. He could envision the shifting of this burden to two strong-willed people like Alex and Frannie.

Armed with a college education, these two would be formidable, Charlie thought. *Armed with the Word of the Lord, they would be invincible!*

15

When Love Takes Over

The lecture was now over, and order had been restored on planet Hillary, not unlike the way in which Hitch described the fraction of a second after the big bang.

Jack's poetry memorization course had become so popular that he had filled and closed the two classes that met on Monday, Wednesday, and Friday, and the one on Tuesday and Thursday. Jack had completed his third full day of classes and was beyond thrilled by what he had experienced. Nothing had changed much as far as the student dynamics were concerned; he was merely looking at them with a fresh pair of eyes until even the neo-Marxists looked good to him.

Exhausted but encouraged, Jack went home and played Legos with Jake and Joey before dinner. He enjoyed Legos as much as his boys did. The best part came after the new model had been built according to the instructions and admired for a day or two. That's when the boys would tear it apart, throw all the pieces into a big container to be mixed up with previous Lego models, and reassemble any way they wished. There wasn't much that could stop a flying pirate ship being piloted by Thor and Spiderman with light sabers. Unfortunately, he was forced to exit the games early after his Guardians Starblaster got shot down by Darth Jake and Joey Skywalker.

"How was I supposed to know that the Hulk couldn't fly a Starblaster and was such a lousy shot?" He complained without getting much sympathy from his two sons, who just laughed.

This was just as well. It gave him time to ask MJ about her day and her thoughts on signing the boys up for Scouts. After dinner, he read a little *Hank, the Cowdog* to the boys before kissing them and their mother good night. Then off to Hillary he went for the first Wednesday night meeting of the school year.

Jack enjoyed these weekly meetings because they combined the study of God's Word with Promise Keepers' strong, unapologetically masculine, God-ordained commission for men that he had craved since he was a kid. The attendees were mostly guys from Hillary, but not entirely. It was an odd sense of curiosity for Jack to anticipate seeing which of the university's major departments would be represented at these meetings by way of their professor's attendance. To keep his findings manageable, he combined two or three departments with similar characteristics or mind-sets. For example, music and fine arts were combined, just as were engineering and technology, science and biology, physics and astronomy, athletics and ROTC, business and economics, English and comparative languages, philosophy and politics, etc. Also included in Jack's accounting were the administrative staff, general facility employees, and the student body, each in its own group. Since he had been coming to these meetings, all of the groups had been represented except for one—physics and astronomy.

Don't see that changing much this year, Jack thought.

The first couple of meetings were usually packed as a result of long-time members bringing along a friend or two for a look-see. It brought a giant smile to Jack's face to see Alex, Charlie's young apprentice, in the room for the first time. From the expression on Charlie's face, this was a pleasant surprise to him as well. It took no time at all for Charlie to make his way over to Alex and begin introducing him to the many courageous young men of faith in the group. Jack also met up with Alex shortly after his entrance and took the opportunity to tease him a bit.

"So, where is your partner tonight?" Jack asked playfully.

"Hello, Professor," Alex replied curiously. "Who's that?"

"Frannie, of course," Jack grinned. "Whenever I see one of you, the other is not far behind."

"Yeah, she wanted to come," Alex grinned back. "Then she got all mad when I told her it was guys only."

"Well, you tell her I'll have MJ call her with some options for the ladies."

"I'll do that. Thanks, Professor."

Because of the strong friendships that had been forged here, it was typical for these first couple of meetings to get off to a late start. Apparently, this night was going to be no different, if the volume of continuous conversation and laughter was the measurement for determining a good start time.

This unbridled camaraderie had gone on for some time, when a hush slowly began to settle on the room. Charlie was still actively socializing with anyone he thought was a newcomer, so there had been no call for quiet to start the meeting. When the silence in the room became more noticeable than the noise, Charlie casually looked up from his small group toward the direction the others were now looking. To his complete and utter amazement, standing in the doorway to the mess hall was the president of Hillary University.

It took a second or two for Charlie to recover from the shock of this unlikely of all occurrences and politely excuse himself from his current conversation. Charlie had no idea how long Peter had been standing there, but he quickly maneuvered through the stunned crowd before the president had a chance to change his mind. The two had spoken several times over the past few weeks about his wife's cancer treatment, and the prognosis was promising. Charlie and Sarah had even visited Peter and Kimberly at their home on two occasions, where they dined, talked, and prayed with the family. But he and Peter had not talked to each other in days.

"Hello, Peter. Is everything all right?" Charlie asked, expecting to hear bad news.

"Kim continues to improve, Charlie," Peter responded, sensing Charlie's anxiety. "I was actually hoping to sit in on your meeting tonight, unless you believe it would be too much of a distraction."

"Heck no, Peter!" Charlie exclaimed with great relief. "In fact, we were waiting for you to show so that we could get this thing going, but first I would like to introduce you to a couple of marine buddies I know."

Jack was within earshot of this unbelievable event. He had never quite understood the relationship between these two completely opposite men, but whatever it was, it easily rivaled the most miraculous redemption story he had ever witnessed.

If I said it once, I'll say it again: Charlie is a man's man, boys, Jack thought.

* * * * *

The professor had proved his relevance once again. His was the first story on many cable news networks and was above the fold on many daily newspapers. Soon most of the major magazines would have his face on their covers, superimposed alongside the familiar face of Einstein. Ms. Brown found it impossible to keep up with the requests for interviews and was forced to hire a temporary answering service just to take names and numbers. Hitch was by no means the discoverer of the superstring model that he had so convincingly described in his lecture. In fact, string theory had been around since 1960, and the big bang theory followed by a big crunch theory had come along before the turn of the century. It was purely Hitch's impeccable reputation and the eloquence with which he presented his hypothesis that propelled it into the public consciousness.

The big story, or the story behind the story that many women wanted answers to, was the true meaning behind this new, softer image the professor had showcased. Evidently, Ms. Brown was not the only person to catch this shift from abrasive tough guy to smooth-talking nice guy. In fact, many of the interview requests were from extremely popular afternoon talk shows that would have little interest in talking about strings, dark energy, or Einstein, but would enjoy getting to know the person behind the big ideas. This had incredible potential, and Ms. Brown knew it. It would have to be a serious topic of discussion at their morning meetings to determine whether her boss was willing to enter this whole new world.

Ms. Brown had noticed that their early morning meetings had taken on a new quality anyway. Ever since the professor had first discussed with her the strange events that suddenly began to happen in his life (and just as suddenly stopped happening), there was a refreshing openness between them. Occasionally, he would interrupt the ceremonial blah, blah, blah to ask her about unrelated matters such as loneliness, fear, love—even religion. She never once felt these detours were an attempt to pry into her personal life. Rather, it seemed to her that he was simply collecting data on subjects that had not yet been thoroughly examined and tested. And the thorough examination of these very inquiries would be absolutely necessary before she put him in front of a million women viewers.

Of course, many aspects of their meetings remained the same, such as the professor zoning out from time to time whenever deadlines and scheduling conflicts required his full attention. Unfortunately, that exact scenario accurately described this morning's meeting and could not have come at a less opportune time. The positive feedback to the university had been so overwhelming since the lecture that Dr. Stansbury gave Ms. Brown carte blanche over Hitch's schedule for this semester, up to and including the cancellation of his advanced physics classes. But there was nothing more she could do to keep his attention today, short of knocking him upside the head with a frying pan. Other than that, she was left with no other option than to leave her boss to his thoughts and come back again tomorrow with twice the workload.

All of this additional work will, of course, require an assistant, Ms. Brown thought wearily. *And a new office*, she quickly added.

The rest of the morning went by as expected, busy with no end in sight. Ms. Brown did, however, receive an earnest apology from the professor for his lack of focus in the morning and assurances that she would have his utmost attention tomorrow. This would have to do. She could now take her frustrations out on the punching bag at the gym tonight—problem solved.

Ms. Brown continued working feverishly on a few workable strategies to bring to the table tomorrow, should the professor want to pursue this other level of fame and fortune. By this time, it was late afternoon and her mind was toast. Whenever things reached this point, it was usually best to close up shop early, go work out to get the blood flowing again, and finalize her thoughts at home. She was about to text the professor that she would be leaving for the day when a good-looking and well-tanned guy walked into the office and politely asked if it would be possible to see Professor Hitchinson.

"I'm sorry, but he is busy right now," Ms. Brown answered politely.

She knew the man had no appointment, and this would have normally been the end of their encounter, but... well... he was ruggedly handsome and wore no wedding ring. They had not met before—she was quite sure of that—yet there was something about him that caused her to hesitate before asking him to leave. She thought that perhaps a few more questions would help her come to some decision on whether or not to work him into the schedule, if for no other reason than to meet him again.

"May I ask what this is in reference to?" she smiled and asked pleasantly.

"Well, my name is Jimi Matsuki," he replied, and returned her smile. "I have been told that Professor Hitchinson is my father."

Ms. Brown was stunned into silence and immobility. Her jaw dropped slightly, and the hand that held her fairly oversized purse opened involuntarily, allowing it to slip off her fingertips and onto the floor with a thud. Fortunately, it also had fairly long straps, so the distance between the bottom of the purse and the floor was minimal. Without moving anything but her head, she glanced at the pictures on the wall of when the professor had first arrived at Hillary... then back to Jimi... then back to the pictures... then back to Jimi... then again... then again.

Noticing that his unexpected news was having an unforeseen and uncertain effect on this stunningly beautiful person standing before him, Jimi moved a little closer in the event she was to collapse.

"Are you all right, miss?" he asked awkwardly.

"Yes," was all she could manage.

It was unmistakable now. He looked much like the professor in his youth.

"I'm sorry if I caused you... to... umm... do that," Jimi apologized. "I didn't know what else to say."

"It's okay," Ms. Brown said meekly as she staggered backward to her desk. "Let me see if the professor... Mr. Hitchinson... your father—I'm really sorry—is still in."

It took several seconds to compose herself and come up with the words to inform the professor that a son he did not know existed was standing in the waiting room. Jimi was content looking over the pictures and awards that occupied the majority of the space on three of the four office walls.

Okay, I can do this, she thought. *Vague... just keep it vague.*

Her text to the professor was just that: "There is a Mr. Matsuki who would like to see you. May I send him in?"

Please answer... please answer... come on... please still be here, she pleaded.

Hitch's text reply was almost immediate: "I know of no Matsuki; therefore, no, you may not send him in."

Thank you… thank you… thank you, she sighed in relief.

"Okay, he says he will see you now," Ms. Brown said with a mischievous smile. "But I will need to escort you to his office, or I'm afraid you'll never find it."

Okay, I can do this too, she thought once more. *Just put one foot in front of the other.*

"Are you sure you're okay?" Jimi asked as they proceeded down the first long hallway.

"Yes, of course. Why do you ask?" Ms. Brown answered nervously.

"You seem to be shaking… you know, like quivering," he replied gently.

"I'll be fine," she responded softly. *Once I get you through those doors*, she thought.

After a few more turns, they arrived at their destination. Ms. Brown gave a few meaningless raps on the door, and they both entered after only a brief pause. She led them to within a few feet of Hitch's desk and waited patiently for him to look up, while Jimi curiously looked around the room. As soon as Ms. Brown made eye contact, she spoke.

"Jimi Matsuki, this is Professor Hitchinson. Professor, this is Jimi Matsuki," she said hastily. "Well, I'll leave you two alone."

With that, she was gone before Hitch could form a word to say. After a brief moment to consider this unprecedented behavior, Hitch spoke first.

"Well, at least I know you're not a ghost," Hitch said glibly. "Have a seat, young man, and please tell me how in the world you convinced Ms. Brown to let you in here."

"Well, I told her you were my father," Jimi said succinctly while taking a seat.

Hitch eased back in his chair to consider for a half second such a preposterous assertion, when suddenly he heard the shepherd's voice speaking clearly in his mind, and he shivered:

"Absolute joy will soon replace sadness, and your seed will melt away your loneliness when he is revealed to you."

This seed is a son? Hitch thought.

"You have an interesting name," Hitch asked in an attempt to gain time so that he might recall the shepherd's exact words.

"My mom was a big Hendrix fan, and my dad's name was Musashi Matsuki," Jimi answered, as if this was not the first time he had answered this question. "They met before I was born and married before I turned one."

"May I ask your mom's name?" Hitch asked politely.

"Sunshine Matsuki," Jimi replied. "That is, after she married dad. It was Hitchinson before that. Shortly after I was born, Dad married Mom and adopted me."

Sunshine, Hitch smiled.

That had been so long ago. Hitch had to smile upon learning that "Sunshine" was actually her real name. He found himself reminiscing on the good times he had shared with his first wife. She was so smart and pretty and funny and kind. But soon his memories darkened, and all he could think about was the cruel way in which he had spoken to her, and treated her, and manipulated her for his own selfish pleasure. The guilt was enough to send him reeling back into reality. Perhaps he could make it up to her, he thought.

"You have spoken of your mother and your father in the past tense," Hitch stated respectfully. "Am I mistaken?"

"Mom died when I was fourteen, after being hit by a drunk driver," Jimi replied somberly. "It was Dad and I until he died from sudden heart failure last year."

After a brief pause to contain his emotions, Jimi spoke again. "A day doesn't go by that I don't miss them terribly, but they are both home now, with the Lord."

"I am sorry to hear of their passing, Jimi," Hitch said compassionately. "So you are a Christian believer?"

"I am a Christian miracle, Professor," Jimi replied. "You see, Mom went to California to abort me and start a new life, but her plans didn't include meeting my dad. When they met, Dad was a missionary student from Japan studying in the U.S. and on total fire for Jesus Christ. When Dad spoke of God's love for Mom—and for me inside her womb—joy soon overcame all her guilt and sadness, and she gave herself to the Lord... and kept me."

When Jimi had finished, Hitch could hear the shepherd's voice speaking to him once again:

"*I tell you this now, so that when it happens you will believe and be saved.*"

"My God, you are real!" Hitch answered the shepherd.

"Very real," Jimi replied, thinking the professor was referring to him. "I know this must be a bit of a shock for you."

"Jimi, what caused you to come here? I mean, now... today?" Hitch asked kindly.

"To be honest, I have no idea," Jimi answered. "Not to be rude or anything, Professor, but I had little interest in meeting you, even as I was purchasing the plane ticket out here."

Jimi condensed the events leading up to their meeting. In the beginning, life was perfect for him and his family. Instead of returning to Japan, his father's calling was to minister to the surfing community in Southern California, so they surfed together all the time. After a long day of surfing, Jimi would sit in the sand for hours and marvel at how easily his father preached the good news to the surf tramps who would stop by and, in their chemically-induced stupor, hang out. There were so many of them, and they were all so lost and broken. Jimi's dad offered them new hope in Jesus Christ, and many were saved. After his mother's sudden and tragic death—and life as he knew it was destroyed by that drunk driver—he watched as his father leaned on the same words of Jesus that he had used to comfort the helpless and hurting surfers. From that moment on, Jimi felt peace and knew they would all be reunited someday, and that day would be glorious.

It wasn't until Jimi was sixteen or seventeen that he discovered how it was that he had been born Jimi Hitchinson, not Jimi Matsuki. It was pretty evident that he was not of Asian descent, but the circumstances had never interested him. Even after the circumstances were fully explained to him by his father, it still did not interest him. Musashi Matsuki was his dad, and that had been God's plan all along.

"All I can say about my showing up here now... today," Jimi said while shrugging his shoulders, "is that the Lord wanted you to know."

"I tell you the truth—my Father loves you, Edmond."

The words were so clear and close that Hitch turned his head gently to the right as if they had come from that direction.

Hitch's mind was racing as he tried to keep up with the information that could finish a puzzle he had previously thought to be complete. The pieces were all together now, and the picture was as clear as day. The veil that covered his eyes had been removed. The burden of disbelief that weighed on his heart was swept away, and a lightness that could only be described as joy remained.

"I also believe the Lord wanted me to know," Hitch replied. "Thank you for coming, Jimi."

After a moment of reflection, Hitch spoke again. "I have apparently been upgraded to rock star status as a result of my latest lecture last evening, but I hope that you will stay for a while so we may get to know each other a little better."

"I could certainly do that," Jimi answered somewhat nervously.

"Is there a problem, Jimi?" Hitch asked, sensing this nervousness.

"Well, without sounding too much like an ill-mannered Californian jerk-face," Jimi began, "but is there a name attached to the divinely attractive secretary of yours?"

"Monica… her name is Monica Brown," Hitch grinned and replied. "And I believe her to have the heart of a true Christian—born again, if you will. But if I may be some-what presumptuous so soon after we have met," Hitch continued, "I'd like to offer you a bit of advice."

"Please do," Jimi replied anxiously.

"Never—ever—refer to Ms. Brown as my secretary, personal or otherwise. You'll have to trust me on this one, Jimi."

Notes:

Chapter 2 – Hitch's Visitor
"Universal obsessional neurosis of humanity": Freud, Sigmund. *The Future of an Illusion*. Hogarth Press publisher *(1928)*.

Chapter 3 – Jack's Visitor
"Invictus": Henley, William Ernest. Book of Verses, Life and Death section. Charles Scribner's Sons publisher (1893).

"The Present Crisis": Lowell, James Russell. Poem published separately in 1844.

"No word in my vocabulary expressed deeper hatred than the word *Interference*.": Lewis, C.S. *Surprised by Joy: The Shape of My Early Life.* Harcourt Brace publisher *(1955)*.

"If I find in myself a desire which no experience in this world can satisfy...": Lewis, C.S. *Mere Christianity.* HarperCollins publisher *(1952)*.

Chapter 4 – Hitch's Dream
"The opium of the people": Marx, Karl. *Karl Marx – A Contribution to the Critique of Hegel's Philosophy of Right.* German-French Annals publisher *(1844)*.

Chapter 5 – Flowers!
"The Raven": Poe, Edgar Allan. Poem's first publication in the New York Evening Mirror (1845).

Chapter 7 – Great Awakenings
"Darkness cannot drive out darkness; only light can do that": King Jr., Martin Luther. *Strength to Love.* Harper and Row publisher *(1963)*. Quote from 1957 sermon.

Chapter 9 – Traveling Partners
"Insight such as this falls to one's lot but once in a lifetime": Freud, Sigmund. *The Interpretation of Dreams.* Franz Deuticke publisher *(1900)*. Quote from the Foreword to the 1932 English edition.

"Well, I said what I meant and I meant what I said": Dr. Seuss. *Horton Hatches the Egg.* Random House publisher (1940).

Chapter 14 – The Lecture
"The First Law of Thermodynamics": Miller, PhD, Jeff. *Can Quantum Mechanics Produce a Universe from Nothing? (2013)* Apologetics Press. Also see; *Evolution and the Laws of Science: The Laws of Thermodynamics (2013).* Apologetics Press.

"ageless universe": Than, Ker. *Greatest Mysteries: How Did the Universe Begin.* Livescience.com posted on Sept. 2007. Also see; Cartwright, Jon. *Ekpyrotic Cosmology Resurfaces.*

Physicsworld.com posted on Jan. 2008. Also see; Mason, Donavan. *The Physics of Everything: Understanding Superstring Theory.* Futurism.com posted on Sept. 2015.

CPSIA information can be obtained
at www.ICGtesting.com
Printed in the USA
FSOW02n0306221116
27557FS